LEGACY

THE LEGENDARY ROGUE trader charters: Imperial warrants of tremendous antiquity, which can bring their bearers wealth and power barely imaginable. Now that Rogue Trader Hoyyon Phrax is dead, his charter is being brought to the great fortress-system of Hydraphur to be ceremonially bequeathed to his son, and already the vultures are circling.

Shira Calpurnia does not want the charter. She can't help wishing she had never heard of the charter. But she has been appointed to ensure that the will and testament of Hoyyon Phrax is carried out according to Imperial law. And that means that when the rival heirs decide that due process be damned and go all-out for their prize, it's Calpurnia and her Arbites who must don their armour, take up their weapons and get ready for action...

D1208068

Also by Matthew Farrer

The first Shira Calpurnia novel
CROSSFIRE

More storming action from the
grim darkness of Warhammer 40,000

• GAUNT'S GHOSTS •

The Founding
FIRST AND ONLY by Dan Abnett
GHOSTMAKER by Dan Abnett
NECROPOLIS by Dan Abnett

The Saint
HONOUR GUARD by Dan Abnett
THE GUNS OF TANITH by Dan Abnett
STRAIGHT SILVER by Dan Abnett
SABBAT MARTYR by Dan Abnett

• SPACE WOLF •

SPACE WOLF by William King
RAGNAR'S CLAW by William King
GREY HUNTER by William King
WOLFBLADE by William King

• CIAPHAS CAIN •

FOR THE EMPEROR by Sandy Mitchell
CAVES OF ICE by Sandy Mitchell

• THE SOUL DRINKERS •

SOUL DRINKER by Ben Counter
THE BLEEDING CHALICE by Ben Counter

A WARHAMMER 40,000 NOVEL

Shira Calpurnia

LEGACY

Matthew Farrer

For B&B

The General Command of the Adeptus Arbites High Precinct of Hydraphur wishes to acknowledge its gratitude to Mr Robbie Matthews and Mr Trevor Stafford of the Canberra Speculative Fiction Guild, Mr Laurie Goodridge of the Australian Studio of Games Workshop, and the members of the Adeptus Arbites and Battle-Sisters Yahoo groups.

A BLACK LIBRARY PUBLICATION

First published in Great Britain in 2004 by
BL Publishing,
Games Workshop Ltd.,
Willow Road, Nottingham,
NG7 2WS, UK.

10 9 8 7 6 5 4 3 2 1

Cover illustration by Clint Langley.

A CIP record for this book is available from the British Library.

ISBN 1 84416 092 0

Distributed in the US by Simon & Schuster
1230 Avenue of the Americas, New York, NY 10020, US.

Printed and bound in Great Britain by
Bookmarque, Surrey, UK.

See the Black Library on the Internet at
www.blacklibrary.com

Find out more about Games Workshop
and the world of Warhammer 40,000 at
www.games-workshop.com

IT IS THE 41st millennium. For more than a hundred centuries the Emperor has sat immobile on the Golden Throne of Earth. He is the master of mankind by the will of the gods, and master of a million worlds by the might of his inexhaustible armies. He is a rotting carcass writhing invisibly with power from the Dark Age of Technology. He is the Carrion Lord of the Imperium for whom a thousand souls are sacrificed every day, so that he may never truly die.

YET EVEN IN his deathless state, the Emperor continues his eternal vigilance. Mighty battlefleets cross the daemon-infested miasma of the warp, the only route between distant stars, their way lit by the Astronomican, the psychic manifestation of the Emperor's will. Vast armies give battle in his name on uncounted worlds. Greatest amongst his soldiers are the Adeptus Astartes, the Space Marines, bio-engineered super-warriors. Their comrades in arms are legion: the Imperial Guard and countless planetary defence forces, the ever-vigilant Inquisition and the tech-priests of the Adeptus Mechanicus to name only a few. But for all their multitudes, they are barely enough to hold off the ever-present threat from aliens, heretics, mutants – and worse.

TO BE A man in such times is to be one amongst untold billions. It is to live in the cruellest and most bloody regime imaginable. These are the tales of those times. Forget the power of technology and science, for so much has been forgotten, never to be re-learned. Forget the promise of progress and understanding, for in the grim dark future there is only war. There is no peace amongst the stars, only an eternity of carnage and slaughter, and the laughter of thirsting gods.

PROLOGUE

THEIR LORD AND master had been carried into the trees at the opening of the day, and instead of the morning clarion, the halls of the flotilla's spacecraft had rung with a single soft mourning-chime. Those appointed to it followed the catafalque into the arboretum deck, through the shin-high mint-grass with the insects around them chirruping in the morning air. The creatures had been chosen from a dozen worlds for the beauty of their sounds, both individual and in choir, and although the lord was too close to death to be able to hear them he would have been happy with the sounds in these his last hours.

Galt stood one rank back from the catafalque, head bowed, the white linen of the cover-cloth glimmering like summer cloud across the top of his vision. He wore the white gown and black shawl that they all did; his face, as all of theirs, was painted with the intricate downward-curving black and white patterns of mourning. The paint was mixed with an anaesthetic that deadened the face and numbed his skin to the feel of the warm artificial breeze, but he could still feel the stir of the cloth and the brush of the grass against his legs and his bare feet. He stood looking at the grass below and in front of his laced hands, and now that the moment they had all been preparing for had come he found that his mind was empty and calm. He welcomed the sensation – he was too tired to carry any more emotion after the past year.

They stood and waited. The two black-hooded senior medicae standing on either side of the catafalque were the only ones to move, following the movements of their diagnostor, a silver replica of a human heart with spidery mechanical hands growing from its sides, as it glided slowly to and fro about the lord's head.

Time passed. The singing of the insects was a soothing counterpoint to the lazy sounds of the carefully-choreographed breezes in the arboretum's trees.

And finally, after who knew how long, Galt blinked as the medicae took a signal from the diagnostor and dismissed the machine, sending it coasting away. Those present stepped away in silent synchronisation, turning their backs to the catafalque and the body upon it. A sigh seemed to run through them all. There were no cries, no staggering or tearing of hair, just that slackening and release. They had all known too well for too long what was coming to respond any other way.

Galt's thoughts were still quiet and empty with the same exhaustion that he sensed in the others. Something had ended, something had moved on, and now they themselves were free to return to their own lives. For now it was enough to stand in the warm still air of the arboretum and sink into reflection, but soon everything would begin to change.

Their lord and master, Rogue Trader Hoyyon Phrax, was dead. It was time to set course for Hydraphur.

CHAPTER ONE

The Avenue Solar, Outskirts of
Bosporian Hive, Hydraphur

THEY WALKED, THE arbitor and the priest, in an amiable
promenade beneath the great shoulder of the hive. Cool
moist breezes set the cages overhead creaking on their
chains, and the occasional shower of excrement pattered
down around them.

At this end of the Avenue Solar, the footbridges connecting the towering urban stacks had grown together
into a roof over the crowded truckways below. It was
ungainly and humpbacked, following the arch that most
of the footbridges had originally been designed with, a
jigsaw of rockcrete, gritty asphalt, flagstones and tiles.
Here and there were odd-shaped gaps where the space
between intersecting bridges hadn't quite been worth
covering over and, even at this distance, Shira Calpurnia
could hear the never-ending rumble of traffic beneath
them.

A splat against the cloth over her head reminded her that it was not what was beneath their feet that concerned her today, and she looked up. The canopy was embroidered with devotional scenes and Ecclesiarchal livery, held above them on poles by six impassive Cathedral deacons. A thick blob of muck had landed on a panel showing an angel of the Emperor blessing the battlefleet. It was taking more and more effort for Calpurnia to keep the disgust from her face.

'We'll be clear of them in a moment,' Reverend Simova told her, anticipating her thoughts. 'It's a little uncomfortable to see, but then a citizen who behaved as they should wouldn't be up there in the first place. Soiling a sacred image is simply one more thing that they will pay for.' As they moved toward the edge of the bridge the deacons shuffled away with the canopy and they looked at the scene above them.

Calpurnia could see why the Eparch had chosen the Avenue Solar for his display. It was a place for awe. Here at the foot of the Bosporian, the capital city-hive of the world of Hydraphur, the towers of the sprawling lower city were the highest and most forbidding, rearing into the copper sky towards the pale band of the orbiting Ring. Classical Imperial architecture had a pattern and a purpose: it existed to symbolise implacable might and everlasting grandeur, and the sky-scraping towers to either side presented sheer cliffs of wall, intimidating overhangs and the stern gaze of statues to cow anyone who looked up at them. The design had been repeated all the way back down the avenue, making it a great deep canyon full of engine-noise that boomed off the high buildings.

And then in front of them, greater and taller still, the sloping side of the Bosporian itself, tier after tier of wall and buttress, glittering windows and polished statues, the steep zigzag of the Ascendant Way climbing up to the walls of the Augustaeum at the mountain's crown. From here the paired spikes of the Monocrat's palace and the Cathedral of the Emperor Ascendant were invisible, but the great mass of the hive was sight enough.

With that sight to arrest the eye, the cages shrank to an afterthought, a cluster of flyspecks. They were strung like party-lanterns on great swoops of black chain, each link so large that Calpurnia could have put her fist through its centre without touching the edges, held up by girders that Ministorum work crews had driven into the skyscraper walls. The metal was still smooth and shiny, the rivets and padlocks on the cage doors bright and new. The Eparchal decree that had ordered the cages strung up was less than a fortnight old.

'There seems to be something about this tradition that brings out the very worst in some of the penitents. I was with the Eparch during his tenure in the Phaphan sub-diocese, and we had exactly the same problem. Hence...' he made a gesture with a red-and-grey-sleeved arm. Calpurnia looked off to her left.

A narrow set of bleachers had been set up at the foot of the arching bridge and when Calpurnia looked at them, she had to rein in a smile. Thirty Ecclesiarchal officers in dark red and bone-white cassocks, Wardens of the Cathedrals Ordeatic Chamber, were crammed in ten to a bench, packed almost shoulder to shoulder, their poses identical: hands laced demurely in laps, faces staring ahead in earnest concentration. By each man sat a little tripod bearing a brass casing no bigger than a pistol-clip, and from each casing a single unblinking metal eye stared. Each was fixed on a different cage, and every man on the bleachers had had their right eye replaced with a receptor for the cable feed; the flesh around the sockets was still raw from the newness of the graft. She suppressed a smile again – as soon as she had seen them she had thought of a row of birdwatchers, all sharing the same cramped hide and now fixated on a flock of some rare specimen preening itself in front of them.

'One for each cage.' Simova expanded his gesture to point at the chains and cages behind them. 'The mechanical eye keeps a pict-record – that's kept in the Cathedral permanently – but the controlling elements are members of our own clergy, not servitors. That's important. Before anyone in the cages is deemed absolved and brought down, the Warden watching his cage has to confirm that they have not compounded their sins in any way. That's how whoever was pelting us with filth is going to be made to pay. I wish I knew what it was about this punishment that makes people do that.'

Calpurnia didn't respond immediately. She was looking at the cages, hands behind her back, face expressionless. In the near cages the penitents were visible, some grasping the bars to peer down at them, some rocking back and forth and setting their cages swinging, some slumped down, the occasional arm or leg hanging through gaps in the floor-bars. One, the nearest, whose cage was hanging above the most soiled stretch of paving, was crouched over the little slop-bucket bolted to the bars and busily scooping something up in its fingers. Higher up the figures were just grimy, ragged silhouettes against the distant hive wall; the furthest cages were no more than dots. She took off her helmet and squinted at the highest, hanging in the centre of the street, but it was impossible to see what, if anything, the person inside it was doing.

It seemed there was still some time left, and keeping Simova talking was as good a way of passing it as any. She pointed to where a knot of junior deacons stood donning rubberised cloaks.

'What exactly are they listening for? A particular chant or prayer? Or does it vary?' As if on cue, the priests began their procession under the cages and the penitents above them let off a chorus of shouts and howls. The one who'd been grubbing in its slops leapt to the cage bars and began scattering filth out and down onto the ground. The priests kept their hoods low over their faces and walked impassively beneath him.

'It varies with the offence, as you imagine. That determines what they have to make heard as well as where their cage is positioned. The ones down the bottom have committed trivial offences – careless misconduct during a religious service, minor disrespect to an officer of the clergy, you can guess the sort of thing. All we require from them is a short oath of contrition. Most of the time they're able to call it out to the priests' satisfaction on the first pass and they're down from the cage within a couple of hours. A little longer for the ones who are tongue-tied or have trouble speaking up. There was a throat-fever in Phaphan one season, and I remember that even the most lightly-sentenced penitents spent days in the cages before the priests reported that they had heard contrition.'

'And that was considered acceptable?'

Simova gave the Arbitor Senioris a sharp look. The cries from the cages and the deeper rumble of engines under their feet floated through the silence between them for a moment.

'The answer to that is the whole premise of the cages, Arbitor Calpurnia. You people deal with the *Lex Imperia* and a traditional system of penalties, but the traditions of trial and sentence by ordeal are almost as old. They remain in the cages until their oath of contrition is heard in full. That's the law of it, pure and simple.'

'You're saying that there's no such thing as being sentenced to six hours in a cage, or a day, or what have you.'

'Exactly. It is not for any lowly servant, no matter how pious, to judge whether a sinner's contrition has outweighed his crimes. That is decided by the Emperor and by the infallible natural moral order that flows from Him. The ordeal simply reveals the truth to our own lesser eyes so that we can act on it.'

'So if someone in the cages has a throat disease and can't make themselves heard, they might spend a month in the cage for stumbling on the altar steps during a temple ceremony.'

Simova gave a polite anything's-possible nod.

'And, hypothetically, someone who'd stood on the High Mesé for an hour screaming blasphemies against the Emperor and all the Saints and primarchs while giving the fig to the Cathedral spire with one hand and wiping his behind on the Litanies of Faith with the other–'

'–would be confined in the highest cages,' Simova finished, pointing at the speck that Calpurnia had been looking at herself earlier on.

'Where it wouldn't actually be humanly possible to be heard at all, I'd think. I can barely even see them up there, and didn't you tell me that the cages on Phaphan were hung even higher?'

'The ones we used for the most serious of crimes, certainly.'

'Was anyone ever heard from those highest cages?'

'Not during my own tenure there.'

'And that to you demonstrates…'

'…that the Emperor looked into their sinning hearts and saw fit not to give them the voice to make themselves heard so that their penance could end,' Simova finished smoothly. 'The received tradition of the Ecclesiarchy teaches us that the blasphemer and the heretic may find absolution in death, and so we may observe that death was the absolution that the Emperor required of them.' Simova's voice had taken on a ringing, pulpit-style quality, and the thought caused Calpurnia another inner smile. The man's tonsured head and broad chest were unremarkable, but where his ribs began the reverend bloomed into a great swell of fat in all directions which held the hem of his cassock well clear of his legs and feet. A ringing voice was not inappropriate for a man who so resembled a bell.

She looked up at that furthermost cage again, squinting as she followed the lines of the chains back to the walls.

The chains were invisible by the time they reached their anchor points, but she could just see the metal catwalk that ran along the girders that held the chains up. She thought of taking the magnocular scope from her belt to look in more detail, but that could wait. Best to play it safe and dumb until things were under way.

'You have nothing to worry about the construction of the cages, Arbitor Senioris,' said Simova, who had followed her gaze and misinterpreted it. 'The girder supports are driven an arm's length into the rockcrete. I'm told that we could safely hang one of the holy Sisterhood's Rhino tanks up next to each cage. You don't have to fear anything falling on you. Well, except for…' He gestured to the filth splattering the walkway. The priests had left tracks through it as they walked about to listen for confessions.

'So this whole array was put up under direct Ecclesiarchal supervision?' It was hard to see, but there seemed to be some kind of disturbance on the catwalk where the uppermost chains ended. Calpurnia felt her shoulders tense.

'Of course. I will not say there isn't much to admire about the Hydraphur Ministorum, but this is not a religious practice that ever took root here. The Eparch wanted to make sure when he instituted it here that it would be done properly.'

'Really?' Calpurnia strolled towards the bleachers where the wardens sat and stared upwards. The identical expressions on their faces had not changed.

'And done properly it was, arbitor,' said Simova, pacing alongside her and once again misunderstanding her interest. 'The only significant blemish on the whole affair was one particular inhabitant of the upper stack levels, who insisted on an above-market rate of payment as well as the granting of Ecclesiarchal indulgences in exchange for the privilege of driving our bolts and rings into the walls of his building. You can see him in that cage there, the one third from the edge.'

Calpurnia made a small polite sound, but she wasn't looking. Two Arbites were walking up to the rows of benches, one with an adjutant's badge and carrying a compact vox-case, one in the brown sash of a chastener.

'I trust this isn't the call of duty just yet, Arbitor Calpurnia?' asked Simova, misreading things again. 'I had hoped you would have time to see the priests arrive back from walking beneath the cages. I'm sure that at least one of the prisoners will have had their full contrition heard, and it's instructive to see the whole process of–'

He broke off. Arbites helmets could make it difficult to tell where their wearer was looking – it was part of the design – but it had become very obvious that the black-armoured figures were staring over his shoulder. Simova gave a disapproving frown and turned.

The blimp coming down the avenue was about fifty metres long, bulbous and dirty. The metalwork along its scooped nose was a clumsy attempt to duplicate the lines of an Imperial warship's prow, and clusters of auspexes and magnoptic emplacements jutted from the long gondola. Its engines were a loud, insectile buzz that counterpointed the seismic rumble of the traffic below.

'How singular,' Simova said. 'Is that an observation gallery built into it there? The Cathedral certainly was not notified of anything like this. I think we shall have to have words with the Monocrat's court. I'm assuming that it's his propagandists who are behind this. Look, you can see the pict-lenses. They must be capturing the cages. Don't you agree, arbitor?'

'No.' Calpurnia's voice was distracted rather than snappish, but it was enough to annoy Simova.

'I'm sure I'm correct. Although I wish they had–'

'The identification numbers on the sides there are from the nautical traffic directorates down past the lagoon. It's one of the blimps they use to monitor sea traffic off the coast and report to the harbourmaster. Haven't you seen them out over the bay?'

'I suppose I must have, arbitor, but what's such a thing doing flying up to the hive like this? Throne preserve us, look! It's barely above the level of the cages! What if it drops?'

'Not *exactly* the problem I'm anticipating,' Calpurnia said calmly. Simova, wrong-footed, gulped air and watched her unholster, check and arm a stub pistol that looked impossibly large for her slender arms.

The arbitor holding the voxer tilted his head as it broke into a terse series of staticky messages. 'East and west teams report that anchors are seized, ma'am,' he said after a moment. 'Repeating that, both anchors are seized.'

Simova looked around and upwards.

'What anchors? What are you talking about? I see no anchors, the thing's… wait, do you mean… Yes, it's lowering a chain, look! How dare they? Where's… Emperor's eyes, there should be a deacon on duty here, where… you. *You.*'

A nervous deacon, who'd been gawping up at the blimp from several metres away, hurried over. 'Give me a magnoc, or bring up a reader so we can look at what that idiot in the blimp is– What? Emperor's light! You improvident lackwit! There is *always* supposed to be a sighting device available at the cages for members of the priesthood to–'

'Use mine if you wish, reverend.' Calpurnia passed across a stubby tube, smaller and plainer than the ornate Ministorum devices Simova was used to. He conscientiously said a small benediction for its machine-spirit and put it to his eye.

It was not a chain that the blimp was lowering but a cable and hook, from a heavy winching scaffold on the rear of the gondola. The blimp lurched back and forth as the pilot tried to keep it in one position in the crossbreezes, and the hook swung in wilder and wilder arcs as it descended. The ragged figure in the cage was standing with its back to Simova, gripping the bars, watching the hook descend. The sheer enormity of what he was seeing stopped the words in Simova's throat for a dozen seconds, and it made an undignified squeak of the voice he eventually managed to find.

'The man's being *rescued*. Golden *Throne*, don't these people realise what they're doing? Have they no idea of the *consequences*?' It took a moment for him to realise that he was talking to himself – the Arbites were conferring with one another and with the rustling voices of their companions on the voxer.

'Anchors cutting, repeating, ma'am. Anchors cutting, both sides. Mast on the move, ETA four minutes.'

'Do we see Helmsman?'

'Tentatively placed with Mast, but not confirmed.'

The hook swung over the top of the cage. The magnoc make it look almost close enough to touch; it was odd when there was no audible clank when the back of the hook bounced off the top of the cage bars. Simova started as the sound of traffic-alert horns blared up through the gaps in the rockcrete.

'I take it someone's going to tell me what that was.' Calpurnia's voice had only the tiniest traces of an edge.

'Mastwatch reports in, ma'am. Mast has developed engine difficulties, probably fake. The horns were from the traffic backing up behind it. They hit their mark exactly, though.'

'I'd expect no less,' said Calpurnia. 'Anchors? If they're too enthusiastic up there then they may save us having to be involved at all, although I'm not sure I'd call that satisfactory.'

Her words crystallised Simova's suspicions, and he rounded on her.

'This is not a surprise to you, is it, Arbitor Calpurnia? What do you mean by allowing this to go ahead? Do you plan on intervening before these prisoners are all loaded up and flying to saints-know-where?'

'I'll have my magnoc back from you, reverend, if you're done with it,' was her reply. 'I'd like to see if that hook has found purchase. Culann, raise Anchorwatch please.'

'Both anchors still cutting. They're... wait... Anchor-watch reports anchors away! Repeat–'

'Thank you, Culann, no need.' She was not looking through the magnoc, but up at the building walls. Simova realised with a sick sensation in his gut what 'anchors away' must have meant. One of the chains had been cut. He watched it curl and flap loose down the rockcrete face of the stack, shattering a row of gargoyles and gouging chunks out of the ledges and balconies it lashed against on the way down. Before it had landed he jerked his gaze back to the distant cage, but Calpurnia had been right: the hook had found purchase and the cage now swung back and forth from the blimp. But the cage was not being raised, as Simova had expected, but lowered.

'Mast still in position,' reported Culann. 'Confirming just one vehicle. No definite sightings of Helmsman. We're having trouble intercepting their vox-bands so we haven't placed his voice yet either.'

'Keep everyone back, Culann. I don't expect anyone to see Helmsman until Captain is... you know, I think we can dispense with the code-name. I didn't like that one anyway. I don't think Symandis will pop his head up until Ströon hits the ground.' Simova gaped.

'That's Ghammo Ströon? That's his cage? Damn, from this angle I didn't...' The curate remembered where he was, and rounded on the ranks of Wardens behind him.

'Who is monitoring Ströon's cage? How is... what...'

'The penitent Ghammo Ströon has not been heard to express contrition,' came the toneless reply. 'My humble judgement records forty-eight offences before the sight of the Emperor and by Eparchal decree, for which penitence must also be made.' The man was silent for a moment, and then corrected himself: 'Fifty-one.' Calpurnia looked through her magnoc: the figure in the cage was making an indistinct but definitely obscene gesture in the direction of the Cathedral spire.

'The... why have...' Simova was trying his hardest, but discoursing about punishment in the abstract in the Chamber of Exegetors had not prepared him for seeing action first-hand. He stepped forward to try and lay a hand on Calpurnia's shoulder but the chastener, who was a head and a half taller than Simova with shoulders as broad as the curate's waist, stepped forward and silently blocked his way. Simova finally managed a sentence:

'This rescue must be *stopped*!'

'Mmm.' Calpurnia folded the magnoc with a snap and stowed it back at her belt. 'I don't see Mast yet, but it won't be long.'

'Mastwatch and Noose are still standing by, ma'am.' Culann's voice was showing an edge of tension.

'Thank you.' Calpurnia had donned her helmet again. 'The cage is on the ground, and I can see Ströon at the door. They had to know that there would be alerts by now. When they move, they'll move fast.' She drummed her fingers against her leg for a moment. 'I think we need to be closer.'

At her words Culann began stowing the voxer in his harness while the chastener gestured to the Arbites who had been waiting in the pavilion that Simova had put up for the Ecclesiarchy's own staff. The curate's mouth went dry as he watched them move up: more chasteners, massive and broad-shouldered in heavy carapace armour, hefting shotguns and grenade launchers. The tramp of their boots was countered by the metallic *tik-tik-tik* of cyber-mastiff feet as the dog-like attack-constructs paced beside their handlers, and the last two chasteners carried shining steel grapplehawks in their heavy launching-frames, the suspensors in their ribcages whining as they warmed up.

As he watched their armoured backs spread out and move towards the hanging line and the beached cage, Simova felt eyes on him. It was the little delegation of priests who had been walking under the cages to hear the confessions. There could not have been a lot to hear: the other penitents had all fallen silent as the shadow of the blimp had passed over them.

Curate Simova did not consider himself a coward. His duties had taken him to more cloisters than battlefields, but the Adeptus Ministorum was at its heart a militant church and its doctrines never shied from violence. Nevertheless, at that moment he felt glad to have the line of Arbites between him and what was about to happen. He snapped his fingers for attention and beckoned the priests over.

'Join with me in raising your voices,' he told them. 'The Adeptus Arbites need our battle-prayers.'

SHIRA CALPURNIA HALF-HEARD the little chorus of plain-song from behind them, and it soothed her. There was always a need for prayer – to believe otherwise was prideful and sinful. The stranded cage was still a good four hundred metres away, and she upped the pace a little.

She flexed her left arm and shoulder and felt a sharp twinge run through her. It had been more than half a year since it had been rebuilt after her shattering injuries atop the spire of the Cathedral, and Calpurnia knew she was healing quickly as such things went. Quickly, but not yet completely. She unsnapped the power-maul from her belt and gripped it tightly in one gauntleted fist.

Three hundred and fifty metres. There were more figures around the cage now, busily working at it. Her detectives had reported that the clique had bought an oxy-cutter with false credit and doctored authorisation, and stolen breaching-charges from a shipment to the Monocrat's personal militia. She had personally suspended the investigations into both crimes: if Symandis had suspected that the Arbites were onto rescue preparations he might have become suspicious.

Three hundred and ten metres. Vox came in, simple and coded. Anchors both locked. The saboteur teams that had blown the chains loose had all been rounded up. That was where most of the breaching-grenades had gone, she would bet. The four teams represented almost the clique's entire field strength, and all of its best, and with the teams codenamed 'Anchor' taken out two of those teams were down.

Two hundred and sixty metres. No one had been able to give her a sure guarantee that the bridges would take the weight of a Rhino, so the strike force spread out on foot, the cyber-mastiffs on the flanks, the grapplehawk tenders in the centre. Two hawks, one for Symandis, one to recapture Ströon. Easy. There was a chastener at each of Calpurnia's shoulders, and it took an effort of will for her to slow her pace to allow the line to overtake her.

Two hundred and twenty-five metres. The targets' discipline was excellent. They had to have seen the force of chasteners, and she was sure they knew the saboteur teams had been taken. But they bent to their work still, and Calpurnia could see the glare of the cutter at the bars of the cage. Let them try. All she needed was for–

'Helmsman!' cried Culann from a pace behind her, but they were close enough now that the vox-torcs in their carapaces had picked it up as well. 'Helmsman! All Arbites, we have Helmsman and Captain! Helmsman and Captain!"

'Maintain pace, please, don't speed up. Remember your orders.' Calpurnia kept her voice level, expecting any moment to have to interrupt herself with the next order. If both Symandis and Ströon were confirmed as being ahead of them, then she didn't think she had long to wait.

A couple of the men around the cage were shooting panicky looks over their shoulders now. They would not have expected the Arbites in such force or so soon, perhaps not at all. Calpurnia gritted her teeth. Their orders were not to open fire until her mark, and she trusted her Arbites to hold that order absolutely, but she hoped that the rescuers would not start shooting before–

There was a blue flare ahead of her – not the steady pin-point of the cutter but the flicker of a power weapon. It flared twice more and the side of the cage fell away. Ströon was free.

'Captain's free!' Calpurnia barked. 'Ströon's free! Close the noose. Go!'

And then everything happened. The chasteners sped up into a run. Lead Chastener Vayan boomed through his vox-horn for the men to surrender to righteous judge-ment and overhead four krak missiles drew sharp white trails from the building heights. Their impacts blew out the blimp's engines and it began a slow, undirected drift; the cable, still attached to the cage, grew taut and dragged the cage away. And then, after a moment, the cage dropped and wedged itself tight in the gap through which the rescuers had climbed, blocking it and anchoring the blimp in place.

And so the Emperor shows His hand for His servants, Calpurnia thought with only a little smugness, before she called into her torc again.

'Mastwatch, the hole is blocked. The cage fell into it. Our targets are trapped, no need for main force in dis-abling Mast. Take as many alive as you can.' And then, heeding the warning twinges from her arm, she slowed to watch the chasteners close.

Symandis's own little taskforce was armed too. They carried punch-daggers, home-machined blades, little foldaway laspistols and stubbers you could hide from the crude traffic-control auspexes if you knew the trick of it. But the Arbites' armour was tough and their wills were tougher: they began weaving as they ran to spoil placed shots to armour-joins and held their guns in a high shoulder position that kept an armoured vambrace over the half of their faces the helmets didn't cover. Not a man so much as staggered as they ran towards the crack and pop of the enemy's small-arms, and then two grenade launchers chugged and the fire stopped completely even before the heavy double-*wham* of the shock grenades. The people they were facing knew more than enough to take cover when they heard launchers.

Not that they had any intention of making a last stand. The burly figure of Symandis was already running up the slope of the pavement. Calpurnia didn't need to give the order: the first grapplehawk went screeching out of its frame, weaving on its suspensor as its handler thumbed the studs on the controller to steer it forwards. It only took a few seconds for its cortex, patterned on the preying instincts of the Avignoran black eagle, to lock onto its prey, and then send it swooping with metal hooks and taser-spikes unsheathed.

Calpurnia swore as Symandis spun at the sound of the suspensor and shore it in two with a stroke of a crackling power-axe.

'Culann! Stohl! Even as the words were leaving her mouth she was in a flat run, champing her jaw shut and ignoring the warning tautness in her shoulder as her power-maul sizzled and spat. She jinked to the left and around the wedged cage, barely registering the shots and sirens echoing up from the roadway below as the stolen scaffold-truck they had codenamed Mast was stormed by Arbitor Odamo and the Mastwatch teams.

Symandis had taken a moment to draw a bead on her, but his snub-barrelled pistol could not give him the range – the shot didn't even pass close enough for Calpurnia to hear it hit the paving. Then he was running again.

'Mastiffs! Two mastiffs on Helmsman, breaking left. Two mastiffs *now!*' She hated to take strength from the fight behind her, but Symandis was just as much a target as Ströon had been. The whole reason they had let the cage be lowered was to make sure Symandis was there before they moved. 'Mastiffs on Helmsman!'

With a clatter of claws two of the hunter-constructs loped past, narrow metal faces fixed with inhuman intent on the criminal ahead of them, their handlers racing to

keep up. Running ahead of them, armoured boots spark-
ing off the pitted and uneven paving, Calpurnia resisted
the urge to draw her pistol: the mega-bore rounds would
wipe out any hope of capturing the wretch alive. The
grapplehawks were supposed to have achieved that –
where the hell had Symandis got a power-axe from?

The handlers must have directed a secondary attack
pattern: when Symandis whirled with a low sweep of the
axe timed to decapitate the lead mastiff, they both shied
away and passed one to either side of him. Suddenly
Symandis was between the two mastiffs and the Arbites.
When he realised this he tried to break right and make for
a different paving gap. One mastiff darted in and there
was a sound like metal shears as its mechanised jaws
snapped the air behind Symandis's heel, a microsecond
away from severing his Achilles tendon. The other ducked
under a stroke of the axe and managed to rake its teeth
along the side of Symandis's knee before he knocked it
scrabbling with the axe haft and put two rapid bullets
into the side of its torso. It lurched drunkenly away as
Symandis backpedalled, sweeping the axe to and fro peg-
ging two more quick shots towards Calpurnia.

As the first bullet whistled overhead, something
crashed into her from behind, shoving her to one side.
She growled and tried to drive an elbow back until she
realised...

'Damn it, Culann!'

'You were under fire, ma'am, I was trying to interpose
myself!'

She opened her mouth, but this wasn't the time. The
two mastiff handlers and Lead Chastener Stohl pelted
past her after Symandis and as she stood she took a
moment to look over her shoulder.

These were no hysterical rioters or brainless slum-
thugs. Ströon was weak from three days in the cage, but
a circle of his men were bearing him in the other direction as fast as they could, trying to make the most of

Symandis's diversion and the way the chasteners had to sight through or fight past Ströon's own men: they had obviously worked out the Arbites were trying to take Ströon alive.

Mast was crippled, and there was no way they could get down through one of the other gaps without the fall splattering them across a busy roadway... but Calpurnia saw in her mind's eye Ströon clambering down his followers as they made a groaning human rope of their interlocked hands – it would only need to hold for ten, twenty seconds – or simply having them hurl themselves through a gap to form a soft pile of bodies on which to land. However unlikely, she wasn't going to take the chance.

'Anchorwatch, do you see captain and his guard? I want you to put a missile in his path every time they make for one of those gaps. Frag load. Well ahead of the pack, we're trying to deny him ground, not kill him.' She nodded with satisfaction at their confirmation – missile launchers were certainly not regular Arbites field kit, but the gunnery teams were turning out to be well worth the trouble she had gone through to borrow them off Arbitor Nakayama's armoury echelon.

The first missile boomed on the rockcrete in the middle distance as she advanced on Symandis again. He was staggering now, on the defensive, unable to face two groups of enemies at once: the Arbites moved in further every time he swung his power axe at the mastiffs, and the mastiffs lunged for his legs every time he tried to snap a shot at the Arbites. One mastiff was missing a leg, and Stohl was bleeding from a bullet-crease to the side of his arm, but Symandis's legs were gashed in half a dozen places and he was treading his own blood into the ground at every step.

Calpurnia shot another look back. Ströon was being forced towards one of the sheer building walls, pressed by the chasteners, hemmed in by cyber-mastiffs and carefully-placed missile explosions. She would be needed there soon.

She doffed her helmet, switched her maul to her other hand and drew her pistol.

'Are we going to play this out to its finish, Symandis? I can kill you now, or we can take you apart piece by piece. Or you can–'

'Or I can surrender and go to exactly the same fate in your cells that I'm ready to meet here now,' he panted. His voice was hoarse. There was sweat on his eyeglasses and sweat slicking the dark curly mop of his hair. 'You want me alive so you won't shoot me. You'll keep trying to knock me down while I make sure I damn well take as many of you as *uhhh*–'

The sentence finished halfway between a grunt and a scream as the mastiffs took advantage of his distraction to scissor through the backs of Symandis's knees, collapsing him to the ground with his hamstrings severed. The hand with the pistol waved in the air and Stohl clubbed it down with an efficient swing of a gun-butt. The power-axe swung wildly and Calpurnia swung her maul in an elegant twisting stroke that came in behind the axe-blade, blew the circuitry in the haft and knocked the weapon flying. Then the mastiffs clamped onto his wrists, razor-teeth retracted but jaws as powerful as ever, and that, finally, was that.

CHAPTER TWO

The Avenue Solar, Outskirts of
Bosporian Hive, Hydraphur

STRÖON, BLASPHEMER AND seditionist and the teacher of
blasphemers and seditionists, was almost in hand. The
mastiffs had broken up the men surrounding him and
carefully aimed Executioner rounds had picked off any
who got too far from their leader. From inside the clump
he was shouting slogans in a voice even more sore and
cracked than Symandis's and waving a combat blade
someone must have given him. The running fight had left
a trail down the side of the humped bridge-slope: blood-
spatter, shell cases, four outlaws sprawling unconscious
or dead and two chasteners, one lying on his side cursing
softly as blood seeped from the shoulder-joint of his
carapace and a companion knelt by him trying to jam a
pressure-pack into place. Calpurnia slowed down to
make eye contact with the wounded man and give him a
nod, then spoke into her torc.

'Calpurnia to lead chasteners. Helmsman is taken. Both Anchor teams are taken. Mastwatch, verify…' she waited for their confirmation. 'Mast is taken. All that's left is Captain. Push them into the wall and let's finish it.'

It took only minutes. A volley of shot sent low to ricochet made the knot of enemies scramble backwards down the slope with blood starting from their feet and shins. When they had spilled down to the flat pedestrian concourse along the stack wall a choke grenade burst on the rockcrete and filled the space with smothering vapour. None of the Arbites even needed to clip rebreathers into place: the cyber-mastiffs didn't need air to pull down the three of Ströon's bodyguards who had managed to stay on their feet, and the grapplehawk didn't need air to glide in on Captain himself. Jittering from the taser-hooks, hoisted up by the hawk's suspensor so that his bare toes just scraped the ground, Ströon was dragged forward into the half-circle of chasteners to where Shira Calpurnia waited to put him in chains.

Simova and his priests had not moved from their spot by the time Calpurnia walked back to them. The prayer-songs were over and Simova simply watched her as she had Culann vox a report; she let him wait, grimacing as she rolled her shoulder to try and work the kinks and aches out of it, not letting on that she had noticed the tiny tremor in Simova's hands from second-hand adrenaline or the quick glances he kept shooting toward the empty space where Ströon's cage had hung. The fighting seemed to have cowed the other penitents for a while – the air was now clear of cries and excrement.

Finally, she sent Culann down to the roadway level to make sure her Rhino was ready for her and turned to Simova, sweeping her damp hair back from her scarred forehead. It was the end of Hydraphur's wet season, cool enough to make people want to move around a little to keep warm but humid enough to make you sweat as soon as you did. The sensation was not pleasant.

'You didn't come here today by accident,' Simova said. He wasn't asking a question, and Calpurnia didn't bother to pretend that he was. 'That was as careful an ambush as I can imagine,' he went on. 'Set up to cancel out every detail of the rescue raid. You knew exactly where those people were going to be and what they were going to do.'

Calpurnia went so far as to nod.

'You knew their plans to the letter. You must have detected their approach, well, how long ago would–'

'A while. Symandis wasn't as good at keeping his activities secret as Ströon. He was too clumsy about getting hold of his equipment and hijacking the surveillance blimp. Things like that find their way to informers.'

'Who were your informers in Ströon's cell?' demanded Simova. It only took a few moments of Calpurnia's level ice-green stare for him to think better of the question and try to soften it. 'Arbitor, if there had been just a little co-operation, well, we could have removed Ströon from rescue's way, or had the Adepta Sororitas guard the cages.'

'Symandis was good enough to know exactly how the Ministorum had set up the cages. You don't think a guard would have alerted him?' Something in Calpurnia's gaze was making Simova uncomfortable again.

'It, well, arbitor, I realise that this is your own, er…'

'We needed to make sure that Symandis was confident enough to attempt the rescue himself,' Calpurnia continued calmly. 'We needed to make sure they believed such a daring exercise would pay off.'

'And look how this turned out!' Simova jabbed a finger at the spot where Ströon had been taken. The choke fumes had left yellow stains on the rockcrete that would take days to fade. 'Ströon was on the ground and running before you got to him! Think of what could have happened! If you had arrested them when they showed their faces they would be safely in irons now and we would not have lost a cage from the array!'

'And Symandis would be free, we would not have their collection of henchmen and dupes dead or slung off a Rhino and Ströon would not be in proper custody.' The louder Simova's protestations got, the quieter Calpurnia's voice became, to the point where he had to take a step forward to hear her.

'I will not have you talk like that to me, arbitor. Ströon was a prisoner of the holy Adeptus Ministorum, as you might remember if you would like to cast your mind back to seeing him hanging over the Avenue Solar in a cage. In fact, by Eparchal decree those cages represent Ecclesiarchal premises just as much as the altars and nave of the Cathedral itself. Ströon should have been no business of yours while he was incarcerated there.'

'Our grapplehawk did not, you will have noticed, pluck Ströon out of his cage,' Calpurnia said levelly. 'In fact, we did not even begin active engagement until Ströon was free of the cage. And a known seditionist running free after exploiting the failures of his captors is most certainly an Arbites matter.'

'It is the role of the Ecclesiarchy to embody and spread the divine word of the Emperor–' Simova began.

'And the role of the Arbites to *enforce* laws and decrees and to ensure that all of the Emperor's Adeptus are in full command of and service to their duties,' finished Calpurnia calmly. 'Which I am quite sure you and your Ministorum colleagues are, of course. All the same, I do not believe in being less than thorough. Although I myself am called to other business, I have deputised Praetor Imprimis Dastrom to prepare a full dossier of inquiry on the business. I won't insult you by lecturing you about co-operating, but I will mention that Dastrom will hold you accountable for the co-operation of all external labour you engaged to put up the cages.'

'You let the rescue happen.' Simova had gone pale, his lips very thin. 'You knew that they had a plan that would get Ströon free. And you allowed it to happen so that

Ströon would be out of his cage and into your own hands.' His words were confident, but the confidence was leaching out of his tone. Calpurnia had found that a steady look could do that.

'The Eparch will hear of this. As will Canoness Theoctista.'

'I shall count on it. The Eparch and I have intended to meet and speak in person for almost six months now, but the opportunity has eluded us. And it will be good to speak with the reverend canoness again. There's no need to delay on my account if you need to set off for the Augustaeum now, sir, I have my own transport waiting.'

And after that it was just a matter of meeting the curate's eyes until he turned and walked back the way they had come.

The Wall, Bosporian Hive, Hydraphur

'IT SOUNDS LIKE he took it well, ma'am,' said Culann, 'considering.'

'He was smart enough to realise that he didn't have a choice,' said Calpurnia, 'especially not outside the hive and with the Arbites outnumbering him. I should have kept some of you up there, actually, to drive the point home. But never mind.'

The giant fortress known as the Wall formed the Arbites barracks and courts for all of Hydraphur and whole systems around. It began amid the building stacks that crowded the base of the Bosporian and ran up the entire side of the hive-mountain to finish at the great fortified Justice Gate, set into the wall of the Augustaeum high above. Calpurnia didn't know how long it would take to travel on foot from the lowest entrances at hive bottom to her own rooms in the Wall's highest bastion, and she didn't think anyone had ever tried. She and Culann were riding in one of the cable cars that ran the whole length of the great bastion, rattling along in the highest space of the building, just below the vaulted roof. Calpurnia was standing at one of the car windows, looking out and down; Culann sat on a bench along one wall

'And he didn't challenge you on the law of it?'

'No. Either he knew we were in the right – and he's a specialist in religious law, after all – or he wasn't sure of his ground and didn't want to force the issue.'

'Do you think the Eparch will? Force the issue, that is?'

'I don't believe so. I hope not.' Calpurnia sighed. 'I don't like playing law games, especially over vermin like Ströon. The Ecclesiarchy were so rapt at catching him for spreading his schismatic books, but I don't think they knew the half of what he was up to.'

'Was that why you wanted him personally, ma'am?' Culann gulped. 'To personally arrest him, that is.'

The cable car was passing over one of the high-roofed drilling concourses. Sixty metres below her, squares of infantry, a hundred arbitrators to a side, stamped and clashed through a weapon drill, whipping heavy *Vox Legi*-pattern shotguns out of the scabbards on their backs and aiming from the shoulder, from the hip, kneeling, then into the scabbard, out, kneel, shoulder, turn, kneel, scabbard, turn, hip, kneel… The drill was one so old that it had not changed between here and where Calpurnia had trained in the Ultima Segmentum, and although she wouldn't have performed it in at least five years she found her muscles twitching along with the remembered moves as if her body still wanted to join in without asking her.

She blinked and realised she owed Culann a reply.

'No. Well, part of the reason, I suppose, but I hope I'm not prideful enough to personally insist on taking in every single outlaw whose warrant declares him dangerous. That's all of them, for one thing.'

'For symbolism, then?' Culann seemed to be taking the conversation for an examination. Calpurnia smiled. The question was not frivolous – the idea of the symbolism and pageantry of the law, that Imperial justice should be seen by the populace to be bearing down in full and unstoppable force, was a philosophy expounded by generations of distinguished Arbites scholars.

'An object lesson for the populace, well, perhaps,' she said, 'although there wasn't much of an audience there today. To focus the minds of the Ecclesiarchy, too, as you probably picked up. I made it very clear to Simova that Dastrom's investigation wouldn't go soft on him because of his office. I don't think they'll find anything – I think Ströon's people got the schematics for the cage anchors and all the rest through their own devices, but I'm uncomfortable with how pushy the Eparch is getting about having Ministorum agents conducting hunts and arrests. The Arbitor Majore and I have been waiting for the right occasion to make a point about knowing their boundaries.'

'A political operation,' said Culann, nodding.

'Not quite,' she corrected him a little stiffly. 'Just the performance of our duty as Arbites that extends some lessons in more than one direction at once. Anyway, that's the second reason.'

'Is there another, ma'am?'

'My own peace of mind, since you ask.' At the words 'peace of mind' Culann noticed her gloved hand creeping up to touch the scars on her forehead. It didn't take most people long to notice the mannerism or recognise what it meant. 'This rogue trader business is going to swallow up a lot of my time, and I wanted to see Ströon and Symandis scooped up with my own eyes so I didn't have to fret about them while I'm supposed to be concentrating on this bequesting I'm signing, or presiding over, or whatever the hell I'm doing with it. And in all honesty, Culann, since I know you're a dependable and discreet adjutant, "bequesting" means taking on those seditionists was the last chance I'll have for quite a time for some good solid boots-on-ground Arbites work. If I'm only going to have one chance to stretch my muscles and see how I'm healing between here and Candlemas then I'm bloody well going to take it.'

Culann took this in solemnly. Another thing that most people found out quickly about Arbitor Senioris Calpurnia was how much she hated leading from anywhere but the front. Opinion on this in the arbitrator barracks further down the wall had been evenly divided between approval at a commander willing to put themselves on the line with their troops, and disapproval at an Arbitor Senioris who put herself at risk instead of riding in an armoured pulpit in the second rank of Rhinos, reading from the Books of Judgement over an amp-horn as befitted her station. Culann had heard there was a small but vocal third faction who contended that the control-freak bitch wanted to be on hand to make sure the arbitrators kept their boots polished and their kits neat while they were being shot at.

'And if I may ask, ma'am, your injuries…?

The cable car passed from the drill hall into a tunnel, and onto a steeper slope that would take them up to the next bastion level. Four more of those to go before they reached the Justice Gate itself.

'Not bad. Thank you for asking, Culann.' He thought that she perhaps was worse than that: they were passing under a series of light-wells in the thick ceiling above them and the brief bursts of yellow Hydraphur daylight made her look tired and hollow-eyed. He knew that she had been on her feet very soon after the confrontation at the Cathedral had wrecked her shoulder and arm. Cynez Sanja had made it a personal point to have his Magi Biologis work minor miracles on her flesh and bones, but her convalescence since then had not been easy. Culann's impression was that Shira Calpurnia did not deal with being a patient very well.

She dropped into a seat opposite him.

'It's the smaller things that bother me, not the big ones,' she said suddenly as though she had seen his thoughts. 'I know I can't carry a shield, my left arm just isn't strong enough yet. Well, fine. What gnaws me is things like having trouble buckling my armour because the fingers on that hand won't quite work the fasteners yet. Or having to spend the time I thought I was going to spend getting back into physical training in the medicae chambers instead, feeling weak and stiff instead of running around a drill-hall like I should have been doing.' Her expression soured. 'Anyway, complaining won't make me heal any faster, even though I know it's said that I never do anything else.' Culann kept gallantly silent. 'Anyway, the Arbitor Majore had a suspicious sort of a "let's see you get into a gunfight on this assignment" air about him when he gave this rogue trader matter to me.'

'Legal theory work, you mean, ma'am?' Culann felt a twinge of relief at the conversation moving to less personal grounds. He had seen the Arbitor Senioris at her forceful best when she had hunted down plotters and saboteurs just before the great Mass of Balronas, and to hear her sound so worn was oddly disturbing.

'Not even that, as far as I can tell. Ceremonial, more like. This man's ship, or is there more than one? I think there is. They're bringing his rogue trader charter back and his son's being summoned from his home by the Pyrmondine Spur. As far as I can tell most of what we're doing is providing a nice warm room where the one can meet the other, and clapping everybody on the back afterwards.'

Despite her air of disdained detachment, she already seemed to be more familiar with the basics of the Hoyyon Phrax affair than Culann was, and he was the one who had prepared the briefings for her.

'Are we overseeing the Naval judicature, or Administratum, or the Monocrat and planetary authorities, or our own, ma'am? I've not studied the underpinnings of Letters of Marque in the *Lex Imperia*.'

'Neither have I, Culann. Because we're arbitrators, not Judges. It's their job to know the cumulative effect of ten thousand years of Imperial decrees on the law we apply, and it's our job to know the cumulative effect of a hundred-shell Executioner volley on a line of rioters.' She smiled at her own turn of phrase for a moment. 'On the other hand, take my advice, Culann, pay attention to any opportunity you have to see how the other pillar of the Arbites works. I like to think I'm versed in both of them, but I get caught flatfooted more often than I'm pleased to admit. Having Judges on my staff doesn't make up for everything.' She blinked. 'Throne alone, listen to me ramble. I've been around Leandro too long. Where was I?'

'Imperial letters of marque, ma'am.'

'That's right, and why this isn't one. We're dealing with something a little over and above the usual planetary governors' marques or the Adeptus wildcat warrants. I'm talking about the true rogue trader charters, the old decrees for the captains who used to fly right clean out of Imperial space, often as not. They would go to places where they never knew what they would find or what they would have to do to survive, so they were given the power to do whatever they needed to.'

'Whatever they...'

'My home was on the Eastern Fringe, you understand. Wild space zones and the Imperial frontier were a lot closer than they are here. There were a lot of stories about the great old rogue traders in the histories of our segmentum. There was one who used his charter to lead a fleet into wild space and raid and strip two xenos factory ships that were mining its asteroids. Then his son used the wealth from that to return and outfit a whole flotilla of ships and return to those systems to drive the xenos out completely. Then his granddaughter used the charter to recruit colonists from half a dozen Imperial worlds and found a permanent fief of her own in this system they'd taken. There was another one who struck a pact with the Ecclesiarchy to transport a missionary taskforce out beyond the Imperial border – the accounts said they loaded an entire prefabricated temple into the hold of his largest ship to deposit whole onto the first habitable world they found, if you can believe that. He went out beyond the border and his grandson came back into Imperial space a hundred and eighty years later with a giant pilgrim fleet in tow. They had found two human worlds lost to the light for more than a thousand years, and turned them into an Emperor-fearing part of the Imperium. That'd be something to be remembered for, wouldn't it?'

They passed out of the tunnel, and Culann blinked at the sudden light. The car rattled up through the high reaches of the spinal concourse of a barrack level; beneath them Arbites bustled in and out of dormitory entrances.

'So these are the rogue traders. The real ones, the grand old ones, the ones that these little pissants with a decommissioned Munitorio hauler and a life warrant from a local governor want to be mistaken for when they boast they're a rogue trader.'

'And so this man, this Hoyyon Phrax…'

'Not Hoyyon Phrax, not any more. His age caught up with him somewhere out past the Anseelie Drift toward the Segmentum Solar.' She stretched and winced. 'There was a riddle in the margin of one of the dossiers that some old clerk apparently thought was funny. "Rogue Trader Phrax never arrives at Hydraphur, but uncounted Rogue Trader Phraxes have left."'

'I think I follow it, ma'am.'

'Well, do some of the talking then. I'm tired.'

'Well, if each new Rogue Trader Phrax receives the charter of trade at Hydraphur, it means that none of them arrive here with that title. And if they all die away from Hydraphur it means they never return here, the charter does, without them.'

'Well done, although I don't see what's so witty about it myself.'

'It's related to the way the hereditary charter works. There seems to be a different principle in operation to the usual Imperial laws of heredity.'

Calpurnia, who had been leaning against a seat back with her eyes half-closed, fixed Culann with a cool, slightly amused stare.

'You anticipated my advice, then, you've been studying already. Carry on then, proctor. Explain to me how it's different.' Culann managed to catch himself a split-second before he audibly gulped.

'Most offices where the Imperium gives a decree of heredity transfer instantly when the previous holder dies. I know that there's often a ceremony or something to cement the transition in, but not like the one that's going to happen here.'

'Go on.' Calpurnia had leaned forward, and the light made the scar-lines in her face look livid.

'It's a quality of those charters, the grand old charters you mentioned, ma'am. No two of them are alike. We police the way governors issue charters far more strictly now, so they never contain anything too outrageous, and the wildcat warrants the Administratum gives out are churned out by a hundred servo-scribes at a time according to templates laid down by the Adeptus, with a space for a name at the top and a stamped-on seal at the bottom. But the old ones, well, they were tailor-made for whatever circumstances led to a rogue trader being necessary at the time. So there were some that gave the traders power to raise troops and make pacts with the Astartes–'

'Well observed. There are at least two famous families who have pacted with Astartes Chapters.'

'–and some that appointed them as de facto officers of the Ecclesiarchy, like the missionary you described.'

'Not entirely the same thing, but parallel, I suppose,' Calpurnia said. 'I keep interrupting. Go on.'

'And there were some that bound the charters, their bearers I should say, to particular areas of space,' Culann went on, feeling a little more sure of himself. 'Possibly to make sure the new rogue trader remained in the area where his influence and skills were needed, or so one might think. And those clauses in the charters have never been amended or repealed, or at least not in most cases, because the charters were originally drawn up by the war-masters, or sometimes by primarchs or members of the Emperor's court or His crusades. So there's no one senior enough to repeal or amend them, and they don't expire on the bearer's death like most of the new ones do.'

'Hence all the rather disreputable folklore on the subject,' Calpurnia said, 'stories of rogue trader charters being stolen, or sold, or forged, or gambled with, which is a disgusting thought. When a charter can be... but I'm interrupting you again.'

'All I was going to add was that the intent of the succession clause was that this charter can only ever be legally transferred in a ceremony conducted within the boundaries of the Hydraphur system. So no matter where else in the Imperium their interests take them, every generation, the Phrax family have to come back to Hydraphur so that a new rogue trader can be appointed.'

'So they do. Don't feel slighted by this, Culann, but I had Praetor Minoris Zbela search some of the oldest records we have in the Wall as well as your own briefings, tracing the Phrax Charter as far back as it would go. That's a long way, too. This charter is for all intents and purposes an Imperial decree and the Arbites oversaw the actual drafting of it, from what sense I've been able to make of the records. Hydraphur was on the very edge of Imperial space back then, and apparently the intention was to use rogue traders to push forward towards the Rim so that the Crusade itself could travel on to Caliban. That was when the line of Phrax was granted its eternal rogue trader charter, bound to Hydraphur. I suppose that the plan was for a few generations of Phraxes – Phraxae? – to have civilised the fringe domains through trade by the time the Crusade returned ready to take them into the Imperium itself.'

'A Crusade-era document,' Culann said. 'I had seen accounts that mentioned its age, but I didn't think about what that meant until now. Ten thousand years. Imagine what the document will be like to look at! Imagine what it would have been like to be there when it was signed! To see, who? Ma'am, do we have a record of whose hand the charter is signed in? One of the Crusading Saints, or the original Lords Militant? Maybe Lord Marshal Wiertalla, they say he was one of the very founders of the whole order of Arbites!'

'Guess again.'

'Ma'am, I'm not sure I know of too many other names. The stories that survive of those times are so broken up anyway, and I remember even at the schola halls they said there was so much myth mixed in that we can't, I mean, guess…'

'This actually isn't a hard one. I doubted the first accounts I read, for exactly the same reasons you just described. But all the later references to the charter in all the old data-arks that Zbela dug up seemed to point to confirmation, so I'm taking it as true. And who are we to question the received word of our predecessors and betters?'

'I don't follow, ma'am.'

'As I said, Culann, it isn't a hard one. Come at it this way. Think back to all the legends and scriptures and gospels and sagas and paintings and pageants you've ever seen or heard about the Great Crusade. Who's the constant, Culann? If the Crusade was resting in Hydraphur at the time that the very first Rogue Trader Phrax was appointed, then who is the one person we can say for absolute certain would have been there to put their hand out to sign it?'

It only took Culann a moment to think of the name, but that moment another dozen times over to realise that she wasn't joking. He felt the colour drain from his face, and the skin on his shoulders and palms start to tingle.

The change on his face must have been visible.

'That's right, Culann,' Shira Calpurnia said. *'Him.'*

CHAPTER THREE

Shexia System

AT SHEXIA, THE flotilla of Hoyyon Phrax came into port to take on certain supplies, make certain arrangements, purge the old trader's possessions and ceremonially kill his concubines.

Disposing of Hoyyon's not especially large harem was a matter of routine for the flotilla and its acting masters. It had been flotilla custom since time well out of mind to greet a new heir with none of their predecessor-parent's possessions of significance. It had been the custom for almost as long for the Phraxes to take concubines – the first that the flotilla histories officially recorded had founded her harem late in the thirty-second millennium – and if the whole flotilla could be considered to be essentially the personal transport, homestead and entourage of the current Rogue Trader Phrax, as the wording of the charter indicated, then it seemed logical that the members of the flotilla who entered the harem of the trader should go one step further, become literal possessions, and be disposed of as such as part of the funerary routine.

So the thinking went, at any rate, and only the occasional malcontent saw any problems with it. Of course, the practice was seen rather differently by the Imperial citizenry at large, whom the flotilla people referred to as 'tikks' (the origins of that term had been lost to memory, the contemptuous way in which the flotilla people used it had not). The fact that almost every tikk who heard of the custom reacted with shock or disgust irritated the flotilla no end. It was the job of tikks to go about the business of being tikks: having things to buy, or things to sell that other tikks wanted to buy, or coming on board to perform the rare piece of maintenance or repair that the flotilla's considerable resources could not manage. It was not their job to pry into the Phrax family, whose job it was to pursue whatever the charter allowed them to pursue, which was, within a few token limitations that the flotilla observed out of tradition, almost anything. The Emperor Himself had said so, had he not?

While the tikks saw the Emperor as some kind of distant but demanding god, the people of the flotilla tended to view Him as a benevolent former patron, the source of a very valuable signature on a document. That was another little fact that it seemed best to keep to themselves: new inductees to the flotilla's petty-officer class were shown bulkheads near the bridge of the *Bassaan,* the flotilla's flagship, where bolt-shell craters had been left unrepaired as a reminder that one of the few things the Phrax Charter did not grant immunity from was the Imperial Inquisition. Folklore had it that whenever the *Bassaan* broke into the immaterium the fifteen-hundred-year-old bloodstains from that terrible affair would for just a moment become fresh and visible again, but then few such communities are without a story of that sort.

So as they flew among the dust clouds and barely-big-enough-to-be-called-planets that made up most of the

Shexia system, the *Bassaan* and its little formation-mate
the *Callyac's Promise* manoeuvred up side by side. *Bassaan*
was the more powerful ship, home to commanders, officers, brokers and fiduciars, a sleek and elegant
ram-prowed cruiser. The *Promise* was nothing more or less
than a floating palace pushed through space on a tail of
plasma, a fat-nosed little block of hull sporting a cox-
comb of steeples down its back. To some it looked like a
claw, to others a small mammal arching its back and
bristling its fur. It had been the private estate of successive
Phraxes since the thirty-seventh millennium when Olen-
dro Phrax had decided that sharing any of his other ships
with pilgrims (even the fabulously wealthy, ostenta-
tiously pious pilgrims he was doing rather well out of
transporting) was beneath him.

Once the two were flying close enough for the
crewmembers clustered at the high-arched windows to
wave to one another, the shuttles launched, crossing the
tiny distance between the hulls quickly and cleanly,
avoiding the usual bravado and fancy flying as a mark of
respect, their doomed passengers wrapped in shrouds
woven with refractor-wires that created fuzzy shadows
over each stooped form and painted face. They had all
known Phrax was dying – the man's final coma had
lasted for more than a year – and most were resigned.
Only a few were weeping, and only one needed to be
physically helped out of the shuttle and down the corridors into the funeral chamber. The air was quiet and
solemn as for any unpleasant but serious duty – similar,
perhaps, to Marking Day, when all the babies who had
been born in the flotilla over the past year were rounded
up to be presented to the trader and receive a ritual brand
across their stomach.

The armsmen stationed in the hall and chamber made
sure that the whole business went quietly enough. The
elaborate and gruesome ceremonies of earlier generations had been dispensed with, and the concubines knew

their role. None fought, in the end, and after their ashes were fired into space they formed for a while a faint haze over the *Bassaan* before vacuum and momentum dispersed them. And so it was finished.

Or so it was thought at the time. It was not until the flotilla was in orbit over Shexia itself that one of the watch officers of the *Bassaan* realised that the concubine inventory was not correctly notarised by his counterpart on the *Callyac's Promise*, and it took the two of them together more than an hour to realise the document had been doctored rather than just sloppily prepared. Two concubines were unaccounted for, and over a dozen shuttles had travelled between the flotilla ships and down to the planet's spaceport already. Already working out excuses to their superiors in their heads, they began organising a search while the word went up to the flotilla masters that the purging had been botched.

It was not unheard of, of course. Concubines recruited from outside the flotilla had a particular tendency to flout tradition and try to run, although most of the flotilla people did not understand it. Concubines, no matter the gender no matter the age, were always given plenty of time to prepare themselves. Fighting or fleeing seemed ungrateful, not to mention graceless and unprofessional. The flotilla had even dispensed with the old rites of live spacing or slow incineration: the concubines had been sent after their owner with a slender needle of instant-acting neurotoxin, as a mark of compassion. It wasn't as if the flotilla were savages, after all.

Foundry Level, Shexia City, Shexia

'As a mark of *compassion?*' Karmine Mitrani was finding it hard to believe his ears.

'Oh yes.' The young man pacing the catwalk beside him took a deep breath. 'Compared to the old ways, which I think we can both be glad we don't have to think about too much, it's remarkably compassionate. That was what everyone kept saying.' He swallowed hard.

Mitrani didn't say anything more, but walked alongside the man, his features downcast. There was something odd about Flag Ensign Nils Petronas's manner that made Mitrani think that more obvious sympathy or horror might be misplaced.

Karmine Mitrani was an orbit-clerk in the service of the Shexia Dockmasters' Guild, and he was good at his job. He should have been – selective augmetics, deep hypnotic therapy and conditioning for fifteen of his most formative years, and repeated physical and chemical surgery to carefully selected areas of his brain, had hardwired and super-sensitised his social reactions. His sense of mood and nuance was uncanny, his ability to grasp and understand odd customs and adopt them seamlessly was confounding. He could keep up hours of the dry, borderline-abusive banter that the farmship syndicates from the Novanjide sub used to test anyone they planned even the smallest commercial dealings with, or remember every tiniest detail of the family affairs of a fiduciary courier who had last come to the system five years ago, and ask after them in the man's own planetary and continental accent, reproduced so perfectly as to bring his guest to tears of homesickness. He could count on one hand the number of times he had had to deal with people whose ways he truly did not understand.

He was having a little trouble with this.

'That's why we're down here, you see. Two of the damned little dollies ran away. Spat in the face of the rest of the flotilla. Pissed all over the respect the rest of us were showing for the funeral rites for old Hoyyon. So now we have to grub around here to make sure they get what we promised them.' Petronas stepped to the edge of the catwalk and peered over it.

Back when this had been a foundry first and a spaceport second, great mazes of gantries and pipes had spread out from the railheads, becoming higher, denser and more intricate over the centuries until now the whole outlying city was a rat-warren of metal lattices rising high above the basalt, endless jungles of pipes and ladder-shafts and walkways in constant vibration from the pounding of the furnace sublevels and the craft passing overhead.

The two men stood on a viewing platform with a semi-circle of exhaust tubes half ringing like organ pipes, echoing the roar of the machinery deep beneath them and radiating dull heat. The air was close and smelled scorched; the valley's permanent ceiling of black cloud and ash looked low enough to be scraped with the fin-gertips.

After a few more moments of surreptitiously watching the ensign, Mitrani tried again, with a carefully-judged change in tone.

'Are they even worth the trouble? Should you not treat the matter dismissively?' He weighed his words; they were well away from the arclight arrays of the central pyramids, and the perpetual twilight was making Petronas's body language hard to read. 'Perhaps the best punishment,' he went on, 'would be to let them lose themselves in a substreet pit of Shexia?'

'They belong to the flotilla. They are its property, which is to say ours. I've been tasked to make sure they die as they were intended to, and to forfeit three square cen-timetres of skin from the back of each of my hands without numbing-drugs if I have not done so by the time we cast off for Hydraphur. I wouldn't expect a t– I wouldn't expect you to understand.'

Petronas untucked an infrascope from the oversized cuff of his elaborate uniform tunic and scanned the plat-form underneath them again. Mitrani thought he saw a slight tremor in the hand holding the scope that Petronas couldn't quite control. Or maybe it was the heat-haze spoiling the infrared view of the platform that made him grunt with annoyance and stuff the scope crudely away again. Below them were bulky, prowling figures: troopers of the dock watch, loaned to Petronas by Second Dockmaster Paich as a gesture of goodwill to his distinguished clients. When Mitrani had been placed in charge of keeping the flotilla officers happy, he had not seen this coming.

As they stood amid the rumble and the low red light, a pair of prop-carriers passed overhead and by their lights Mitrani saw Petronas scrub a hand over his eyes and face. His shoulders slumped for a moment, and then he gasped in a lungful of the smoky air and snapped himself back to attention when he remembered he was sharing the platform with someone else. In the better light the orbit-clerk got his best look at the ensign's face since they had left the ornithopter: pale dun eyes, lantern jaw, a birthmark curling under one side of the mouth. It wasn't hard to see where the tears from Petronas's eyes had left marks down both his cheeks. Despite the ensign's crude attempts, their tracks were still as clear to read as the cocktail of expressions he was trying to hide. Agonised frustration, grief, and poisonous rage.

During his career Mitrani had encountered behaviour that he understood in a cerebral way but knew he could never fully feel in his guts. He knew about the intensity of emotions within families, and there were times when he had visited client ships and seen families together that made his own feelings ring like a bell, but he himself had been taken from a foundry crèche at five to begin his conditioning and could not imagine what such a life might be like from the inside.

Master Paich liked to amuse himself by locking Mitrani away by himself every so often, where the lack of human company was torture as the clerk's heightened social cognition starved for input. Each of the nights that he wept himself to sleep in an empty room, Mitrani knew it amused Paich to see how much isolation hurt him. But that was not

the same thing as knowing what made such casual cruelty
so appealing. Mitrani had tried to imagine inflicting cruelty
on another person and the thought had revolted him.

So it was easy for him to know what the ensign was
feeling, but Karmine Mitrani was still trying to understand how that meshed with his words when there was a
shout below.

'Hear that?' cried Petronas. 'The lift-platform, they're
trying to get down the shaft! Run, come on! I knew the
little bitches couldn't have gone far!'

The metal lattice under their feet rattled as Petronas
bolted across the platform and down the narrow stairs.
Mitrani, wishing not for the first time that he had not
drawn this assignment, picked up the hem of his ash-coat
and ran after him.

The *Callyac's Promise*, Docking orbit, Shexia

THEY NEVER TALKED about the little vault in the depths of
the *Callyac's Promise* as a conference chamber. The conference chamber was where old Hoyyon had called them
together to wait upon him, the place where all their
advice had to be pitched to his ears, the place where they
all were required to begin every meeting standing in
stylised positions around Phrax's throne so as to reproduce exactly the earliest known painting of a Phrax
delivering orders to his underlings. As the whims of
traders went that had not been the worst, and it had been
bearable while Hoyyon had been younger and lucid and
still full of steel, but as he had aged the conferences had
changed, and not for the better.

So now they met here instead, a little room where the
truth was told between colleagues and equals. None of
the masters brought in their retainers, none attempted
formal greetings or rites. They all understood that the
flotilla required traditions and ceremonies – but occasionally it also required this.

'Have we got the last of them yet?' Halpander asked. He was the flotilla's Master of Logistics, the controller of provisions, loading, unloading, crewing, repairs. Things being out of place bothered him.

'We haven't had the final report yet, but it won't be long,' answered Kyorg. Kyorg controlled the Office of Envoys aboard the *Arrow of Magritta*, supervising diplomacy with whatever authorities the flotilla was required to deal with. Most of the others had a low opinion of him: as rogue trader, Hoyyon had been his own figurehead and first envoy and had left Kyorg with little more than formalities to take care of. With Hoyyon dead, Kyorg had shown little inclination to pick up the slack, and always had a delegate to blame for anything that went wrong. 'I gave Rachen the job of getting authorisation to hunt them down and he said the dockmasters had waved us in and given us a clerk to help it all go smoothly. I think he sent an ensign down to finish it off. I'm sure they've got it in hand.' The others around the circle exchanged glances.

'We must have the full account of the escape documented for punishment and suppression, too. And quickly.' That was the papery voice of Mistress Zanti, skin as white as her tunic and eyes as black as her skirt and shawl. The grey silk scarf over her head showed the outlines of the ridges of data-sockets that covered it from ear to ear. Zanti had the unusual ability to genuinely unnerve most of the flotilla masters: she was as cool, ruthless and unerringly precise in her thoughts as one of the logic engines she presided over. Her craft, the *Kortika*, was the newest of the flotilla, added seventy-eight years before, all from the way she had built up her own agencies and her own turf. Nobody could remember the last time someone had become that powerful in the flotilla through nothing but their own efforts. 'I have not ordered the eidetor-savants to begin the scribing processes yet,' she went on, 'and I will not do so until I can know that they can record that the escapees were brought home and their accomplices punished.' Such a statement in such a tone should have been grossly out of line for someone in Zanti's position, and it was a measure of the force of her personality that the rest of them simply stared at their fingernails or at the table.

'We have managed our affairs for centuries, I think we all know,' put in Galt smoothly after the silence had stretched out for several minutes. 'This is an unfortunate untidiness that will soon be over, and which I am sure we do not need to spend any more time on. Perhaps the charged situation we have found ourselves in since the death of our old trader is persuading us that such setbacks are larger than they are?' Looking around the table, he saw that he had hit on it. They had spent so much time on the minutiae of the escape because no one wanted to come out and say what they knew they were all here for.

Galt had been Hoyyon Phrax's major-domo, his master of chambers. Officially he was probably the least powerful man in the room, even with the fluid, personality-driven way that the flotilla masters measured rank, but in personal terms he had been closer to the old man than any of them. So, he supposed, it came down to him.

'It's time we admitted it,' he said. 'Not all of you may know how strongly the feeling runs, but I have spoken now to every one of you and I know that all of us here feel the same way.'

He watched them look at each other. The masters of the Phrax flotilla were tough and seasoned. They had been in their jobs for decades at the least; many could remember a change of trader, some of them two. Between them they had seen the flotilla through warp-tempests, radiation and meteor storms, excursions into wild space and through Imperial interdicts, pirate ambushes and xenos raids, the attentions of rival rogue traders and rare internal intrigues.

They had even bluffed, connived or deceived, or on one occasion outright assassinated, their way through clashes with Imperial governors, the Adeptus and the Inquisition. But the introverted little microculture of the flotilla could be oddly sensitive about certain things. Like…

'The matter of the succession.' It was no surprise that the voice was that of D'Leste, the man with whom Galt had spent the most time in secret talks. A squat man with the craggy red face of a brewhouse thug and the deft hands of a born surgeon, D'Leste commanded the flotilla's Apothecarion and had been Hoyyon Phrax's personal physician. 'More specifically, the matter of the heir.' There were uncomfortable stirrings around the table, but no one contradicted him. Galt would not have allowed the subject to come up had he not made sure that everyone at the meeting would hear the matter out. But they went one better.

'Phrax the Younger. Varro Phrax.' Behaya's thin, mobile face and reedy voice always made her seem nervous, even when she was simply thinking aloud as now. Her title, according to the old and quaintly-worded flotilla documentation, was 'Supervisor of Pertinent Bodies and Labours'; she was universally addressed by the shorthand title of 'Crewmistress'. 'I suppose we've all had time by now to form an opinion of him.' Behaya had charge of the network of 'friends and correspondents', as the flotilla referred to its spies and informants through the major systems of a dozen sectors. The responsibility had technically been Kyorg's, but he had been outwitted by Behaya and had lost the responsibility to her after he had not displayed the wit or ambition to retain it. By that stage Hoyyon had been entering his final illness and one of the first things Behaya had done with her new powers was to establish a dossier on Varro Phrax. Neither she nor any of the other flotilla masters had liked what they had heard.

'The man's useless,' ventured Trazelli, the flotilla's captain-at-arms , once again voicing the room's opinion.

'I don't remember him as a child the way I suppose some of you do, but let's be honest, we've all read the reports from Behaya's people. The little wastrel's done nothing but drift and spend since he parted ways with his father. No stomach for the role. Oh, I don't doubt he's got a gut hanging to his knees, but no stomach for the role.' That was what passed for humour with Trazelli. The others ignored it.

'I do remember Varro as a child,' said Galt. 'He left the flotilla at ten. His father thought it would do him good to grow up on Gunarvo. There was talk at the time of a major migration into the worlds beyond it in the Deunoff Sub-sector after the second Hadekuro Crusade cleared the orks out. Full Imperial colonisation and reconstruction edicts, very profitable for rogue traders providing we moved in time. Hoyyon wanted to make sure there was a way in for us if we needed it, so he left Varro and his mother there so the boy could grow up making some good contacts.'

'He's wasted his life, then,' snapped Zanti. 'Literally.' One of the things she also handled was the flotilla's contracts and commercial bonds; if anything at all had come of the Deunoff Sub she would have known it.

'Admittedly it's been forty years,' said Galt as though he had not been interrupted, 'but I remember Varro as being a very... *passive* boy. He wasn't short on brain, and he seemed to like pleasing his father, but I watched him carefully and I never saw him with that light in his eyes. Never saw him want to reach out and clutch something and change it.'

'A withdrawn little man, would you say?' asked Halpander.

'Not as a child, no. In fact, I remember him as not being shy in making use of the finer things we provided him with. No qualms about making sure his life was good.'

'Has that changed?' Zanti asked Behaya.

'Not at all,' the crew-mistress answered. 'He and his mother became quite the darlings of Gunarvo, by all accounts. That push into the Deunoff sub never came about, but Gunarvo grew prosperous anyhow. And Hoyyon made sure Varro and his mother were very well set up to begin with – he wanted them sought after so they could get established in the right kind of way. Pity we never got around to going back there, really. We might have made a difference.'

Zanti flicked her hand as though she could physically brush the irrelevant thoughts away.

'So it's out in the open, then, isn't it?' she said. 'We don't want him. We're without a trader and in the shit, because our trader-in-waiting is an indolent little playboy who's going to come on board with favourites he's built up after forty years of being allowed to indulge himself.'

More thoughtful silence.

'We were not always a flotilla,' said Galt, who had often heard Hoyyon talking about this. 'We were a single, small ship. Then we were two, then three, and as the line of Phrax built itself it built us. But how many times have we talked about this? How many of us have not had the dream that our grandchildren or our great-grandchildren will not be masters of a flotilla but of an armada? Other rogue traders have commanded them. Is the Phrax Charter not the equal of any and the superior of most?'

'I know what our charter says,' said Kyorg, as if everyone else didn't. 'It might let us look down our nose at the Imperium, Galt, but it won't let us spit in their eye. Remember those craters on the *Bassaan*? Our trips back to Hydraphur are the one time when we're really under the Adeptus' thumb. We don't get to pick and choose which successions we like and which we don't. The charter says that–'

'Thanks, Kyorg, we follow you,' D'Leste cut him off with little grace. 'We know this is not a good succession. We have had bad successions before. There are sometimes ways around them, but not this time. Varro's not old, so just dropping out of communication for however long it takes him to die and blaming it on a warp storm won't work.'

'We did that?' asked Halpander.

'Succession of Saitiri Phrax from his brother Rukkman, 347.M37,' said Zanti. 'The fleet wasn't able to reach Hydraphur until after Saitiri had passed away. His daughter Mietta succeeded.'

'Letting Varro succeed and simply running him as we run... as we administer the fleet in the temporary absence of a trader is not an option either,' said D'Leste. 'I won't bother with details now, but it's clear from Behaya's reports if you want to read them. He's not the man Hoyyon was, but he's no pliant little custard-brained figurehead, either. He'd fight us if we tried anything. Even if we kept control, the flotilla might not last in any form we recognise.'

'You and Galt seem pretty confident you know your succession problem inside and out,' said Kyorg, giving D'Leste an appraising look. 'If I said "I suppose you have an answer for us too", would I regret it?'

D'Leste's and Galt's eyes met, and the same thought was in both of them. There was no point in dancing around it any longer. D'Leste fingered an amulet at his throat and the room lights dimmed; a holo-cage of tiny wires hissed down from the ceiling to hang in the air and wove a net of light-threads that grew into a picture. A holo-pict of a young man's head, pale dun eyes, a lantern jaw, a birthmark curling under one side of the mouth, the collar of an ensign's tunic just visible where the picture truncated.

'Well then,' said D'Leste, 'I would like to move the discussion on. And so here, my colleagues, is our subject.'

* * *

Foundry level, Shexia City, Shexia

THE ALLEY THEY had found themselves in was a hewsink, which came from 'HW-sink', which came from 'human-waste sink.' The human waste was humans themselves, outcasts whose age or injuries stopped them working in the foundries, and who had so far eluded the Urban Purity Patrols who chased unproductive citizens out into the sewage marshes to die. As the pursuit party stampeded down the narrow space the shadows around them were full of furtive shapes slipping between the pipes and pylons – in a hewsink, if you saw a weapon or a uniform you ran without another thought. As Mitrani gritted his teeth and followed the troopers through the slippery muck underfoot, he could hear scuffles breaking out behind him as the braver outcasts emerged again to fight over food scraps or heat-taps abandoned in the rush.

Underneath the ash and warm mud the alley floor was a bundle of broad pipes with not even a grid laid over them, and Petronas and Mitrani both found themselves slipping and stumbling. The troopers, who had the advantage of cleated boots and experience moving around the lower levels, were pulling ahead of them, and that meant that they were drawing closer to their quarry. Mitrani's guts knotted at the sound of a woman's voice, a young one, sobbing out prayers and pleas ahead of them.

The alley suddenly dipped down into a slope and zigged through a ninety-five degree turn. Their quarry was already through it and the troopers, laughing and calling to one another as though they were on a treasure hunt, rounded it easily. Petronas, just behind them, skated on the ash-mud and clanged into the pipes in front of him, then went down on one knee, cursing, as he tried to pull away from the hot metal and unholster his pistol at the same time. Mitrani, almost piling into him, saw the pistol come out and before he could help himself blurted 'oh no.'

'Oh yes, clerk,' Petronas snarled. His eyes and teeth shone in the ruddy foundry-light. 'Don't think you can do a damn thing to stop this. If you do I'll kill you myself and tell your oily little boss that someone down in the slums had a pistol we didn't expect.'

Ahead of them one of the women was caught, crying out as she kicked armoured shins and bit gauntleted hands. Petronas regained his feet and walked towards her, and the light was bright enough for her to recognise him. Mitrani heard her scream 'Nils! Nils for pity's sake, you of all of them–' and then there was the snap of a las-round and her voice cut off. The troopers, finally starting to be disturbed by the work they were about, let her body slide to the alley floor as the second woman was dragged back.

The trooper who had her in a brutal hammerlock was also a woman, her face grim under the uniform bandanna and ash-goggles as the concubine talked quietly and urgently to her. Finally, when they were alone in a clear spot of mud together and the trooper still had not answered, the prisoner spat full into her face.

'Look at me,' Petronas told her as he walked up to them. Neither woman moved. 'Look at me, Aralye,' Petronas said again, and when she still refused, walked around behind her, put the hellpistol to her head and pulled the trigger. Then he stepped away, faced the alley wall, and stood there for a moment shuddering so violently that the muzzle of the pistol chattered against the gemstone edging of his holster when he tried to put it away. He pulled two heavy plastic parcels from a satchel at his hip, fumbled with them for a moment trying to open them, and then let them drop from his shaking hands and made a curt gesture for the troopers to pick them up and unfurl them.

'Corpse-sacks,' he said to Mitrani. 'Flotilla custom says they have to be burned onboard ship, so we need them easy to carry. Get on with it, we gave you orders!' The last was a bark at the troopers, who were standing and staring at him; after a moment, two of them drew serrated combat knives and knelt down by the first corpse.

'One of them knew you,' Mitrani whispered. 'I heard it in her voice, there was no mistaking it.'

'We knew… each other. She was a friend… of my mother's.' Petronas's voice was dry; he had to gulp and lick his lips before he finished each sentence.

'Then *why*?' Mitrani was almost screaming, all thoughts of service and diplomacy forgotten. He had never, never seen anything like this. 'Why did you kill them? Why hack them limb from limb? Nobody would have known! Why didn't you help them?'

Suddenly Mitrani was half-sitting on the warm ash-slurry, blinking at the way his mouth suddenly felt wet and stung. He had never been punched before. Petronas stood over him for a moment, then crouched down to glare into the shaking clerk's eyes.

'Because the third of the women to walk into that chamber aboard the *Bassaan* was my mother. Do you understand that? My mother. Walking in there with her head high. And there was nothing I could have ever done to help *her*. So if I have to lose my mother because that old bastard saw fit to finally die, well then no one else, *no one* else is going to go running away from their duty. Do you understand?'

He stood up and turned away, shouting at the troopers again, and Mitrani rolled over, scrabbled away on hands and knees and vomited again and again as from behind him came the sound of knives sawing into flesh.

The Flotilla of Rogue Trader Phrax, Docking orbit, Shexia

'DO YOU THINK he'll do it?' Galt asked D'Leste as they walked away from the meeting room. They both understood what the question was. Galt was asking if their subject would manage the deception. The question of whether he would decide to co-operate with them would have puzzled both men. What the subject thought he might decide to do was irrelevant. But D'Leste was not going to be drawn.

'It's something to try,' he said, as he always said when he was unsure of whether the thing to be tried was going to succeed. The look they exchanged said all that was needed: a select circle of pragmatic people had considered their position and taken the only option they felt they had. What else to say?

As the ships began to vibrate with the power of the plasma coils and vox-hails flew from ship to ship and from ship to dock, they went to their posts. Halpander stood on a platinum pedestal surrounded by a holo-sheet of green crystal on which fiscal and logistical algorithms flashed and swam butterfly-quick – it was traditional for the Master of Logistics to begin every voyage surrounded by the signs of his post. Zanti's spindly frame settled into a deep-cushioned linkage niche as the ports on her skull spoke to the ship's logisters and sent transmissions sleeting through her skull like chilly white lightning. D'Leste, no longer needed on the household decks of the *Callyac's Promise*, retreated to his chamber and began planning his letter to Magos Dyobann. He knew that the Mechanicus cabal would be on the flotilla's side, but the magos would be insulted were he to simply assume it. Certain formalities had to be followed.

Galt was left on the *Promise*, the only one of the conspirators with no traditional or required place to be, but there was one thing he thought it fitting he should do. And so he walked down the ramp from the speaking room, weaving slightly every so often or adjusting his gait without conscious thought as the ship's gravity didn't quite cancel out the ship's manoeuvres. As the flotilla powered away from Shexia and out to where they would break warp, Galt walked down the long promenade that ran down the spine of the ship, connecting the base of each of its spires with a tunnel of crystal-clear armour-glass reinforced with rows of carved rockrete arches like ribs.

In the heart of the tallest spire he sat on a stool of pink and grey marble while thrumming augmetic drones analysed his scent, gene-print, walk, breathing patterns, brainwaves. When they were satisfied they flew ahead of him down a hall of chilly, unadorned steel and spat the blood and breath samples they had taken into the eyes and mouth of an intricate gargoyle embedded in the hall's far wall. The trial was passed, the terrible devices in the walls spared Galt's life. There was a hiss as parts machined to near-miraculous tolerances slid over one another and then one of the steel walls was gone.

Galt walked forward to stand on a little square of black steel on a floor polished to mirror-brightness. In a steady voice he began reciting each of the oaths of loyalty he had taken to the line of Phrax, begun on his tenth birthday and added to in each of the twelve decades since then. He found himself wondering, as he spoke each ritualised line, whether his doubts were showing in his voice, whether the listening machines were capable of deciding that what they were planning to do would trample on those oaths. But if there was anything to show in his voice, the machines did not hear or did not understand. The automata at the far end of the room, patterned after great men and women of the First Crusade whose names no one now remembered, bowed in unison and said his name in flat voices. There was a crack of power as the void-shield lowered and then the final wall parted like a curtain. And after so many trials and barriers the space beyond it was comically simple: a little metal nook with a table sitting under a bank of polished glass.

Galt knew the stories and the rumours, and knew they were stupid. No dire curse-runes, no pages of human skin or ridiculous incantations to appease dead spirits. It was a small, plain parcel of cloth cover and creamy paper, the writing across each page the regular, even hand of a competent scribe. What ornamentation imaginable by a human mind could go a hundredth of the way to doing justice to what was inside?

The book was held in a neutral gas formulated to prevent the material from ever decaying; the stasis field that filled the room whenever there were no visitors made sure of it. It had acquired scuffs and creases in its days as a working document, but it would acquire no more. Fine wires rested between the pages and in theory the machine could turn the book to whatever clause a reader needed to look at. Galt could not remember it ever being used. The flotilla had plenty of transcripts and copies to use day to day, the masters knew the whole document to the letter. There was only one thing worth coming into the chamber to see. Galt crouched down and looked at the last page of the book, the expanse of stiff paper untouched but for three marks.

At the top of the page, in an antiquated hand that made the letters barely recognisable, the signature of Beleusa Phrax. And below it…

…below it, a single letter, written down the dead centre of the page with five beautiful, elegant strokes of a nib: a cross-slashed letter *I*.

And below that, a little mark, a smudge, a dot on the page. Looking at it, as always, Galt seemed to feel the air shudder around him, growing close and thick as though before a storm.

He stayed there for nearly an hour, crouched before the case that held the Phrax Charter, staring with meditative intensity at the page and the twofold mark that signed it: the *I* of *Imperator* and the single pressed-in drop of blood.

CHAPTER FOUR

The Phrax Manor, Asterine Lock, Gunarvo

VARRO PHRAX DIDN'T seem to want to talk about business, but Domasa Dorel found that less irritating than she had expected. That morning she had risen early and taken an hour longer than she usually did to go through her physical and mental exercises. And if all else failed she had brought a little flask of sweet-perfumed liqueur concealed in the fold of her mantle, a sip of which she knew would relax her if she needed it. But she had been lucky: the visit to Varro's estates had been exactly the diversion she needed after nineteen dolorous months as a junior Navigator with an Adeptus Ministorum pilgrim fleet, surrounded by pious mutant-haters who refused all contact with her whenever they could and kept staring at the bulge on her forehead and making the sign of the aquila when they couldn't. Varro seemed barely to have given her genes a second thought, and his home offered far more diversion than the cramped cell aboard the *Song of Righteousness*.

The giant enclosed garden they were strolling through now, fully half again the size of the manor itself, was a case in point, even if some of its diversions were more than a little unnerving to a spacefarer unused to wildlife.

'Now this,' Varro said, 'this is the sort of thing that the charter will be very handy for indeed. Take a look here.'

'I see a very interesting stretch of churned earth between two large, rather dull trees,' Domasa replied. She was confident enough now to make wisecracks; something about Varro tended to put people at their ease. He laughed delightedly and pushed a hank of hair out of his eyes.

'Just earth now, Domasa. But here's the thing. The Emerald tripleaf – that's those two plants on either side of it – they're very social plants. They try to co-operate when they sense another growing nearby. They produce waste as a result of metabolising their prey – you remember the picts I showed you of them in their native system? – and they pump that away through their roots. Careful!' Cherrick, one of Domasa's entourage, had stepped closer to look at the tripleaf. 'See how the leaves are quivering? That's how the higher-order mammals on Stavron know to back off. You saw the way they lunge on the picts.' Domasa shook a playful finger at Cherrick, and he went red under his visor and made fists as Varro waved at the empty ground. 'So they've spotted the empty ground and they're pumping out the exhausted haematic fluids they can't use, and guess what the Tygranese pufferfruit uses?'

'Uses as in eats? Hmm, could it be the kinds of, er, things found in exhausted haematic fluid from the, er…'

'Emerald tripleaf?'

'Of course, there's no way I could have guessed that.'

Varro was laughing again.

'The pufferfruit are amazing. I've only seen one myself apart from in picts, a tiny little one in a glass bell in a botanical exhibition on Lynia three years ago. Then last month I paid through the nose for an original copy of

Euseby Riva's book on Tygranese plant life, and you should see the size they can grow to. There are all sorts of edicts about what flora you can transport to where, of course, and the Imperial mercantile controls are pretty strict. One of my best agents in the Kozya sub has told me that he won't be able to send me specimens any more, because the whole quarter has been closed off by some kind of quarantine. But with the family charter, you see, well, what's the limit on what I can do?' He grinned at Domasa and clapped his hands.

'Almost ready!' called Rikah from behind them, making Domasa jump. Rikah was one of Varro's close retainers, tending to the same sort of uncritical jolly humour as his master. The sides of his head had been implanted with vox-receivers, the receptor vanes incorporated into ornamental frills that ran from his face around to the nape of his neck. Domasa thought them tacky beyond words, but Rikah was obviously tremendously proud of them – he had confided to her that when Varro had the charter he was hoping someone on the flotilla would put in augmetic muscles that would let him flex the frills up and down. Domasa had smiled politely while she doubled over with laughter inside.

'Hear that? We really should get going. Do you all have your cards? Have you all given your picks in? Everyone?' Varro looked past Domasa to her retinue, who were unused to being directly involved with their mistress's conversations and shuffled nervously. 'Dreyder's been after me to organise another of these for months, we can't let it start late. All ready to go up to the gallery? Rikah, let them know to bring some more drinks to the gallery, will you? Kolentin knows what we like.'

The twisting skyways that ran this way and that through Varro Phrax's rambling garden of horrors were not directly reachable from the ground, and they had to wait for one of the little platforms to come rattling down on its silver chains before they could be winched up to the nearest one. Gripping the railing to steady herself, Domasa finally took an opportunity to talk business.

'Varro, we're going to need to talk about the charter at some point.'

'I'm looking forward to it,' he cut in. 'I know it probably looks like I've been dodging my responsibilities here, you know. When I lived on the flotilla they made sure I knew every day that I was going to grow up to be Rogue Trader Varro Phrax.'

'Good. But–'

'I don't take it lightly. But don't you think I deserved a breathing space before I take it up? I think it will make me a better trader, don't you? Living in that weird flotilla, I can't see how that makes you a rounded person. Wealth for its own sake, I mean, it's stupid. I think I should use those resources *for* something. Do you have a garden, Domasa?' She shook her head and went on quickly before he could start up again.

'I know you're excited about the possibilities it gives you for all this,' and she swept a hand out over the garden, 'but I'm worried that you're making too many plans too soon. I'll be honest with you, Varro, you're going to have to give some more serious thought to your succession.' This was the kind of conversation she was used to having in sealed rooms that had been swept for auspexes and spy-flies, wrapped in privacy fields with an astropathic choir drowning them out to any scrying or spellcraft. But she was proud of her adaptability.

'The trip to Hydraphur, do you mean? I don't believe there will be any problem with getting there in time. Anyway, the ceremony can't start without me, can it?' Varro stepped onto the elevated gallery-path that snaked through the garden and held out his hand. After a moment's surprise she took it and was impressed when he didn't flinch: like most of the Navis Nobilite her physique was skewed in more ways than just the warp eye in her forehead – her hands had only three long fingers each. It was the only oddity of her appearance she was really self-conscious about – the others were all invisible under her gowns and robes, and most other Navigators didn't care about them.

'No, the trip wasn't what I meant,' she said, looking around. Like all of Gunarvo's trading gentry, Varro kept a manor embedded in the ravine wall over the Asterine Lock and it loomed over them now. But his garden ran on over kilometres of canal-bank, an ungainly range of arboretae and ribbed domes on the outside, a lush mass of plant life on the inside, all of it hostile. Further on there were domes of elaborately engineered climates for dangerous flora from the more exotic worlds which she was hoping to avoid seeing; walking the elevated paths over the predatory greenery in the main gardens was more than enough for her.

Now some of the plants below were starting to quiver as the gardeners began to stimulate their attack responses with scent-puffs, electromagnetic shadows, tiny patterns of vibration on the ground. The tripleaf thicket they had walked past was shivering, the edges of the plate-sized leaves hitting against each other with a faint chinking sound.

'The laws, then? I don't imagine that dealing with the Arbites will be a problem. Nobody told me it would. Rikah, is everyone ready? Is Dreyder ready?'

'He's bounding about like a puppy, Varro. He's been sprinting in and out of the garden for the last two hours. He's told everyone he's scouting for the runners, he's been taking them little tips and reports. They're playing along. He's fine.'

'You let him run in and out of the garden like that?' Domasa asked, curiosity getting the better of her annoyance. The dynamics of Navigator families were very different to those of mainstream humanity, and sentimentality towards children was something she didn't begin to understand, but she found it interesting nevertheless.

'Dreyder's seven,' Varro told her, 'and that's more than old enough to know his way around the south wing. The plants there are all passive hunters, so he's in no danger if he keeps clear of them. The gardeners won't let him anywhere he might be in over his head. He'll own this garden one day, remember. He needs to start young! I was twenty before I discovered predator-plants.'

'Speaking of inheriting, though, Varro…'

'Yes, the Arbites. I looked at the last succession when father got the charter. There was some kind of ceremony with a general.'

'Arbitor General Actte.'

'That sounds right. Have we written to him?' They stepped aboard a little viewing-carriage, barely more than a flat platform, designed to skim along right at the edge of the gallery. It glided toward the southern end of the garden; the viewing levels were all packed with chattering spectators and drums were beating.

'He's no longer on Hydraphur. Arbites change more often than rogue traders do. There are four Arbites General commanding on Hydraphur now. One Majore, three Senioris. But no, the problem isn't with them.'

'I see.' Varro was waving to a slender woman in yellow who was carrying a squirming little boy through the throng. 'Ksana! Here, come up on the car with us.' Ksana and Domasa exchanged cool looks – she did not have her husband's expansive nature, and had kept at arm's length from the Navigator ever since her arrival. The boy Dreyder paid no attention to her, although when he had first seen her he had cried and complained about the 'cold ice lady'. Domasa had shrugged and avoided him as much as she could after that. Being around Navigators affected people in different ways, that was all.

Watching them now, Varro bent over the boy exclaiming over his accounts of the 'scouting' he had done, Ksana smiling at them both and adding details that Dreyder was too excited for, Domasa decided that she wasn't going to be able to get the man to concentrate on business matters any time soon. She looked down into the garden again.

Ten athletes, eight men and two women, had emerged from the staging-rooms and stood in a rough line while the starter capered up and down before them: his glittering suit included suspensors just powerful enough to let him dance on his toes and turn oddly slow-motion back-flips. The racers' hair had been dyed to match the clinging gymnastic uniforms they wore, brief and glossy affairs that finished just short of elbows and knees. They jogged on the spot, ready for the signal.

Domasa idly wondered how many variations of this were being played out today across the Imperium. Navigators tended to quickly acquire rather jaded palates for entertainment, and Domasa liked to pay attention to how the connoisseurs amused themselves wherever she went. Wearyingly often, 'elite entertainment' boiled down to cheering people on while they tried to kill each other. But apparently these people were volunteers, and the race was only through those parts of the garden that would be challenging rather than deadly.

The runners got a round of applause, and Dreyder got another one when he was hoisted on his father's shoulders to give the signal. Domasa slipped her pick-card out of her sleeve. Not knowing anything about any of the runners she'd chosen orange and black, the closest to the russet-and-black robes of House Dorel. Orange was a thick-necked man with a great shock of hair and skin the shade of creamy caffeine that rather clashed with his running colours, and black was a slender, snake-hipped young man who was finishing off his pre-race stretches with some poses that had moved several of the female spectators to thoughtful silence.

Domasa had come prepared to bet extravagantly – normally that was the way to a host's good books on occasions like this. She had been a little surprised to find that it wasn't expected. All she was supposed to do was give a small token if one of them finished. Well, she was equipped for that, too. Another old trick was to bring arrays of flashy but basically expendable jewellery and trinkets to meetings like this, to be given away as presents if that looked like it was going to make things easier. Domasa's appreciation for physical beauty had been stunted by a life spent among Navigators, whose appearances tended to range from odd to grotesque, but as she watched the runner in black finish off his exercises she found herself thinking that perhaps getting up close to him to hang a gem-thread around his neck might not be such an ordeal.

Then Dreyder suddenly threw both of his arms in the air and screamed 'GO!' The drums gave one almighty beat and Domasa grabbed the railing as the car surged forward to keep pace with the runners.

IT WAS HALF an hour before they all came back down the gallery, the younger spectators trotting ahead and laughing, the more sedate ones walking behind with drinks in their hands. Varro's little son was with the six runners who'd finished, riding on the shoulders of the tallest, kicking his heels and crowing. Domasa walked a little behind the slowest of them, keeping a stately gait, hands shrouded in her long sleeves and tucked demurely at her back. When Cherrick met her the disgust in his face was the first thing she saw – she shot him a warning look and he had the wit to keep his voice low when he finally fell in alongside her.

'No fatalities! What the hell was everybody supposed to be betting on? What sort of nursery school have we fallen into the middle of, lady? What next, are we going to take turns making each other flower-chains?'

'No, no fatalities. I made the mistake of talking to our host as though there were going to be and he gave me this look and said "I'm not a savage, you know." But it was diverting enough and it's put our host in great good spirits and therefore I will *not* hear you take that tone again while we are here and in earshot of anyone, Cherrick, you or anyone on your team. I don't care what the provocation, there's a flogging in it for you the next time at the very least.' Despite the venom in her words she had kept her tone light and conversational: anyone standing over a couple of metres away would have thought she was sharing an exciting moment from the race.

'In fact, just to make a point about diplomacy and to make sure we stay at the front of our host's mind, I believe I'll take you with me to meet the runners. Paste on a smile for me, now.' A smile seemed to be beyond Cherrick – he made do with cordial nods to the people they passed, while Domasa silently wished she'd been born with too many fingers instead of too few, so it would be easier to count the days until she could start a new assignment on which he would not be tagging along.

Although Varro's physicians were waiting back at the starting line, none of the runners had been seriously injured. The woman in green had welts running across her thighs and shins from the stinging tendrils of a lasher plant she'd been too slow to hurdle, and cords stood out on her neck as a nurse plucked out the little thorn splinters and squirted on a sterilising mist. The man with the dazzling silver suit and hair had misjudged the reach of a scissorleaf creeper, and a quick shoot had caught his ankle. Once the rest of the field had passed him the gardeners had gone in to help, but by that time the horn-plated leaves had succeeded in twisting his foot to a nasty angle – he now sat and stoically watched as the swollen joint was bound up.

Over by the garden door itself the lithe young man in black whose card Domasa had drawn was sitting on a bench surrounded by nurses and well-wishers, all female. Domasa had missed whatever it was that had happened to him but it didn't seem all that serious. On the other side of the gate the wounds on the finishers were being tended to – the winner, the man in blue, was the only one unscathed.

Varro and his wife and son were sitting around the last of the non-finishers, a man in early middle age, stocky and sallow, dressed in bright white and riding out the last of the jitters from the stingmoss juice that still stained his hands and bare feet. As they came off the bridge over the garden's central pond the runners had had to run holding their breath for about half a minute through a cloud of soporific pollen. The runner in white was the only one to have misjudged and taken a breath, which had sent him staggering over the stingmoss to fall to his hands and knees. Dreyder sat cross-legged in front of him and watched with huge eyes as the man's legs and arms jumped and shivered. For some reason the movements reminded Domasa of the shivering of the tripleaf when they had gone too close to it.

'Domasa!' Varro called as they drew near. 'I was wondering where you were! I hope you enjoyed the race. These people are quite something to see, eh? Aetho here is one of the trainers at the Whitroc Citadel up on the Escarpine Lock, where they train the PDF officers.' Varro shot a grin at the twitching Aetho, whose answering smile was a little strained. 'I'm sorry your corps colleagues had to keep pace on foot. Hopefully we'll be able to arrange a spectators' car for them if you're here for the next meet.' Varro caught himself and laughed. 'What am I saying? We've got a voyage ahead of us, haven't we? Ridiculous of me.'

Instead of agreeing, Domasa gave Aetho a regal nod.

'Your race certainly made an impression on Cherrick, my head of entourage,' she said. 'He claims never to have seen anything like it.' Both statements were technically true, she thought, wondering what Cherrick's face looked like at this moment. 'Varro, the part of the classic business-obsessed, world-hopping trade envoy is one I hate to play at a...' she blinked as the stung woman behind them let out a pained yelp '...happy occasion like this, but I really would like to continue the conversation we were having before the race. There are things you need to be thinking about.'

Varro nodded earnestly and gave Aetho a reassuring clap on the shoulder.

'Perhaps Cherrick can wait here and go over the finer points of the garden race with Aetho?' Domasa suggested sweetly, steering Varro away from the other guests with no particular subtlety.

'Will you navigate my ship?' Varro suddenly asked, catching her by surprise.

'I... no. No, I'm far too junior for the responsibility of a voyage as important as this.' She'd made herself sound like a bloody novice, too, which hadn't been her intention, but if playing the helpless-junior card was the way to keep Varro's guard down, then fine. 'I'm here for *you*, Varro, to help and advise you and to make sure that my family helps you too. You've got three whole Houses of the Navis Nobilite and their allies and friends looking after you, Varro. Don't you go doubting your ship will have the keenest eye we can provide.'

'Three Houses? I thought you said it was just yourself and some associates.' Varro was looking back to see what his son was doing, and Domasa ransacked her memory for anything she might have said that she couldn't contradict now. She had only had a few hours' notice of her change of assignment, and she had been too taken up with skipping out on the pilgrim-hauler and actually getting here to be able to concentrate on her story.

'There are a lot of people who want to see this charter pass smoothly from hand to hand, Varro,' she said before he could notice her concentration. 'My own family as well as the Krassimal and Yimora. I won't pretend that we are great Houses in the scheme of things, certainly not with lineages like yours, but we are working hard on your behalf to–'

'Really?' She had his full attention now. Varro wasn't stupid, she reminded herself, however he might appear.

'What needs doing on my behalf, exactly? I had assumed that a little thing like ten millennia of tradition would be enough.'

Domasa's family had been founded before anyone named Phrax had even heard of a charter and had survived the toxic politics of the Navis Nobilite by never, ever assuming anything. Oh, Varro was a puppy alright. But puppies could be trained, provided you didn't get too sentimental about them. Now, how to word this...

'The spacefaring class is one of the oldest in the Imperium,' she said after a pause. 'The Navigators, the rogue traders, the officer classes of the Imperial Navy and the explorators and others. The regrettably spreading habit of granting low-level charters and so-called "wildcat warrants" is creating a callow breed who don't really grasp the ventures they're taking on, but I believe the core of the Imperium's essential travelling aristocracy remains. We remain because we... understand things. We have values like tradition. Continuity. Order. We believe that there is a way of doing things.' She was quoting from one of her uncle's lessons, back in her days in the Segmentum Solar when he had been her tutor. 'The inheritance of the charter is important to us just because of those values, as a point of principle. You want it to pass to you at Hydraphur, and of course you are fully entitled to do so, and so that is why we are on your side. My family and my associates and I.'

Varro was staring at her. Behind them there were cheers and shouts: the second stage of the entertainment had begun, with acrobats leaping and swinging and vaulting around and over spiny cacti and thorn trees. Coloured paper lanterns were appearing overhead, strung from tiny wires, and the drumming was back: a light, fast beat that the guests could clap to. Domasa and Varro walked deeper into the garden again, where the light was dimmer. When they reached the point where the plants were starting to rustle at their approach, Varro stopped and turned to Domasa again.

'I'm not completely naïve, you know,' he said. 'I am a member of the Gunarvo Mercantile Chamber and I'm a rogue trader-in-waiting, too. You've told me that yourself enough times, Emperor knows. So come on. You've been so frantic to talk business to me all night and now you won't get it out. What aren't you telling me?'

There was a cry behind them as an acrobat did something amazing. Or maybe fell on his face and died. Domasa didn't care. She was watching the look on Varro's face.

'There's been a counter-claim.'

Varro blinked once, twice, then stared back at the party. Domasa looked the other way, less trusting than Varro of what the assortment – five hundred and sixty-eight species, he had boasted – of carnivorous greenery was doing.

'Impossible,' he said, finally.

'If you think so,' Domasa replied, 'you only have to wait a day or so until the message reaches you. It's an Adeptus communiqué, authenticated by the Arbites command precinct on Hydraphur. The flotilla will go before whoever the Arbites have appointed to oversee this thing, as they're supposed to. But what they're going to do then is announce that there's someone with a better claim on the charter than you who should become the new Rogue Trader Phrax instead.'

'Impossible.' Varro's voice was not angry, just disbelieving. 'How idiotic do these people have to be to think that someone else can walk in and have the charter handed to them? The Arbites supervise the succession to stop exactly that.'

'The charter stays in the Phrax family, Varro. That's all. What do you think happens when more than one heir contests the succession? That was why the Arbites were written in. If there's more than one viable heir the ruling between claimants is theirs.'

'Yes. Well, maybe that's so. I never really paid much attention to how the succession would work with more

than one heir, Domasa, because I am the *sole* heir. The
one and only.' Varro's voice had risen enough to set a
nearby Kendran feather-tree groaning as it tried to spit
still-unripe spores in the direction of the noise. Domasa
shot a warning look over at the party, and Varro took a
deep breath while he got his equilibrium back.

Finally, Domasa spoke: 'Sole heir you might have been,
Varro, but you're going to have to change your thinking.
You're going to have to get a lot less comfortable about
the idea of just putting your hand out and taking the
charter. Now I'm going to say this again. Some very powerful people believe you are the rightful heir whose claim
must be protected. They found out about this communiqué and they arranged for me to see you, to let you
know that we're on your side and to make sure you're
ready for your voyage. You're going to be facing a challenge from Hoyyon's other son. Your half-brother.
Petronas Phrax.'

CHAPTER FIVE

The Flotilla of Hoyyon Phrax,
Deep Space outside the Antozir Proxima system

THERE HAD BEEN chop and eddy in the immaterium on the long, looping route from Shexia towards Hydraphur. Not enough to be dangerous, but the flotilla masters were grim about taking any chances at all, so at the great empty shell of Antozir Proxima with its beautiful, sterile garlands of gas clouds, the flotilla broke warp and rested. As always, the vox-traffic danced between the ships as they drew in and coasted through Antozir's fringes; the occasional shuttle, too, as those with errands or cargo that couldn't wait to move between vessels took advantage of the freedom of real space.

Two teams of cooks and slaughtermen had come over to the *Bassaan* from the *Proserpina Dawn* with a shuttle-hold full of fattened verdikine from the sprawling pastoral decks, to be slaughtered in the *Bassaan's* own kitchens. Eight of those cooks had visited the *Bassaan* for

a single day just before the flotilla broke warp on the outskirts of Shexia, and that made them the targets of Flag
Ensign Nils Petronas, who waited hidden in the shadows
in the flagship's vast galley with vomit down the front of
his uniform coat and his right fist taped shut around the
grip of a punch-dagger.

Two hours ago he had haltingly, blearily looked over
the weapons rack in his stateroom and decided that he
was too sick to reliably use a gun, and he had nearly lost
his balance when he took a test swing of his rank-cutlass.
The dagger was the least risky, the hardest to miss with.
Petronas could tell his vision was beginning to blur, so he
probably would not have been able to see to use a pistol
anyway.

It had started within hours of the dinner for two dozen
or so flotilla personnel, all about Petronas's age and
including several of his friends, hosted by Petty Officer
Intendant Gensh.

Gensh, the vain little poisoning bastard with the little
blond beard he was so damned proud of. Petronas
squeezed the dagger grip until his hand tingled. He could
hear the man's voice in his head, wet and smug as though
he were gargling his words through cream.

'Why've I invited you all here?' he'd asked. 'Isn't it obvious?' No, a couple of voices had answered. Few of them
knew Gensh personally. 'Meetings like this are a new direc-
tive from the masters of the flotilla, Crew-mistress Behaya
is enthused by the idea.' Rubbish, they had agreed later as
they ate. The fact would have been better known. 'The
flotilla goes to meet its new trader,' Gensh had said, 'and
Emperor bless Trader Varro! This is a time to come together
as crewmates and brothers and sisters,' he had said, sloshing drink. 'We shall make sure that every soul on this fleet
knows he is part of a brotherhood, a united crew...'

That was what had struck Petronas as the lie, although
he didn't think at the time that Gensh knew it was a lie.
And all the stirring, wine-fuelled talk of the golden days

of Trader Varro soon to dawn only served to keep his mother's face hanging in the front of his mind. He hadn't dared let his anger out at the dinner, but walking back to his quarters afterwards he had found a pair of deckhands he didn't know and roared that they had been looking at him insubordinately. His friends had held one of them back while Petronas had torn into the other, and he had finally returned to his room with his knuckles raw and bleeding and his head ringing with exhaustion. There was none of the beautiful calm he normally felt after finishing an evening that way, but with the state his thoughts had been in since the alley on Shexia a night of dreamless sleep had been reward enough.

The verdikine meat in the pot flared and the cooks laughed and clapped at the bursts of yellow flame. Petronas started shuffling between the two slop-chutes, but his knees folded and the dagger point squealed against the chutes as he toppled over. He lay slumped in the cramped space, feeling his stomach roil – the last of the food had come up two hours ago, but he had still been bringing up bile every few minutes. His eyes felt like coals, and no matter how many times he squeezed them shut or worked the eyelids with his fingers he could not get them to water and give him some relief.

Waking up like this, he had known straight away Gensh was responsible. When he had lurched out of his bed, throat bubbly with vomit, he had realised even through the cramps in his gut and the spike that twisted behind his eyes that it had been deliberate. Rengill, Rengill his dear friend since the days they had played along the ornamented garden-decks of the *Callyac's Promise*, who had sat beside him at Gensh's dinner, was sprawled in the doorway of her own stateroom, convulsing. Her own mouth and chin were smeared with bile, but it was mixed with blood and mucus, and as Petronas had staggered toward her blood began to drip from her nostrils and ears as well.

Beyond her, Lead Ensign Omya sagged against a wall and wept from the pain that was doubling him over as pretty, dark-haired Atith tried to help him move. Omya had sat opposite Petronas and argued with him about the merits of the wines, and had helped hold the unlucky deckhand's friend back while Petronas had worked off his anger afterwards. And behind Atith, a sprawled shape that Petronas barely recognised as Nimmond, against whom he had boxed until they both collapsed from exhaustion and with whom he had learned the strange lilting Low Gothic dialect they spoke on Spaeter Relixas so they could read the stirring warrior-poems of its militant priests. They had even given a recitation at the dinner, clanging their pewter wine-cups together as they roared out the verses. He recognised Nimmond by the swept-back way he wore his long hair and the broad gold belt he had won for his gunnery – he would not have recognised the young man's distorted face, bloody where muscle had torn the skin apart and twisted itself free of the bone.

His surroundings now matched those grim memories, as bloodied scraps and bone were dumped into the chutes with clamour and echoes from the metal walls. The racket shook Petronas back out of semi-consciousness and gave him enough energy to drag himself to his feet. His balance was still bad, though, and he could not stop his forward lurch. But the interruption had been timely, because ahead of him, walking around the seasoning tubs, was the moustachioed senior steward who had served them their dinner. Their poisoned dinner.

Petronas erupted from his niche in a wild-eyed run, the kitchen crew yelping and scattering out of his way. In the hot fog of his vision the steward turned, his eyes widened and he scrambled backward. The point of the punch-dagger caught in his tunic but only made a shallow gash from hip to shoulder. He howled and grappled at Petronas's arm as the ensign made graceless stabs at his face and eyes.

Petronas heard a voice, cracked and crazed, screaming over and over again and when he saw the man's mouth move in reply he realised it was his own. When he stopped to suck in a tortured breath he had a chance to realise that he had been shouting, 'Your life for Gensh! Your life for Gensh!' over and over.

The steward, groaning, hit the side of a tall carving-block and slid down it as a sudden burst of hot, liquid pain in his abdomen made Petronas double over with a cry and go down on one knee. When it slackened again he spiked the point of the dagger into the floor to steady himself and looked the steward in the eye.

'Gensh… Officer Gensh… I can take you to him! We didn't know! We didn't know! Please! I bear you no ill-will, sir, you know that! I was *pleased* for you, I was happy that such a fine young man…' the steward gulped and clutched at the wound across his torso, 'such a fine officer had been invited…'

'You poisoned me.' Petronas knew his words were coming out slurred, but there was no time to slow down to try and talk properly. So many of them must have been involved, there were so many of them to track and find. 'You all did. Rengill and poor Nimmond. Why Nimmond? Who poisoned…'

'No, no, not we! Food and celebration are our, our, *calling*!' The steward was gabbling, his hands held out. Dimly, Petronas realised why no one was coming near them: to the ones who knew no better he was carrying the marks of disease. Better to let him stab a colleague than get close and risk the flotilla's ruthless internal quarantines. He drew his arm back and the steward screamed.

'No! We were driven out of the kitchen, the red-robed man, that was him! He never eats! The red-robed man and the trader's doctor! They came in with staff and–'

Petronas let his weight drop forward and aimed the dagger carefully at the steward's eye. It went in true; the man shivered and died. After a moment slumped against the corpse Petronas pushed himself back and staggered upright to look at a grey-uniformed blur in the centre of his melting, throbbing vision.

'Gensh.' For a moment Petronas was thankful almost to the point of prayer that his nemesis had been miraculously placed here for him. But he was confused. There were more? The trader's doctor, D'Leste, an ugly man Petronas had only seen once or twice, and the red-robed man who never ate, that, that had to be... Suddenly Petronas saw everything clearly.

'Here's the last one. Light of Terra save us all, but look at what he's done! It's a good thing we got to you, Petronas. When we heard you'd gone over the edge we feared the worst.' The blur that was Gensh turned to the indistinct masses behind it. 'Get him down and restrained, and get that grox-sticker off his hand. We're lucky we were vigilant, it looks like he only got one.'

The thing about the punch-dagger was this: Petronas already knew that he could kill with a simple forward fall to put his weight behind it. He tottered a step, then another, then as someone started to say, 'It's alright, sir' he let his final collapse pull his arm forward and heard the shocked whoosh of air out of Gensh as his weight bore them both over in a cascade of cries and shouts from around them.

'Two,' Petronas gurgled contentedly into Gensh's face. And although he felt strong hands gripping his arms and hair, he was deep in unconsciousness and never felt them dragging him clear of the dying officer's body.

Private Offices of Shira Calpurnia, The Wall, Hydraphur

'SO WHAT THE hell is this about a counter-claim?'

Normally the briefing conferences of the senior Adeptus Arbites followed a detailed and traditional protocol, which was why when Shira Calpurnia needed to get quickly to the pith of an issue she held a less formal and more forthright meeting somewhere away from the meeting-vaults around the Arbitor Majore's tower. The Arbites who made good use of the freer, blunter-spoken environment tended to be the ones who found their way onto her growing personal staff; the ones who were scandalised by it or allowed it to make them sloppy were quickly and firmly rotated out. Now in her little set of chambers were three of the staff she liked and trusted the most: Culann, her personal aide, the grizzled Arbitrator Odamo and Umry, the quick-witted praetor-cognatis who'd distinguished herself in the Anstoch trials the previous year.

'Received by communiqué sent by flotilla astropaths from Shexia system, repeated again at Antozir Proxima. Authentication reads "Zanti", that's one of the flotilla masters. Shexia and Antozir-Prox are successive steps on the route to Hydraphur from the border sectors where the old man died. Time-stamps on each of them show the flotilla making good time.' Leaning against the table by Calpurnia's door, Praetor-Cognatis Umry was twirling the data-slate in her fingers but rattled off the report without referring to it.

'Good time? Hurrying, are they?' Kyle Odamo was a heavy-jawed aedile senioris with thirty-two years on arbitrator strike teams, including eight on an Arbites intercept cruiser until a shipboard accident had cost him both his legs. The augmetics hadn't taken well enough to return him to full combat assignments, but on his planetside posting he still took an interest in spacefaring. 'Don't know much about that direction firsthand but I've heard it's not hard to hurry through. They'll have an easier time of it than that other poor fellow. Fearful rough it gets coming up the well past Knape and straight out from galactic centre.'

'We can't know,' Umry replied, tossing the slate and catching it. 'That message is pretty much all we've had out of them. We've got no informants on the flotilla. The really old traders have had these whole sealed communities grow up around them. Just try getting one of your own people in or turning one of theirs. Next to impossible, I'd think. Unless the Emperor willed it,' she added piously.

'But someone's got an insider,' said Calpurnia. She was out of armour and in simple duty fatigues, sitting cross-legged on a soft mat in front of her bookshelf. 'We know that because we're monitoring the Varro end, or so Culann tells me. Culann?'

'Yes, ma'am. Things are as rough between here and Gunarvo as Arbitor Odamo said, and our communiqué from the commander of court there took a few attempts. But, well, the flotilla may not be hurrying but the heir, this Varro Phrax, is moving like a scorch-arsed blasphemer. A representative of Navigator House Dorel visited him and he was making tracks out of the system within twelve hours. Rather a lot got spent to make sure he had a ship in a hurry. More than we think Varro can afford, although he's not badly off.'

'Is this House Dorel behind any of it?' Calpurnia asked. In her experience, very little that the Navis Nobilite did was as it appeared on the surface.

'I don't know about that, ma'am.' Culann was the only one to still call her ma'am in the private meetings – he seemed to find the habit hard to get out of. 'But we do know that the rush-requests on some of the exit permissions for the ship that they're taking out of Gunarvo weren't paid for by Phrax himself. One of the astropaths travelling with them is part of the precinct commander's collaborator networks, so we have a couple of insights from what he was able to send. The money came from an exchequer to a shipping syndicate with ties to the House Yimora, not Dorel. There's been more money moved around in the financial houses at the Gunarvo docks that the Courthouse there is starting to pull out into the open, but it looks like bribes may have been paid to get the right traffic patterns for the *Gann-Luctis*, that's their ship, to get out of the system and break warp as soon as it possibly could. No formal communiqué is recorded in Gunarvo's astropathic logs about any counter-claim.'

'And I assume we didn't tell him ourselves?' Calpurnia asked. 'Of course we didn't.'

'We didn't,' said Odamo. 'I used your delegation to demand confirmation of that. Our own Astropathicae chambers certainly didn't pass anything on, and the Chancellor of the Witchroost confirms likewise. Oops,' he added.

'Oops is right,' Calpurnia told him. 'I've made my feelings on that clear. Use one of its more respectful names, please.' She looked over at Umry. 'So... This counter-claim...?'

'I'm sorry to say it, but I think at this moment we know exactly as much about it as has just been aired in this meeting and we're going to have to wait to find out any more. The older a charter, the cagier its holders tend to be about letting any Adeptus hooks into them.'

'That notwithstanding,' Calpurnia put in, 'I wanted us to sweep for information. How far along is that?' Umry glanced at the slate and tapped a key.

'Transmissions have gone out to every Arbites leader on the list I gave you and the secondary list is with the Arbitor Majore's cryptomechanics prior to transmission.' She turned to the others. 'To keep you up to speed, the prime list is every taskforce and precinct head on every world and patrol route that we know the flotilla has had dealings with in the last thirty years. The secondary list is a range of possible but unconfirmed stops. We're asking all of them for any records or observations that may give us an idea of who this new mystery counter-heir is and how strong his claim on the charter might be.'

'What we need,' said Odamo, half to himself, 'is some way of forcing these people to share their records with us.

Now, if they had to supply us with information on every change in events that might impact the charter…'

'I believe there are some like that,' said Calpurnia. 'There were several major rogue traders in the Ultima Segmentum whose charters required them to co-operate with inspectors and archivists. Unfortunately, that provision tends to have to be built into the charter from its creation.'

'If we have the authority to oversee the charter, ma'am…' Culann began, but Calpurnia was already shaking her head.

'Oversee is exactly what it is. We can enforce the possession of the Phrax Charter by the rightful successor, and where the succession is unclear we can judge and rule and enforce our ruling. That's it.'

'It's kind of the point,' said Umry. 'It's the exact things about the old charters that make them so sought after – antiquity, tradition, exalted legal status – that make them so hard to interfere with. And they're next to impossible to amend. I don't think alterations to any of the really old charters have ever even been considered.'

'Whose mark do the oldest charters bear?' asked Calpurnia, and the question hung in the air for a while. For a citizen of the Imperium, a subject of the Emperor, a worshipper at the altars of the Adeptus Ministorum, how could the idea even be countenanced? How did you set yourself up to rewrite and tinker with words penned and sealed by a walking god? Calpurnia watched the same thought go through the minds of the others: Odamo's eyes had gone hooded, Umry was staring at the floor and Culann was actually shivering. She knew exactly how they felt. She had only been able to concentrate on the details of the succession ceremonies because she had kept the nature of the charter out of her mind. When she allowed herself to think about it the weight of it was almost physical. It made her feel too small, too young.

But duty was duty, and only in death did duty end. She picked up the jug and refilled her water glass, poured more for the others and picked up her data-slate.

'Well,' she said, 'whatever the details of the claimants and their cases, the fact of it is we're going to be conducting a hearing, not a ceremonial handover. So let's start getting ready for one.'

The Flotilla of Hoyyon Phrax. In transit

'–USELESS IF HE–'
Blackness.

'–INK HE'S GOING to be able t–'
Blackness.

'–ATCH WHAT YOU'RE doing, I don't kn–'
Blackness/a moment of pain/blackness.

'–E THOUGHT IT best, magos. But Doctor D'Leste, sir, I should tell you that the codes–'
Fading away more slowly this time, but still…
…blackness.

SLOW FADE UP, blurry light. Something wedged in his mouth. Needs to get it free, needs to–

'Gods, but he's thrashing! Get over here! I don't *care*, just get over here and hold the little bastard down, get him, get his arm!'

Blurred movements in the blurred light. Pressure bearing down on tender muscle and skin. Pain. Have to get the pressure off.

'How can he be so bloody strong, look at him! Damn it, get D'Leste! No, get the magos. Yes, bloody well disturb him! Do it! Give me that slapneedle–'

A startling cold sting through the fog of raw pain.
Blackness.

Dreams, for the first time in a while. Not good dreams. Wandering through the decks and halls as a child again, dead bodies bleeding through their skins littering the floors and piling up in the arches and hatchways. Mother's voice echoing through the ship. She's singing a lullaby, except that she's trying not to cry at the same time. Hearing her aches.

Blackness.

LIGHT. NOT BLURRED this time. A white, concave ceiling and figures, way up in the distance, looking down on him. Faces he knows from shipboard musters and offi-cers' gatherings. He knows there was something about them that was so clear, so clear, back before all the light and the blackness and the dreams and the pain.

There is still pain, though. His brain seems to float in a strange, unearthly cup of it.

Rich red at the foot of the bed. Hard to see. He knows he stabbed someone. Did they live? Couldn't have. Did they die and come to tell him they're dead? They must have. In the tilted fever-logic that is all he can think in now, he decides this must be the only explanation.

'Can you hear me? Can you understand me?' The voice is odd in cadence, beautifully warm and soft, but soulless with it, like the voice of an actor who can reproduce all the appearances of a human voice but believes none of them.

'Ensign Petronas, can you understand me?'

A rich red robe with odd, geometrical gold trim, charac-ters that he doesn't recognise. A steel chain at the neck. And above the neck, the face, the face of pale flesh and glittering metal and a single red-rimmed eye…

'His cognition seems to be returning,' says the voice from that face as he thrashes and the hands grasp his arms again. 'Sedate him. Another day of rest and we'll see if he's ready to meet with us.'

Blackness.

* * *

Council Chambers of Kostazin Baszle, Eparch of Hydraphur. Level 47, Ducatine Spire, Cathedral of the Emperor Ascendant, Hydraphur

REVEREND SIMOVA GLOWERED about him as they filed through the door and each priest touched the amulet at his neck to the feet of the marble statue of the Emperor set into the far wall. As was the habit in many Ministorum chambers it had been set deliberately off-centre so that it could watch over all the room, not stare out from behind the Eparchal chair. Moving from the statue, each kissed the aquila stitched into the end of the Eparch's prayer shawl. It was done in green thread on blue at the moment, reflecting the sacerdotal colours for the celebration of the Hydraphur's wet season and the turning of the year.

It was four minutes before they were all done and kneeling before their seats, repeating the Eparch's brief High Gothic blessing. Then they rose, settled into their seats and waited to hear what was on their master's mind.

'No, it isn't about Reverend Simova's continued clash with the law,' Eparch Baszle said, to dutiful murmurs of amusement from everyone except the man he had named. 'Although perhaps, brother, you could hazard a guess as to exactly how long that affair will take?'

'There is little left for them to do,' Simova said with as much dignity as he could. 'This arbitor they have set in charge is obviously anxious to prove himself to the Calpurnia woman, and he seems to feel that the way to do that is to subject the Adeptus Ministorum and her priesthood to all manner of pointless legal delays. Their real targets are the cell whose leaders we were punishing.'

'Or leader, at any rate. You only had one in the cages, didn't you?'

'One, yes,' said Simova, bristling inside. It had been the Eparch's insistence behind the reintroduction of the old Phaphanite cages, but anything going wrong of course was Simova's fault alone. But he knew better than to start trying to defend himself in front of all the other clerics. He would wait and plead his case another time. Except that the Eparch did not seem minded to let it drop.

'The matter I want to discuss is an important one, important enough to require you all away from your afternoon duties. It will involve placing this Cathedral in the way of a certain amount of attention from the other Adeptus. In particular,' Baszle turned his handsome, angular head to stare at Simova again, 'it will bring us the attention of Imperial law. And will involve questions of law both spiritual and temporal, so I must say, Simova, this is a particularly poor time for one of my senior exegetors to lock horns with the Arbites.'

'I am not on trial, your eminence,' Simova replied, flushing a little. 'Praetor Imprimis Dastrom has made that clear. The investigation is into the infiltration of the construction and guarding work on the cages. Aspects of it that do not concern myself,' he added after a moment, conscious that he had been the one technically in charge of the whole affair. The supercilious Dastrom had made no secret of the fact that he considered Simova at least a little culpable. 'But I am faithful according to my powers, and what they lay in my way I shall overcome since I know that the Emperor is with me.' He sat back in his seat, a little happier. 'Your eminence, I must say that I am curious about this important matter that you say you wanted to discuss with us.'

The Eparch's deep-set eyes stayed on Simova for a moment before he too decided to move on.

'Brother Palomas, will you please list for me the latest additions to the reliquary of our Cathedral?'

A short man in a simple brown habit at the far end of the semicircle read from a faxscroll.

'Two shell casings from the pistol of Saint Csokavi of Tamar, obtained as tithe from the Diocese of Chigand. They await their reliquary case; Demipater Ushiste will be blessing it at tomorrow's sunset mass in the Bell Chapel.

A vial of soil from the landing-field where the Four Bishops of Phael were martyred. It's been authenticated by the Chamber Pronatus you authorised at the end of last year, your eminence, and the ship carrying it broke warp at the edge of Hydraphur yesterday. It should be here within the week. Lastly, the Reverend Baragry has sent word from Iskaza-Maru that he has recovered nearly all of the fragments of the skull of Sister Elidas the Demi-Sainted. I understand he will be returning here as soon as he is able.'

'Excellent, and thank you for the news of that last, brother. Our sisters in the Order of the Sacred Rose will be pleased that a relic of one of their own is on its way back to them. And I convey the Reverend Baragry's apologies to this meeting, of course, but you all knew he was absent on my errands. Apparently there were certain parties on Iskaza-Maru who were reluctant to allow such a relic to be taken off their world.

'But all things unfold for a reason, my friends and brothers, and we can reflect on our brother's exploits under a different sun to remind us that the ways of worship are often harsh and must at times be ruthless if our faith is to spread its wings and raise its spires.

'I know I've spoken to you all about my desire to make Hydraphur the brightest beacon of the Imperial faith in all the sectors around. Hundreds of worlds and billions of souls, all looking back to us as we reflect the Emperor's light to them as Luna shines the sunlight down on holy Terra. I want the walls of the Cathedral to groan with the trophies of the Ecclesiarchy and the relics of her holiest saints. And I have said that there is much that the Emperor will smile upon in such a holy cause.'

Ah, Simova thought. That was why Baszle had gone off on the tangent about Baragry. It wasn't a tangent – he was preparing them. There was something they were going to have to do.

'Let it never be said,' Baszle told them, 'that I saw glory for my Cathedral and my Emperor and turned my back to

it. We have the chance now to take a wondrous relic of
the time when the Emperor Himself set His eyes to
Hydraphur, to fetch it from hiding in a prison of iniquity
and set it high in the Cathedral where it belongs. A token
of the Emperor's true life, that will have our faith
strengthened as steel. Something that will place us at the
head of an army of the faithful, pilgrims and priests and
crusaders, as it ought always have been.'

The priests shifted in their seats and looked at each other,
but Baszle himself had fixed his eyes on Simova again.

'We will not be tithing for this. It will not be brought here
by a war of faith and force of arms. No matter what we
demand of our Eparchy it could not furnish us with this.

'No, the way we are going to acquire this relic is
through *you*, Simova, you and your chamber. There is a
very precious relic being brought to our very doorstep
here at Hydraphur, and the Emperor, all-providing, has
seen fit to set its owners against one another. They will
come before the Adeptus and they are going to try to
argue that the Arbites should rule them the rightful owners of this relic, as if there could be any kind of rightful
owner but the Emperor's own Adeptus Ministorum. That
is what we are here to plan. Curate Simova?'

Simova was about to cross his arms defensively and
argue when he realised that Baszle was no longer accus-
ing him but appointing him. He ran through the Eparch's
words again and blinked. A great relic, a relic that was to
be fought over by law. The importance of his new task hit
him so hard he almost gasped.

For a horrifying moment he thought he had run dry of
words. And then, as it had so many times in the days-long
debates in the chamber, his mind clicked smoothly into
motion.

'I will begin,' he said, 'by outlining the writings of Pontifex Militant Orgos Arnck concerning the right of the
Adeptus Ministorum to take possession of any object, person or territory which meets the definition of a holy relic.

We shall also consider the definition of a holy relic as originally addressed in the writings of Ecclesiarch Chiganne IV and formalised by the Four Thousand and Eighty-Second Ecclesiarchal Conclave. We must also consider the Eighth Edict-Spiritual of Terra and its implications for clashes between religious and temporal law; there are over a dozen recent and relevant precedents in the Segmentum Pacificus. And I believe, your eminence, that I should also touch on the epistles of Confessor Luzaro of Sirius which, according to the deliberations of the Eparchs Solar in M38, is considered canon for Ecclesiarchal actions where holy items must be claimed from fellow Imperial subjects by brute force of arms.'

With the Eparch's permission, he stood, then closed his eyes for the few breaths it took for him to find his orator's voice and lay out the points of law in his head. This was what delighted Simova as few other things did: he could almost see it in his mind, an interlocking web of points and counterpoints, tracts of text and decrees of religious law, forming constellations and webs of duty and obedience.

He opened his eyes and began to speak. They listened, they questioned, they discussed, as outside the yellow Hydraphur sunlight ebbed away into a long, chilly, rainy night.

The Flotilla of Hoyyon Phrax. In transit

WHAT HAD BEEN simply and luminously clear to Nils Petronas while he was killing Officer Gensh was not clear any more. It had come back to him with time, as treatment brought the spasms and pain under control and thinking was no longer like trying to pick up spilled oil in his fingers. He remembered the realisation clearly: the purging of the flotilla went far deeper than he had believed, that he and all his friends had been sentenced to death by some arcane tradition that the seniors and masters had kept from all the rest of them. It wasn't as though there weren't plenty of those.

That insight had had the force of a hammer. All he had been able to think of was striking back, taking as many with him as possible. If there was to be a hole in the flotilla where he and his friends had been, then he would make that hole a little bigger, leave a scar that the masters would have to remember.

But he no longer thought that was true. He no longer knew what was happening or why. He still knew something was going on – the scraps of memory of what he had heard in the kitchen and the Apothecarion saw to that. But he could look around him now at the luxurious chair that they had shifted him into from the survival-bed, the diagnostor hanging silently in the air over his right shoulder (it was built into a beautiful butterfly sculpted in silver and stained-glass, a holdover of an infatuation old Hoyyon had had with insects some decades ago), and the slender weave of tubes and lines that were nourishing his ravaged muscles and strengthening his flesh. He could not believe that they were nursing him so extravagantly just to put him to death again. If he were so valuable to the flotilla masters, that gave him power. At some point he was going to have the chance to hurt them.

Just that morning (as far as there were any mornings in the whiteness of his chamber) Petronas had found that he had enough strength to make fists of his hands again. They were weak, and he could not maintain them for more than a few moments, but when he made them he could see the last of the red roughness on his knuckles from the beating he had given the deck hand, and that made him feel better. He had even started to grin when he found that out, until he realised that someone was probably watching him. So he kept the grin but hid it inside his head, stoked like a little hot coal, and bided his time.

CHAPTER SIX

The Sanctioned Liner *Gann-Luctis*. In transit

THEY HAD RUN into trouble right from the start.

Gunarvo lay at the edge of a band of perennial riptides and whirls in the immaterium that followed the line of worlds trailing out of the Broadhead Cluster. To accurately scry and catch those tides was work for a skilled Navigator, and most craft that left the system took on extra supplies and endured a ten-week haul through real space before they broke warp where the conditions were calmer. The Navigator that Domasa's backers in House Yimora had assigned for Varro's voyage was tough and skilled enough to make even Domasa feel deferential, but it had still taken three attempts to properly break through into the currents that grabbed them from Gunarvo into calmer warp flows where they could come about and lay in course for Hydraphur.

Ksana Phrax had travelled between the stars exactly three times in her life, and had counted herself lucky for it. Not just because her husband had told her so, either. Although she remembered him picking up a tiny pinch of gravel from the riverbed at the bottom of the Asterine Lock one night before their first voyage and holding it out to her. 'If the riverbed is everyone on this whole world for the past hundred years,' he had said, 'then this is the number of them who will ever manage to look down on Gunarvo and see it hanging in space, let alone how many of them will ever look down on another world the same way. The people who never travel between worlds never think about it; the people who do usually take it for granted. But it's an incredible thing, my love, to look on a world so far from yours and taste its air. You'll see.'

Ksana had believed him, and remembered her privilege. This should have been a greater privilege still: she still had to tell herself that, after so much anticipation, she was leaving Gunarvo as the wife of a rogue trader-in-waiting, to return, if she ever did, a merchant princess with a flotilla and a ten-thousand-year old legacy behind her. Varro had once told her about how the charters had been signed and sealed by the Emperor Himself, and although she had thought he was exaggerating she also believed she was coming into whatever destiny the Emperor had for her.

Alone in the beautiful stateroom, with its blue velvet drapes and cushions and its purple-trimmed furniture of ebony and gold, she told herself again that she should not be so disturbed, that there was no reason for her nerves to be so taut or for her hands to want to lace and unlace themselves – she had even put on gloves of thin blue silk when the skin between her fingers had become red and sore.

But there were things to disturb her. Plenty of them. Varro had told her with a smile that they were in good hands, that Dorel and Yimora and the rest were worthy allies who understood how important the charter was going to be to him. He had shown her letters from the first controller, the Imperium-appointed governor of Gunarvo itself, who would help them make the case for his proper succession. As they were leaving they had been joined by another delegation, Imperial Administratum representatives bearing seals from the subsectoral prefect on Baryatin II. The delegation leader, haughty in his formal gown and high, intricate collar, had told her that the Administratum would be pleased to place its resources 'at the disposal of the Phrax succession and its orderly and correct resolution.' They had not said much else to her after that, and that had not surprised her. She knew how most of Varro's new associates thought of her: the little heir's trophy-wife, ignorant of the Imperium beyond the walls of the family compound, standing well back and smiling benignly at whatever her husband did.

But Ksana Phrax was the daughter of a Gunarvite merchant guilder and the sister of two doctors-at-law to the planetary Congress of Selectmen. She saw much and suspected more.

There was a plate of meats and spices on the table next to her, but she had little appetite. Her nerves had robbed her of it. She slipped off her shoes and padded carefully to the sleeping alcove to move the drapes carefully aside with a hand: Dreyder was still asleep, more quietly than he had been when they had been trying to break warp and he had twitched and cried out from the dreams. Ksana resisted the urge to pull the blankets up around him – the room was warm enough, and she didn't want to wake him. She let the drape fall back into place.

What she had seen was the way that Domasa Dorel spoke to her husband, either artificially gruff as though she were a better friend than she had the right to consider herself, or a contrived singsong lilt as she pretended a respect for Varro she clearly did not feel. And that bright, steely, calculating look never left her eyes. Ksana had watched to see how Domasa dealt with the way she frightened their son – and there had been no reaction at

all. The look in her eyes as she had watched Ksana con-
soling her son after he had cried at their first meeting had
been cool and dismissive.

She knew about the whispered conferences between the
first controller's men and the delegation from the Administratum. She had gone walking the decks and visiting
what few diversions the ship offered – the little library, the
promenade stairs around the base of the bridge-tower, the
rows of idols to the Machine God that lined the halls leading to the enginarium – and time and again she had come
on them, little knots of turned backs and low voices, that
broke up to shower her with sunny greetings and then
silently waited for her to move on. She knew that mes-
sage-runners had been working the corridors between
their suites night and day, special Administratum-trained
couriers who were hypno-conditioned to remember nothing of what they heard and recited. She knew that she and
Varro had dined with the *Gann-Luctis's* officers at a table
half-empty because the others were meeting privately in
rooms that even the ship's personnel had been barred
from.

She knew that the first controller's men wanted a copy
of the charter's wording, and resented Varro for not providing them with one. She suspected that they were
looking for ways to distort those words: she knew enough
about the controller's dreams for Gunarvo that trying to
tie the charter to their world instead of Hydraphur
seemed natural when the prism of ambition was applied
to one's vision.

She knew that Maghal, the Adept Prolegis who was sec-
ond-in-command of the Administratum delegation, was
already trying to negotiate with Varro to attach a ship to
the flotilla under an Administratum charter. The ship
would have a captain appointed by Maghal or his superiors and its relationship with the rest of the flotilla would
be governed by contract – it would collect tithes of pop-
ulations, resources and data from the Imperial worlds the

flotilla visited and the Administratum adepts on its crew would have a voice in determining the flotilla's itinerary. And in return, subsidies and favoured-trader status on merchant routes all through the subsector. Ksana could well imagine what they were planning: get Varro fat and comfortable on a regular run across routes the Administratum already controlled, use his charter to flout the vigilance of the Arbites, use him to venture into the wild space south of Gunarvo where the prefect desperately wanted tithe-paying Imperial rule to spread again.

And the Navigator. Even the memory of her pallid face and her fierce, somehow feverish eyes chilled Ksana. She did not know and did not want to speculate what Domasa Dorel might want, but she did not think that it would stop with taming a rogue trader to a pet run in a favoured subsector or to a certain world. She did not think that at all.

'THAT PRYING LITTLE rodent of a wife is going to be a problem, too, you mark me,' said Cherrick, hefting his hellgun.

'What makes you think so?' Had they still been back on Gunarvo Domasa would have dismissed the remark out of hand, but even this early in the voyage she was uneasy. The turbulence in the warp was bad – as a Navigator she understood just how bad, and what that might mean for the voyage. She was trying to put it out of her mind: the man who was navigating them was far more accomplished than she, and she had other priorities. Hers was the thumb that the thrown-together syndicate wanted on the pulse of whatever was going on around Varro and that was what she was trying to concentrate on.

With the glimpses her third eye was showing her of what was going on outside the hull, she had a feeling that was going to be hard.

'I don't like her. I don't like her at all. She's got this nasty, ratty, watchful look to her. I bet she's got it all planned out in her mind, wants the charter for herself. It fits, doesn't it? And she doesn't like you.' Cherrick grinned.

'I suppose I see why. She's smart enough not to trust me, and I think she's got a good idea of what I want out of her husband.' Domasa shrugged. 'Plus, I scare that little brat of hers, so I suppose she dislikes me for that. Rather sweet of her, really. Have you got the conduit covered?'

'What?'

'The crawl-way. There's meant to be a crawl-way along the roof of this whole corridor.' Domasa's voice slowed and dropped into an ice talking-to-an-idiot cadence. 'So. Do. You. Have. It. Covered?'

Cherrick glowered upwards, trying to think of something smart to come back with. The two of them were standing at the head of the central utility corridor that ran through the *Gann-Luctis's* lower decks, whose maps Domasa had spent half a day memorising: it would not be wise to walk about the ship with blueprints under her arm that she was not supposed to possess. She stood patiently as Cherrick muttered into a vox-set and watched as two armsmen came hurrying down the stairwell. She had obtained an amulet-key that could speak to nearly every security plate on the ship, and when she directed it at the hatch above them there was an avalanche of screeches and clatters as it slid aside and a rickety metal ladder unfolded. The two men exchanged a sour look, ignited shoulder-lamps and began climbing.

Domasa closed her eyes and brought up her mental deck plan again. The crawl-way was the last way out of this level. She and Cherrick blocked the corridor, other armsmen were guarding the liftwells off the utility deck and covering the compartments to either side. Domasa had experienced a single small flash of annoyance when they had found their quarry gone from the Psykana dome, but it was something she had been prepared for. It was fine. She had control.

'So, were you listening?'

'Hmm?' She hadn't been. She needed to concentrate. If they didn't do this seamlessly things could get messy.

'The wife. She's going to get in the way. I think we can run him, but we might not be able to run him with the wife around.'

'Leave the diplomacy to me, Cherrick, you've already proved that you can't do it. What you can do is make sure that toy of yours is charged so we can get started.'

'If weapon-handling is something I'm meant to be better at, my lady, then maybe I should just check to make sure you're properly equipped yourself?'

Domasa glared at him and slipped her sleeve back. A bundle of fine golden rods rested against her forearm and the back of one malformed hand: her long fingers were curled around a trigger-grip and the ammunition tank was anchored at the inside of her wrist. Cherrick sniffed.

'Useless if he's armoured, of course.'

'He won't be,' snapped Domasa, 'and this is much better for taking him alive but incapacitated, which I'll thank you to remember is our priority.'

'Fine.' Cherrick tapped the chime-stud on his glove for the teams to start moving and got half a dozen steps down the corridor before he realised Domasa was still behind him. 'Are you coming, ma'am? You're the one with the non-lethal weapon, after all. Are you really going to let me laz him full of holes?' Domasa began to follow, slowly, weaving back and forth to make sure Cherrick was between her and door or alcove they passed. She was confident that Symozon was no fighter, but physical confrontation made her edgy.

Oafish as Cherrick was most of the time, now he was silent and focused, his steps so controlled that Domasa realised she had to listen hard to hear each footfall. Domasa tried to do the same – her feet were as elongated as her hands, only touching the floor at the balls and toes of her feet, her heels jutting like a big cat's, and that made it easier.

From Cherrick's vox-plate she could hear the faint rustle of voices from the other men. The whole formation was moving now, slowly, thoroughly, unstoppably. Domasa almost tripped on the leading edge of her gown, and realised she was walking hunched over. This was stupid. She found herself wanting to straighten up and shout out. How did the man think this would end? Where did he think he was going to go?·How long did he think he could hide?

As long as he can, she thought to herself, and when he's brought out of hiding then we can damn well expect him to want to take a few of us with him. So be careful, Domasa Dorel, and don't give him the chance.

The Flotilla of Hoyyon Phrax, in transit

ALTHOUGH HE HAD been expecting it ever since he had properly regained consciousness, Petronas's heart still gave a lurch when they came filing into the room.·He was still in the chair, still nauseous and always tired, but his thoughts were razor-sharp and he could make fists and hold them for a count of seventy-three before the pain made him stop.

He recognised Crewmistress Behaya straight away – he had spoken to her once or twice before, on special occasions when she had toured the lower tables at feasts. And after a moment he was able to place Kyorg as well, the old fool who purported to run the Office of Envoys. It had been Kyorg's orders that had led to him going down to Shexia to – to do a thing he didn't like to think about. He tucked his hands under the blankets so that the masters would not see him making fists.

Halpander he had dealt with a few times, when he had been assigned to run loading of cargoes and provisions. And there were faces he couldn't quite put names to: the lipless woman in the black and white shawl, the little bald man with the sad-hound face… and the figure in red. Petronas's eyes locked onto it and did not move.

'I find it difficult to believe that you never knew anything at all about Magos Dyobann.' That was D'Leste, who was dragging a stool over to sit by Petronas's chair. 'He's a regular associate of mine, of course, but aren't I right in thinking that the whole fleet knows about the monster-man who lives on board the *Gyga VII*?'

Petronas kept staring. Just like all the other flotilla children, he had listened to, made up, embellished and passed on the myths about the *Gyga VII*. It was the ship that almost no one travelled to and that anyone who had seen inside was not allowed to discuss. Although he had scoffed at the stories of the red monster-man, those stories had still kept him awake after lights-out, and when Nimmond had made up extravagant fantasies about what lay in that ship he had listened along willingly enough. When he was older he had learned that the ship was something to do with engineering and workshops and had barely given it another thought. The flotilla was full of things it was useless to wonder about.

But now the red-robed monster-man was here, and Petronas was surprised to feel no fear in the presence of the flotilla-children's favourite bogeyman. He kept staring.

'Time for you to be introduced, I expect,' said the sad-looking little man. 'This, Mister Petronas, is an honoured member of the flotilla, a member of rather more years of service and standing than yourself if I might say so. As Doctor D'Leste has said, he is Magos Dyobann of the Adeptus Mechanicus. He joined us as a magos errant after the Explorator fleet of Pontifex Mechanis Hvel was disbanded some, what was it, one hundred and twelve years ago, by my count. Near the beginning of my service, in fact.'

'I thought we were supposed to be independent from such as that.' Normally Petronas would have stopped at the thought, but the words were out before he realised. He wondered if the drugs in his system were blunting his edge.

'Our great flotilla could travel the galaxy for a long time on our own resources,' said Galt, the reproach stronger in his voice now although Magos Dyobann had not reacted to the shot at all. 'Perhaps a lifetime. But there come times when we must conduct rites of engineering or medicine or other things that are simply beyond us. The Adeptus Mechanicus knows this. And even as we have need of their services, there are things that we offer in turn. We are a rogue *trader* flotilla, after all.'

'Our contract with the Adeptus Mechanicus is a simple deed of exchange, with no date of expiry,' said the woman in the shawl, pinching each word off with her lips as though she resented having to expend the energy on it. 'We have the right to call upon the services of the Mechanicus to meet what needs our own lay techmen are incapable of meeting. In exchange, the magos errant… travels with us.'

'There has to be more to it than that,' said Petronas. The realisation that he had not been punished for the way he had first spoken was making him bolder. 'What is your stake in this, Magos Errant Dyobann?' His voice, he noticed, was still weak, even hoarser than the woman's had been. Then his gut lurched as suddenly the magos bore down on him with a disturbing, gliding gait.

'There is much all across the cosmos to interest and draw a disciple of the Omnissiah,' came the voice from under the scarlet half-veil that hid the magos's lower face. It was the voice Petronas remembered from his sickness, simultaneously warm and affectless. 'And its charter allows this flotilla to travel in places that might attract attention or be simply forbidden. There are certain discoveries that my ancient and holy order consider are better studied in privacy.' The magos bent over and then, to Petronas's revulsion, the corner of the man's right eye bulged and birthed a slender metal worm that stretched from the place where the eyelids joined. It swayed in the air for a moment, then lunged out to meet and snap onto one of the antennae of the butterfly-diagnostor at Petronas's shoulder. The machine began to quiver as though the magos's tendril were sucking it dry.

'There will be the occasional need, for example,' Dyobann went on, his face centimetres from the ensign's, 'to ensure that a… setback for the Imperial military does not lead to the loss of rare and consecrated technology. There may be times when a traveller of independent means such as a trader flotilla comes into contact with devices fashioned at xenos hands, or specimens of value to our Order Biologis, which it is prudent to extract and place into Mechanicus custody as a priority. Fortunately the flotilla has permitted the construction of excellent laboratoria aboard the *Gyga VII*, over which our treaty allows me full control. Or perhaps there is an artefact of our own construction, lost in the way that so much of what the Imperium once was has become lost, rediscovered by our scouts and agents or by purest chance…'

'I think I see,' said Petronas as the worm suddenly uncoupled from the butterfly and snaked back into Dyobann's face. It did not completely vanish, he noticed now that he knew to look: it still hung at the very corner of the eye like a tiny silver tear. 'That detour we made out into that dead cluster a couple of years back. Fourteen-month round trip to a world none of us were allowed off the ships to see. Was that you?' The magos didn't respond. 'And that xenos meeting post out in Lucky Space in the Segmentum Obscuras, and the stop at the Wulanjo system forge-world straight after. Alright.' He suddenly winced, looked down, and could not stifle a cry.

The magos had brought his arm up and the sleeve of his crimson kimono had slipped back to his elbow. His arm was a tangled braid of metal cables, twisting over and around and through one another, of some dark metal that gleamed with scented ceremonial oil. The whole array was in subtle motion, each cable pulsing and shifting against its neighbours. Petronas looked down in panic. At a point a little past where the magos's hand would have been the cables plaited together and locked into a shining gold collar then splayed out like a hand: the dozen metal dendrites that were its fingers had slid under the thin sheet covering Petronas's body. The ensign gawped silently into Dyobann's augmented eyes as each tip slid coolly over his skin, then stopped, pinched and slid a needle home.

'You demonstrate a perceptive and assertive nature, ensign. I approve.' The magos's tone had not changed in the slightest. 'Yes, the missions you have mentioned were performed at my request. The decision to keep the nature of the *Gyga VII* from the rank and file of the flotilla was made by your own masters, but I admit to occasional curiosity as to what the crews of the other ships made of the errands that my own masters occasionally require us to make.'

Petronas fought to control his breathing and think. Every instinct he had told him that something big was about to happen to him, something *big*, and that he had to get onto the front foot and be ready for it. With an effort of will he pushed away the sensation of the needles wriggling in his skin.

'And I'm no longer rank and file, am I? They've brought you out into the open and introduced you. So you're about to kill me or about to promote me. Which is it?'

There was silence in the room. The dendrites squirmed and left pale-orange oilstains on the sheet; the needles withdrew and the magos dropped his sleeve over his snakes' nest of a hand, then straightened up and stood there with his eyes closed. Looking at him, Petronas thought of one of Galt's sommeliers tasting a wine before pouring it out for a dining-party.

'The diagnostors are correct,' Dyobann announced a moment later. 'The preliminary doses have all taken and been absorbed. You did well to recommend this one as the most likely, D'Leste. I approve.'

Petronas fought down another wave of revulsion. He had been right. The magos had been tasting his blood, with whatever inhuman senses he could extend through those cables.

It took a moment for the other word to hit.

Doses.

Under the sheet, his fists were white and aching.

'What do we have to straighten out?' D'Leste asked. 'Didn't he cause a little trouble before we got him?'

'He thought it was the cooks who were behind what was going on and went after them,' said Behaya.

'Killed a couple of them, didn't he?' asked a tall, stately man Petronas recognised as Captain-at-Arms Trazelli.

'A steward named Rheo and a junior officer named Gensh,' said Behaya. 'Nobody important.'

'More importantly,' put in Kyorg, 'how many of the other potential subjects actually survived the dosage anyway?'

'Technically?' D'Leste asked. 'Four. To all practical purposes, none. Two are comatose and fading fast, their metabolisms have lost the ability to process nutrients. They won't last two more days. One will probably be gone by the time we get back. Every single cell in his body seems to want to become a tumour. And there's one last one, Omya, another young officer. He has developed some rather interesting instabilities. The magos and I are going to keep him on the *Gyga* as long as we can, out of curiosity.'

'We cut it very fine indeed, then,' rasped the woman in black and white. 'You ought to be thankful that this one survived. I didn't realise we were going to be taking this much of a chance.'

'Omya…' Petronas whispered. 'Omya. My friend. He's not dead?'

D'Leste snorted. 'I'd forget him were I you, my young friend. You're not going to see him again, and you're going to have plenty of other things on your mind.'

Petronas stared at him until Galt finally stepped forward.

'Spite's sake, let's just out with it and tell the man, shall we?' He turned to Petronas. 'We have a duty for you, my young ensign. A new office we want you to take on. One that perhaps won't be pleasant at first, but which is vital to the survival of the flotilla as we know it now and which will reward you in ways you cannot imagine.' He stopped, made to speak again, stopped again and laughed.

'And even I find myself balking at saying it outright,' he said to the rest of them. 'You'd think we'd all be a little numbed to the enormity by now.' He turned back to Petronas and took in a deep breath.

'Nils Petronas, how would you like to be the new Rogue Trader Phrax?'

The Sanctioned Liner *Gann-Luctis*, In transit

'HE WAS HIDING in the winch-wells on the utility decks. He hurt a couple of Cherrick's troopers but we flushed him out with a microshock grenade and gave him a needling for good measure.' Domasa Dorel's normally flat, hard eyes were shining and her voice was excited – she looked as though she should have been flushed, but her skin was as pale as ever. Behind her Cherrick, the man in charge of her bully-squads, held a leash whose other end was cinched around the wrists of a kneeling man with the sunken eyes and green robes of an astropath. Behind them, one of Cherrick's men quietly closed the door of the *Gann-Luctis's* ready-room.

'Hurt? How did he hurt them?' Varro looked past her for signs of injury among Cherrick's men. Domasa waved the question off.

'They're not here, they're off resting up. He didn't have any weapons, nobody but the ship's own complement is supposed to carry weapons during a warp-voyage,' said Domasa, cheerfully ignoring Cherrick's hellgun and belt of grenades and the needler whose trigger-grip she was still clasping. 'But psykers don't dare work their wills too hard on a warp voyage either, there's only the thickness of a Geller field between them and the Worst of Seas.'

'And the beneficence of the Emperor,' put in Ksana Phrax, standing behind her husband's shoulder with her arms folded.

'Alright, and that too,' Domasa conceded. 'But still, grabbing up power with your mind on a ship at warp is like firing krak missiles back and forth when you're sitting in a shuttle. That was why we waited until we broke warp to go after him, except we got to the Psykana dome and found he'd already gone scuttling off.'

'What did he do?'

'We were taking a bit of a chance with the microshock, weren't we Cherrick? But it was worth it, we needed to make sure that his concentration would be scrambled.' Domasa was almost gabbling – it was the most excited Varro had seen her.

'What did he do?'

'But I don't think it was really too much of a chance, I mean, if he had been somewhere else, but the winch-wells, that's pretty heavy machinery and the microshocks would barely scuff the metal, we judged it a worthwhile risk.'

'That was my judgement, yes,' put in Cherrick, with a not particularly subtle emphasis on 'my'.

'What did he *do*?' The snap in Ksana's voice was finally enough to register with the others. Domasa caught her reflexive sneer and bowed.

'Apologies, my Lady Phrax, events have me a little keyed up. He sent an astropathic transmission just as we passed the cometary zone. Not enough of the signal was caught by anyone actually *loyal*,' her speech turned into a spit for a moment, 'for us to know about it word for word. But we know that our friend Symozon here has been harvesting information on our voyage and our ship's complement, and he was careless enough to leave some ghosting around the telepathica chair he used that one of our *loyal* astropaths was able to catch before it evaporated, so we know at least some of the names in the transmission.'

'I don't see why you're doing this,' said Varro. His hands were clasped in front of him, taut with distress. 'What have we to hide? You told me yourself that this counter-claim is just rubbish. If we have the stronger claim, then who cares who knows what about this? About us?'

Domasa's mouth opened and closed for a moment.

'Prolegis Maghal has shared some of the Administratum's knowledge of our destination with me,' she said after a moment. 'And one of the things he said was that this arbitor who'll preside over the succession – at which she'll judge whether you even succeed to the charter, I'll remind you – is a straight arrow. Not like some of the Arbites my House has encountered, the ones who love their secret informants and midnight raids. This Calpurnia's apparently a fussy little bitch. If a woman like that wanted to know our complement she'd have an Arbites herald bang on the hull until we handed over a list. She just loves barging in where she's got no right and throwing her weight around, that's what I heard.' Domasa turned, and the hem of her russet skirt twitched as she jabbed Symozon with her foot. 'No, if our friend here was doing any spying then it wasn't for the Arbites. It was for whoever is trying to pull your family's legacy out from under you. Is that honestly the kind of thing you'll sit back and take?'

'How are you going to confirm all of this?' asked Ksana as Varro stared at Symozon's slumped form. 'What has he told you? Wouldn't there be some sign we could find that he has ties to… to some possible other interests?'

'Nothing on his person, nothing in his cell,' volunteered Cherrick. 'But he came on board as a last-minute transfer by the Telepathica chambers at Gunarvo. It's not the kind of thing they do too regularly. Strings got pulled, you mark me.' Domasa nodded agreement.

'We have to deduce, because of where we are. If we were out of warp, then this would be a lot easier. We could peel back the little rat's brain until we found what we wanted. There are certain ways to use a warp-eye that I've even been keen to try out myself, although I'm no psyker in any kind of way that would let me do a thorough job. But we're in warp at the moment, and it's rough out there too.' Her face grew sober and she took a breath. 'Things can ride in storms like this. Pulling a mind, especially a psyk-mind, inside out in conditions like this, when our protection is already strained… no,' she said more loudly, as if convincing herself. 'We're not going to risk that. I don't even want to take a chance on a mind like his in pain or drug-weakened, not when the warp's like this.' She flared her narrow nostrils. 'And I'm certainly not taking the risk of having him fire off some kind of distress call after we break warp. He's not going to be communicating then.'

'I think that this ship has psyk-cages,' Varro began, 'so if we need to imprison him…'

'Imprison,' snorted Cherrick, cutting him off. 'Did you hear what Lady Dorel was saying?'

'We need to be able to confront these counter-claimers with him as evidence for what they've tried to do,' said Varro. His mouth was dry. There was something in the eyes of both the Navigator and her trooper that he didn't like. 'I would have thought that the evidence of wrongdoing, espionage, like this, would weaken their case at law. If this Calpurnia is such a stickler for above-board legality…'

'It would have about as much effect on them as their producing evidence of a spy of ours would have on us,' said Domasa. 'And if the arbitor-woman is surprised that it's happening then she's even dumber than Maghal's reports made her sound. If he just doesn't transmit again then we've got them wondering. Did we catch him? Did he get left behind? Did he turn? Has he just not got much to report?'

'So it's the psyk-cage, then,' said Varro. 'I'll have one of the stewards paged and they can make the arrangements.'

He stood up from his seat, but no one else moved. Domasa was staring at him. Varro looked to his wife for support, but she had gone pale and was looking away.

'I think, Varro, that I need to provide a demonstration of the way your mind is going to have to start working from now on,' said Domasa, raising her needler. One of her elongated fingers curled around to work a stud on the trigger-grip nestled in her narrow palm.

'Lethal dose,' she said briefly, and lowered her arm. There was a tiny sound, no louder than a sniff, and Symozon slumped forwards. As Varro watched, his gorge rising, he saw the little sliver of crystallised toxin that had embedded itself in the back of the astropath's high-crowned head melt and soak the rest of the way into his skin. He dropped back into his seat as the strength seemed to go out of him.

'The nature of my mission here has been made very clear to me by my backers,' Domasa said. 'I am to help you in whatever way I can to fight the counter-claim and have you succeed to the Phrax Charter and the mastery of the flotilla. You need to travel there, so here is a ship and a Navigator. You need protection for your own good, so here am I and here is Cherrick. You will need aid and support for your future work as a trader, and so worthies of Gunarvo and of the Administratum are with you.' She raised her arm and Varro flinched, but she simply released the grip of the needler and folded it back into her armband. 'All you have to do,' she told him sweetly, 'is claim your inheritance and remember your friends. That's all you have to do, Varro. We'll take care of every-thing else.'

They left him, then, left the silent tableau: Varro Phrax, pale and clutching the arms of the seat; his wife in her yellow gown, turned away with her face in her hands, and at their feet the sprawled corpse of Astropath Symozon.

CHAPTER SEVEN

Arbites Fortress of Trylan Tor, Hydraphur

THE ADEPTUS MINISTORUM arrived at Trylan Tor on the fifth day of Shira Calpurnia's stay there, on an afternoon when she was distracted and irritable and in absolutely no mood for uninvited visitors at all.

It wasn't the tor itself that she disliked. Both island and fortress were rugged and powerful: like all Arbites architecture the tor fortress was designed so the mere sight of it intimidated any onlooker. It took up the whole crowning plateau of the tor for which it was named, sitting on an almost sheer-sided pillar of rock that jutted three hundred metres above the waves. Even from the air it radiated power and immovability; she thought it would be even more impressive from the sea.

Inside, away from the constant wind and the booming of the waves, the warm air and narrow corridors made the place feel almost like some giant burrow. Through most of the building the halls were only just wide enough for

two Arbites to pass, and even then it was only Calpurnia's
slender build that meant she could move through them
easily. Even Culann, not a heavyset man, was noticing the
cramped quarters when he was in armour and Odamo,
manoeuvring his broad shoulders around the tor on two
canes and his sticklike metal legs, had resigned himself to
having to wait while anyone he met coming the other
way either backed up to a niche or a cross-corridor, or
plastered themselves against a wall.

The tor was not a conventional precinct fortress. The
archipelagos were lightly populated, and the sea and all
the surrounding island-tors were kept empty for a hundred kilometres around by Arbites interdict. Some
long-ago Arbitor General had decided that the Arbites
presence on Hydraphur could not be crippled by a deci-
sive strike on the Wall: pockets of strength were carefully
cached around the planet and the system so that, should
the unthinkable ever happen and the four thousand year-
old citadel at Bosporian fall, the surviving precinct
houses would not be without their most essential tools:
weapons, personnel and the *Lex Imperia*. The fortress at
Trylan was one of those specialised bases, keeping within
its thick black walls copies of the most vital core of
Arbites scripture and dogma.

It was the custom for Arbites to come there to study or
teach, the fortress becoming over the years a kind of
miniature university. There were texts there of which
copies existed nowhere else in Hydraphur except for the
Wall itself, and while the tor had its garrison of arbitrators guarding the walls, crewing the sentry posts on the
surrounding tors or patrolling the interdiction zone in
armoured flyers or snub-nosed submersibles, most
Arbites on Trylan spent their time by lamplight in hon-
eycomb of tiny reading-cells in the lower levels of the
central bastion.

Judges were the most common, bent over bound papers
or flickering data-arks as they explored ten millennia of

ever-expanding, ever-complicating Imperial laws. But there were chasteners there, too, standing out from the rest in their bulky uniforms and brown tunics, usually posted to Trylan to build their knowledge of the rarer and more obscure treatises on the capture, handling and breaking of prisoners. Verispex officers came to wade through the forensic notes of cases a thousand or more years old. Garrison preachers studied the texts of their forebears, sharpening their understanding of their religious duties to their fellow Arbites. And the arbitrators themselves would go down to the reading levels when they were not walking the walls with magnocs in hand, to read about techniques the Arbites of generations past used to break a crowd, or a bunker, or a seditious parade; the weak points of a house, a palace, a tank, a cargo-dray, an unarmoured rioter; how formations of arbitrators could best work to lock down a hab-block or bring it down in rubble, storm a spaceship or commandeer one, defend a power-plant or detonate it from within.

Calpurnia approved of the bookish atmosphere. Two Calpurnii five generations before her had both been Arbites General in border systems on the Ultima Segmentum: she had read their diaries and the remark of one of them that force without understanding was of no more service to the law than understanding without enforcement had stuck with her. Under almost any other circumstances at all she would have found a spell at Trylan tor restful and inspiring. But not when she was being badgered by uninvited visitors on a day when her hands were full dealing with her invited ones.

'Arbitor Senioris Calpurnia, I fully understand, I assure you, that I stand on sovereign ground of the Adeptus Arbites.' Genetor-Magos Sanja spoke carefully and formally. 'But arbitor, you must understand that I just do not have licence to throw off the laws and traditions of my own Adeptus, which are not only binding by decree of the Mechanicus but sacred in the sight of the Machine

God. This *must be* how I work here. There *can be* no other way.'

'But I have to respectfully repeat my question, magos. Can I know, please, the specific requirements on your rituals? If your laws are against anyone outside the Cult of the Machine setting eyes on your–' she had been about to say equipment, but she knew that some Mechanicus considered such a term for their sacred devices derogatory '–on the homes of your machine-spirits, then we have no conflict. A screen can be erected, or curtains, or a simple veil or blindfold on all the non-Mechanicus present in the room whenever the machines are in the open. I'll allow one of your own servitors to do the blindfolding. I'll stand in the room and allow myself to be blindfolded first–'

'The matter is not one of beholding,' Sanja told her. As far as Calpurnia could tell he was accoutred identically to the first time she had met him on the steps of his own shrine in the Augustaeum. He made a vivid splash of colour in the fortress's dark, austere little courtroom: a crimson Mechanicus kimono, his head hooded and veiled with only his bright blue eyes and hooked nose visible, a skull-cog emblem around his neck in black steel and diamond, the red and white sash decorated with the helical livery of a genetor in tiny gems. Behind him stood one of his junior acolytes, also in scarlet, his head completely hidden by a hood of red chainmail and his hands bulging with shrouded augmetics. Shoulder to shoulder behind him in turn were four dwarfish servitors, resembling obese, blank-eyed children balanced on hoofed, reverse-jointed augmetic legs that gleamed under the lamps. Sanja's luminants, the gold-plated skulls of Mechanicus dignitaries that accompanied him around his shrine, had not followed him here.

'The ark of the Helispex is one of the most revered engines of the Genetor cult on the whole of Hydraphur,' Sanja said. 'To consult with it is to perform an act of religious significance. Even on consecrated ground, the rituals of calibration and initialisation take over an hour to please its anima to the point where it will bring the engine to bear. To remove it from our shrine is something I have done before, and the engine itself is built for travel, but in every case we travel to ground that has been sanctified by a member of our cult before our arrival.

'That is the issue here, arbitor. I don't care to think about what might happen to the Helispex engine should we attempt to rouse it on unsanctified ground. The possibility that its spirit might be angered or damaged beyond our ability to repair does not bear contemplating. If this is where you wish me to examine the gene-samples from these two heirs, then some part of this fortress must be handed over to one of my liturgical mechanics for consecration as sovereign Adeptus Mechanicus ground. There is no other course of action. If this is impossible,' he went on as Calpurnia opened her mouth to reply, 'then I shall provide every assistance that I am able without the engine. Or, if you prefer, I shall return to the Augustaeum and rouse the Helispex there, so that the work you require can be done and the results communicated to you here. I shall do this with no animosity and with my respect for you undiminished, as it goes without saying.' Sanja finished his words with a bow.

'What we have here, you see, magos, is a clash of sovereign territories. I am just as bound as you are. Every precedent for a contest between heirs has said that the claimants remain in the courtroom while their blood is taken away, brought before the Helispex and the engine's verdict brought back before the court by one of your order. Trouble is, all the precedents are for trials conducted in the Wall, where your shrine is not much more than walking distance.' She sighed. 'You don't want to be the man who broke the Helispex engine for all time, and I don't want to be the woman who created the precedent for an outside organisation to claim sovereignty over an

Arbites fortress.' Her fingers had found the scars over her
eye and were lightly tracing them. 'I can't lie, even by
omission, and leave something like that out of the
records. And once it's recorded into precedent, magos, it's
a devil to get out again. Things don't just un-happen.'

'I understand. We are at an impasse, one that is the creation of neither of us.' Sanja had nothing against the
Arbitor Senioris, and his willingness to help was genuine.
But for a moment he could not help but be amused.
While its control over its own jurisdictions was absolute,
the Mechanicus had little ability to simply move in and
overrule other arms of the Adeptus as the Arbites did, and
he suspected that such impasses happened to him more
often that they did to her. He tried again.

'Where are the engineering functions of the fortress carried out, arbitor? Do you have tech-priests ministering to
your systems, or laity?'

'Laity. It's the same here as in our other fortresses, there
are lay tech-adepts granted indulgence by your priesthood
for the duty. There's no tech-shrine on the tor that will
meet your needs, I thought of that.' She looked around.

The room was probably the biggest one in the whole
fortress, and it was barely bigger than some of the meeting chambers back in the Wall. That was unusual for an
Imperial building, which tended to have at least one soaring, vaulted space in it, although at first it seemed bigger
than it was because the ceiling and far walls got lost in the
dimness of the light. The light at Hydraphur's equator
was brighter and less fusty-yellow than further north at
Bosporian, but they were far too deep inside the fortress
for windows. Although while she thought of it...

'Is outdoors out of the question? The surrounding tors
have sentry posts on them, but nothing else. There
should be enough open ground to put up some kind of
tabernacle...' But Sanja was already shaking his head.

'The engine's physical form is as delicate as its temperament,' he said. 'I cannot chance exposure to the

elements, even under conditions better suited to it spiritually. I suspect, arbitor, that if I am to use the engine to verify this succession as you wish me to, then it will have to be done either back at Bosporian or at one of our shrines on the southern coastline of Nyherac. There are perhaps some there that would be suitable, although I would be obliged if your own arbitrators would assist with fortification and security while the Helispex was housed there.'

'Hmm.' Calpurnia was brooding as she took a message chit from a runner who had shuffled in and was looking nervously at the tech-priest and his retinue.

'If I may be so bold as to wonder, Arbitor Calpurnia, I can't help noticing that no similar problem to this appears in the Mechanicus's own archives on the Phrax succession, although I confirmed that we assisted in verifying the genes of contesting heirs. Now although I don't wish to be less than tactful...'

'No offence taken, magos. As I said, the precedents are for hearings at the Wall, and holding the hearing there is one area of tradition that I want to get away from. There are already signs of possible foul play and I want this hearing somewhere we control absolutely, not where both parties can play hide-and-go-backstab through the Augustaeum for days before and afterwards. I found out the hard way how much potential there is to be mucked around by all sorts of interests when you're sitting in the middle of Bosporian Hive, no matter how safe you think you are.'

Sanja, who had been caught up first-hand in Calpurnia's experience of the Bosporian's brutal intrigues, bowed agreement.

'And I got caught out,' she went on. 'Had I thought about complications like this I might've stayed there.' She grimaced. 'Actually, no I wouldn't. But I wouldn't have had you fly a third of the way across the planet on an errand that turned out to be a non-starter, magos, and for that you shall have a written apology over my seal. I had no business being that careless.'

Sanja waved the words away. 'Fault attaches to me, too, since I should certainly have made sure before my departure that you understood everything that the Mechanicus would require of you.' They were moving towards a narrow hall door; the arbitrators standing guard there presented arms as they passed through.

'And I am sure that the problems need not be fatal to the endeavour, in any event,' said Sanja as they turned into the passage outside. It was narrow enough that only the four little servitors could comfortably walk two abreast. 'There are a number of ceremonies of diagnosis that I could perform in the fortress as it stands. They will not have the ceremonial weight of the Helispex, whose formal stamp I accept is a traditional part of the succession. However, if you are after simple genetic confirmation so that you can move on to legalities, I should be able to meet your requirements. Who are these two again?'

'One a son by his late wife, one a son by a concubine on board the flotilla itself, according to our information.'

'Well, I can guarantee that given a day or two with their samples I can – arbitor?'

Calpurnia had come to a halt in the middle of the corridor and was reading the chit under one of the brighter ceiling lamps. As she finished her arm twitched as if she wanted to throw the thing away down the passageway.

'I don't believe this. What does the idiot think this is, some kind of bloody carnival? What the hell is he doing all the way out here?' She set off again, at a pace that Sanja found difficult to match with dignity. 'Why isn't he back where I told him to be?'

'Arbitor, may I ask who you're talking about?'

'Simova! That pompous, gawping Reverend Simova.'

* * *

The *Gyga VII*, In the flotilla of Hoyyon Phrax,
Batrista midsystem docks

SOMEONE HAD TOLD him they were in-system again, one last stop at Batrista, as much a regrouping stop as anything, before the ride down a cascading warp current to Hydraphur. Nils Petronas, no longer ensign but rogue trader-apparent Nils Petronas, didn't care. He had almost forgotten there was a flotilla, a system, an Imperium out there. His world had narrowed to the vaulted wardchamber on the *Gyga VII*, and the wide four-poster bed on the dais in the centre of it, directly beneath the tall dome in the ceiling, and his own body, and pain.

He tried to tell himself every so often that not truly knowing what was happening to him before had made it worse, that now he knew what was wracking his body he could deal with whatever else might happen. But there were times when it got so bad that this didn't help at all, when the pain got worse and he lost the ability to think clearly enough to tell himself anything. They would not help him through the pain, either. Your system must grow into its changes, they had told him. If we numb you even a little your body may lose the ability to govern the changes, they had told him. We will not risk you, they had told him.

Maybe that was it, and maybe it wasn't. Petronas thought it wasn't all of it. The magos didn't seem to care, but Petronas had seen D'Leste's eyes light up and his tongue creep into the corner of his mouth while he watched the spasms light Petronas's nerves up like a sunflare.

When there was no pain at all he would sleep as much as he could; indeed, those times he often dropped straight down into exhausted unconsciousness, or at least into a blissful drowsiness in which he wanted no troubling thoughts at all. It was when there was just enough pain to run along his nerves like a whetstone and make his thoughts cool and sharp that Petronas closed his eyes gently and worked on his plans.

Once his treatment was complete, he would succeed to the charter and become the new Rogue Trader Phrax. On that he believed them. The guests at that fateful dinner had not been selected to help the flotilla bond – as Gensh the (dead) idiot had told them all – it had been a way to get all the promising subjects that D'Leste and Behaya had identified between them, a way to administer the first stage of the serum.

Nobody in the flotilla knew if the gene-treatments Dyobann had designed had been tried before, anywhere, ever. The magos had based them on scriptures he had found in the wreckage of an explorator ship that had been studying a mercenary xenos breed, combined with treatises on the transformative gene-seed of the Astartes that no one outside the bio-forges of Mars was supposed to own any more. But the treatments themselves were an unknown quantity, and they had needed an inconspicuous way of exposing their candidates to the trigger-serum.

And Petronas was the one who'd survived, although D'Leste had told him in a less guarded moment that they had clawed him back from the edge more than once. He was the one they had been the most confident of, the one that they had actually been hoping to work with: the fact that he looked more than a little like the young Hoyyon Phrax was a bonus.

'Does that mean I'm really Hoyyon's son?' Petronas had asked hesitantly when he had heard this. There had been a bundle of serum tubes running into his mouth at the time, making him careful as he shaped his words. But D'Leste and Trazelli, who had been watching over him at the time, had both burst out laughing.

'No, you cheeky little…, you're not the child of the trader,' Trazelli had told him. 'Didn't you know that his whores were allowed to roam a little in the old man's later years? He was never very randy in the first place. I've heard tell in some quarters that Galt even needed to progle him along a little to make sure there was any kind of heir at all, although if he'd known then what we all know now I suppose he wouldn't have bothered.'

They had all fallen silent for a little while as one of Dyobann's servitor-aides detached the tubes from Petronas's gullet. When the coughing had died down and the water he swilled and spat no longer had any red in it, Petronas had dabbed at his eyes and cautiously asked what Trazelli had meant. They told him amiably enough – by now they didn't seem to care what he learned. What threat could this sweating, gulping little creature in its thicket of medicae devices be? And that was fine.

'Varro Phrax, you've probably heard his name,' said D'Leste. 'He's the target here, or at least his claim to the charter is. It's a claim that has to be knocked over, for the sake of the charter and the Phrax name and the flotilla. Harsh decision, maybe, but our first loyalty is to the line of Phrax as we see it. Varro is unacceptable. An overindulged little playboy who has not done a thing to earn a claim on the charter other than have some Phrax genes sloshing around in him. And if a succession is so weakly constructed as to be based on that rather than true worthiness, well then we can challenge in the same way.' The look on the apothecary's face had been just a little too carefully composed, and as he had listened to him Petronas had realised that D'Leste was forcing himself to believe in what he was saying. Since that moment Petronas had no doubt: this was a power-grab, nothing more. And that was fine too.

'Anyway,' said Trazelli, 'if there were no other direct heirs this'd be a lot easier. The key is blood proximity, do you see? You're a reasonably bright boy. Now I don't know much about this – well, I know about drawing blood, but not playing with it, ha – but the idea is that if we show blood proximity then we're all but there.'

Blood proximity. It was a good term. Petronas had remembered it and held onto it as he lay in the four-poster now and watched Dyobann's servitors, with their spidery limbs and inlays of pearl ivory and ruby. They glided between biotic vats and sample-vials, centrifuges and arrays of pipes and dishes. Occasionally one would extrude a worm from a limb or face and slide it into one aperture or another in the banked lecterns that housed the cogitator engines. Petronas understood that then they were talking to the engines beneath their fingertips, and maybe more elsewhere on the ship, although he didn't fully understand how. Dyobann's pulpit was behind his head, although the bed and his own weakened body meant that he had not been able to twist around to see it. The magos stood there when he was overseeing the servitors and some kind of machine-witchery allowed him to see from their eyes and control them without any commands that Petronas could hear.

Beyond his feet, hanging over the door to the chamber, was a great pict-plate that showed a constantly rippling mosaic of images: elegant patterns of lines and circles etched in green light, strange greyish ovals and ellipses that seemed to move and swim, and strange strips of oscillating colours and spinning runes that Petronas couldn't read. On Dyobann's previous visit he had mustered the courage to ask what those images were and the magos had replied, 'that is how I see your blood.' Something about that had disturbed Petronas so much that he had lain back with his eyes closed and not opened them again until he knew Dyobann had gone.

Had there been no direct heir, no son Varro, the flotilla could perhaps have escaped with little or no tampering and this whole exercise might not have been necessary at all. But contesting the succession in a court of the Adeptus meant they would have to produce not just a tissue sample but a challenger whose blood would show genetraces of Hoyyon Phrax himself. He supposed, then, that it could be expected to hurt when artificial viruses and alchemic serums were working their way through his metabolism, twisting and rewriting his fundamental blood-print to show that he was the son of someone whose son he was not.

So he let Dyobann and D'Leste work on him. When they were satisfied, he was told, he would be moved to the *Callyac's Promise* where Galt would work on him too, making sure he could talk about Hoyyon as a father, talk about the flotilla as his own, and never arouse suspicion even from one who really had spent his first ten years living with Phrax as a father. When it was over he would be the little merchant prince, decked out and properly primed, ready to dance on the flotilla masters' strings while they got themselves a charter and to be their pretty figurehead after they had it.

And that was fine too. Really. All of it was fine.

Nils Petronas as-was, Petronas Phrax as-was-becoming, didn't know if Dyobann could pull it off. He had taken in more through the pain and the occasional delirium than he had allowed them to see, and he knew the flotilla masters were taking a roll of the die on whether his rewritten blood-prints would fool the Arbites and steal Hoyyon's legacy away. But he had already decided that, whether they got away with it or not, whether they got the charter or not, he owed something for his mother and Rengill and Nimmond and Omya and all the others.

Petronas lay under the sheet and made his hands into fists. He could hold them, now, for a count of five hundred and he grinned as his nails sank into his palms and drew little red arcs of his strange, changing blood.

Nils Petronas would ride with the flotilla masters to Hydraphur. And at the end of the voyage – this he vowed to himself yet again – Petronas Phrax would kill them all.

Arbites Fortress of Trylan Tor, Hydraphur

REVEREND SIMOVA WAS standing on the sloping top of a tor at the edge of the interdiction zone, underneath the high

grey walls and watchful gun-slits of one of the Arbites'
observation strongpoints. Beside him stood a herald
from the Eparch's Nunciate office, without much to do
except hold up a scroll since Simova seemed to have
decided to do most of his own talking. Behind the herald
was arranged a single rank of white-armoured Adepta
Sororitas, Sisters of the Order of the Sacred Rose that
Simova must have drawn from the Cathedral garrison
back in the Augustaeum, in full-face Croziat-pattern
helms that hid their faces from the stiff sea-breeze.

Calpurnia leaned over the holographic pict-relay and
watched the scene as it was captured by the sentry-post's
opticons, eyes narrowed with anger as the little holographic Simova jabbed a finger at the miniature arbitrator
in front of him. There was a sound pickup at the post, but
the wind on the tor and the natural noise of the transmission swamped the voices into incoherence.

'Do we have any idea what he actually wants?' she
asked, and Arbitor Thesalka, the comms technician,
shook his head.

'Our visitor is rather insistent on his protocol, ma'am,
so once he was face to face with the senior officer of the
post – Proctor Ammaz there – he went through a presen-
tation of credentials and so on first. Full and formal. Now
he's demanding passage to the tor itself. He says he's got
letters of errand from the Eparch. Ammaz told him no,
but the priest didn't look like he was gong to take that for
an answer. Started talking about how his office was divine
and wouldn't stand for mortal sanction. Then Ammaz
told him that if they flew into the interdiction zone without express grant of passage and an escort they'd be shot
down before they'd gone two kilometres...'

'Good.'

'...and so now he's back to trying to talk his way in
again. He's saying that he is here to follow up business
with you and that you're going to punish the crap out of
Ammaz when you find out he kept the priest waiting.'

'Good work Proctor Ammaz, and more fool the priest. Are you passing instructions back to him while he's out there?'

'Yes ma'am,' said Thesalka. 'His torc is active but he's got a helmet pickup that the priest can't hear too.'

'Good,' said Calpurnia, straightening up. 'Tell him he is not to give any ground. Literally. Not a millimetre. If they try to force their way forward then he's to react exactly as he told them he would. No arbitor ever makes an idle threat.' Her left hand rose uncertainly, moving to touch the scars over her eye, then her expression firmed and the hand dropped to rest on the hilt of her power-maul. 'Culann? Have the transport flier we came in prepared for departure, please, and notify our respected guest Magos Sanja that he should make similar preparations. Have one of the patrol fliers prepared too, for a trip out to that sentry post. You'll be flying in that one, by the way, so you might want to take your pick of the hangar in person. The Reverend Simova didn't appear to take a point I made to him when we last met. I think I'm going to have to add a little emphasis.'

CHAPTER EIGHT

**Coronet Triatic MRA-47; Imperial Navy sentry gate,
Outlying Hydraphur system**

THE FIRST PERSON to see the flotilla break warp on the outskirts of Hydraphur was an opticon rating named Jarto, who saw the tiny, distant pinprick of light as the ships came spilling through the gap in reality, surfing their momentum and setting their prows toward Hydraphur's bright sun.

Jarto dutifully slid the bronze measuring rods into place and charted the co-ordinates of the sighting, called them up the speaker-tube to the Opticon Intendant's control cabin high above him, and punched them into a grey card that was sucked into the slotted mouth of a gargoyle on his viewing-deck's central pillar and carried smoothly to the gate's archive stacks. He never thought any more about it, as he never thought any more about any of the tiny warp-flares he recorded. Everyone knew Hydraphur was too well fortified and too deep in the

Imperium for hostile traffic – Jarto's priority was earning enough commendations for a transfer off this crowded, Emperor-forsaken little pocket of tedium and back to one of the big planetside bases, where the fortifications went deep under the crust and there were warm rooms, and women, and forgotten little passageways where a man could run a still.

So if the first man to see the arriving flotilla did not, perhaps, accord it the importance its masters would want, that would not last for long. The astropath in the top spire of the gate's slender metal spindle sent a hail to the flotilla which was courteously returned, and then a message by both astropathy and vox to the naval squadron of Captain Irian Traze, the nearest node in the complex web of warship patrols that prowled all through Hydraphur.

The Navy's goodwill toward the Phrax flotilla tarnished quickly. Despite an invitation, then a request, then a demand that it halt one hundred and fifty kilometres out from Coronet Triatic MRA-47 to await escort, the flotilla grudgingly dropped its velocity to a little under cruising speed and set a course that would take them between Hydraphur's two ecliptics, around the star and toward the planet itself. Offended by the flotilla's rudeness and unimpressed by the repeated and unsubtle references in its communiqués to the privileges the charter granted it, Traze took the opportunity to give his squadron a little live close-manoeuvring drill.

So the observers on the flotilla decks were startled to see the high, crenellated prows of half a dozen Battlefleet Pacificus warships bearing down on them, fast enough for some of the more nervous flotilla commanders to issue orders to brace for collision. The Navy formation speared into the side of the Phrax flotilla and then, in a beautiful display of piloting and discipline, the powerful warships wheeled around onto the flotilla's course, effortlessly matching speeds. The flotilla crews, used to looking out of their viewports to the comforting sight of other flotilla ships blazing with light, now looked out at the pitted grey hulls of the battlefleet vessels, their arched gunports and the venomous, hulking shapes of lance turrets.

This time there was no invitation, request or demand, but an order. Navy pilots would come aboard with data-plaques and vox-links to guide the flotilla through the maze of minefields, sentry gates, gravitic tides and patrol squadrons that would, it was made very clear, wipe out every one of the Phrax ships if they tried to fly into Hydraphur on their own. Flag-Captain Traze boarded the *Bassaan* himself, and the first thing he did was walk onto the bridge and up to the captain, and send the man sprawling on the deck beside his own command pulpit, his lips split and bleeding from the swipe of Traze's pistol barrel.

The Navy, as a rule, did not like rogue traders much.

The Flagship *Bassaan*, Flotilla of Hoyyon Phrax, Hydraphur

AND THE FEELING was mutual.

'Interfering grox-loving...' growled Zanti. She stood with Kyorg on a catwalk before a great circular window, looking out at the great flank of Traze's flagship *Diarmid's Redemption*. A runner had brought them news of the orders and of the indignity the Navy man had inflicted on their poor captain. 'I don't understand why we're letting them do this. The charter means what it says. We should be able to sail through their lines and be damned to the lot of them. You people lack spine.'

The flotilla masters had conducted a brief but heated meeting when the Navy squadron had closed in. Zanti, who had been listening carefully to Dyobann's reports on Petronas's health, had wanted to speed straight to Hydraphur and demand the charter. She was none too pleased at being outvoted, and less so at getting one of Kyorg's lectures about diplomatic realities. Zanti was a woman who lived by the letter of the law, and the human complications that surrounded it were things she had never mastered.

'On the contrary,' Kyorg told her, 'I have a spine. And guts, too, which was the other thing you said I didn't have any of. Oh, and brains, you made remarks about those. I have brains.'

'Pah.'

'I also have bones, eyes, lungs, muscles and even toenails, and I'm fond of all of them, and that's why I wanted us to co-operate with the Navy and not try to bluff any outrageous behaviour with a charter that they resent having to honour in the first place. I'd rather that all those parts of me stay parts of me, and not end up floating around Hydraphur in a cloud of vapour.'

'I told you,' snapped Zanti, 'the charter's passive protection is considered to apply to the flotilla even when a trader is not present to wield it. The codicils referring to–'

'Yes, but do the Navy agree with that interpretation? You admitted yourself, that particular boundary of the charter has never been tested.'

'It doesn't matter,' snapped Zanti. 'Our interpretation is *right*. The whole point of having the charter in the first place is so that the *tikks* can't boss us around.'

'I don't even understand why you're impatient,' Kyorg told her. 'Explain to me where there's a hurry. We're here now, we're at Hydraphur. We'll be shaking hands with the arbitor before you know it.'

'I know this full well, thank you.' Zanti was suddenly trying to understand why she had allowed herself to be drawn into conversation with a man she so detested.

'And has anyone told you that the real heir is still labouring through warp storms off Santo Pevrelyi? Storms bad enough to send out ripples that even made our own astropaths nervous.' Zanti glared at him. The flotilla's astropaths were one of her responsibilities.

'They're going to be ages yet, Zanti. Think of all that time we'll get to work on the Arbites. I'm sure we'll come up with some way to lay the groundwork in our favour.'

'You're the Master of Envoys, Kyorg, you're supposed to have plans to lay the groundwork now. And backups and contingency plans. What preparation have you done, exactly, to make the most of the time?'

'There's plenty of time yet,' Kyorg told her loftily, sauntering away.

He had done nothing, then, as usual. She wondered if he understood how precarious his position in the flotilla was, and how he seemed to be wilfully making it worse.

She shook the thought off, made an irritated flap of her hand at the giant warship outside the window and stamped off in the opposite direction. If he wanted to make such a poor bed for himself, let him; after he was gone the role of Master of Envoys would sit neatly within her own portfolio. She just didn't see why people had to be so stupid all the time, that was all.

The *Gyga VII*, Flotilla of Hoyyon Phrax, Hydraphur

D'LESTE WATCHED THE shape under the veil uneasily. Petronas's eyes seemed to be getting more sensitive, and he had demanded veils to keep the light on the bed dim. D'Leste was rather grateful for that now. Dyobann's retrogenetic treatments were taking a toll on the boy – he was barely recognisable as the arrogant young ensign they had looked at in the speaking-chamber's holographic display.

'He's stable,' came Dyobann's voice as a tickle in D'Leste's ear. They had taken to using microbeads around the bed, especially when they were discussing their patient's condition. 'If you obey my teachings, allow my servitors to do their work and stay vigilant, then he will remain stable.'

'For how long?' D'Leste asked. He was not looking forward to this. Something he would not have admitted to anyone was that he was frightened by the idea of being in charge. He had become used to the magos's sure touch and preternatural calm. The idea of having no one to take a problem to was bothering him.

'For long enough. Until I return,' Dyobann informed him coldly. 'You will not need to initiate any new stages of treatment. Should I be delayed, we have in fact brought our subject to the point where his tissue will at the very least be able to contend as a Phrax relative. We shall not know specifically what this Arbitor Calpurnia will require until we reach the moment of her decision.'

'We're trying to find out what that will be,' said D'Leste, although he didn't hold out much hope. Kyorg's handling of it so far had involved delegating a clerk whom D'Leste was pretty sure was his mistress to send a message ahead. He wasn't even sure if the message had gone.

'If she does require a live tissue-draw then I leave it to yourselves to improvise a solution,' said the magos. 'I, however, shall do my best to lay the groundwork for it. This is why it is best I go. I trust myself more than I trust Kyorg.'

'Don't we all.'

'That is not my affair,' said Dyobann. 'I am no envoy, but I am best placed for this errand. Genetor-Magos Sanja is the one who will conduct the rites of analysis and he will be flattered by the fact that I have made a point of bringing him a sample in advance. The fact that I only need to alter a small sample rather than a full living being allows me to make more comprehensive alterations on the specimen I shall bring before him–' he held up a metal flask in one gleaming hand '–but should my additional work be insufficient to convince him, I am also best placed to make the case for the flotilla's continued ownership of the charter. The relationship between this flotilla and the Mechanicus has been most constructive for us both and Magos Sanja will realise the new heir cannot be trusted to let that continue.' D'Leste felt proud to hear that. Nobody had any idea what Varro would make of Dyobann's status in the flotilla, but he had told the magos that Varro was known for antipathy to the Mechanicus and apparently he had been convincing. He pointed to the bed again.

'Galt will not be delayed any longer, I understand?'

'He won't,' D'Leste confirmed. 'Navy protocols will mean a delay of quite a few days travelling into Hydraphur, perhaps more, and Galt says he needs all of that time to make sure Petronas can comport himself like a proper trader-in-waiting. He's more than a little angry that he's had to wait as long as he has. That's why I need your word that Petronas will be fit.' He glanced at the bed. 'Will he be fit to deal with people? Learn things? He's no use to Galt if he's in a haze all the time.'

'The subject,' said Dyobann, starting to move towards the door, 'is lucid and in control. I have had him perform certain verbal, physical and logical exercises, and used pain relief to provide small rewards. You may convey to Galt that he should need no concessions to any supposed dimunition of our subject's capacity.'

D'Leste grunted. He hadn't known about the exercises. The double doors swung wide for Dyobann, and the magos marched away from D'Leste with two servitors behind him. The apothecary didn't know what clout Dyobann had had to use to commission a dromon system-ship to carry him ahead of the flotilla, but he was glad of it even as he was nervous about the wrecked man behind him being left in his care. It meant something was happening, at last.

He turned back to the white curtain and put his face up to it, but all he could see was a faint hint of sluggish movement in the bed. He supposed he should go and notify Galt that his pupil was ready. Petronas would have to appear before the Arbites soon, after all, and Galt had promised he would have him acting the part.

* * *

From inside the curtain, Petronas Phrax watched the burly doctor walk away. He lay half in and half out of the covers: his lower body had developed regular, painless spasms that were continually dislodging the bedclothes. Even through the curtain the light was unpleasant for his eyes, which had become almost black, tinged with yellow, but he made himself stare after D'Leste until the doors had closed behind him.

Something had happened to his hearing, and words often seemed to pick up an odd, metallic, double-echo, but he had made out the conversation well enough. D'Leste's part of it, anyway – the man hadn't got the hang of subvocalising into the microbead link.

Soon he would be out and among the other officers. Soon he would be back with his brothers and sisters in uniform. Odd, discoloured tears seeped out of Petronas's eyes at the thought, staining the pillow beneath him. He did not doubt that he would be able to make his plans and his needs clear to them. He did not doubt that they would side with him, not Galt.

He did not doubt that they would help him have his revenge.

The Sanctioned Liner *Gann-Luctis*, Docking orbit, Santo Pevrelyi

Domasa Dorel, normally chilly of emotion and tightly controlled of gesture, wanted to throw back her head and howl.

She clutched the communiqué from Hydraphur in one malformed fist, written out onto flimsy ricepaper in the same coded syllables the astropath had fielded it in. The cipher was a custom one, designed for this particular informant; learning it from the file her Navis Nobilite backers had provided her with had kept Domasa from fretting during the turbulent warp-passage it had taken them to get here.

The news was bad enough that Domasa had suppressed the urge to shred the paper in her fingers out of spite – she wasn't sure that she wouldn't need to show it to Varro at some point. If he wasn't yet convinced of the voyage's urgency, this would do nicely.

So where the hell was Varro? Domasa had spent half an hour prowling the upper passenger decks under bitter mental protest: a minnow she might be in the world of the Navigators, but she was not accustomed to having to run errands like this. She had rousted Cherrick and his squadmates out of bed and set them to checking the lower hab-decks and the utility levels, and haranguing them over their private vox-link helped her mood a little. But too much was starting to go awry, and she hated the feeling that her assignment was going off the rails in ways that she seemed to be powerless to stop.

She tried to keep from pointless fretting, but as she passed like a robed shadow down the arched passageway to the formal dining hall, she found her thoughts returning to the problems like a tongue to loose teeth, like fingernails to a scab.

The warp storms were the greatest and least of her problems. She did not take lightly the fact that turbulence between Santo Pevrelyi and Hydraphur was building into a tempest of a kind she had never had to navigate anywhere near before. She trusted old Auchudo Yimora. He was a good Navigator. But no matter how good the man was, Domasa thought darkly as she stood in the shadowy forechamber of the dining hall, there came a point when even the keenest warp eye was useless except to set its owner to soiling himself with fear at what his ship had caught itself in. No matter how skilled the Navigator, he could no more steer them through a truly lethal storm by sheer skill than an athlete could learn to run through a brick wall by agility alone.

She thought she heard a movement behind her where the long passageway stretched off into the gloom, but when she turned it was empty. Domasa gritted her teeth and gave herself a mental kick – this was no time to let her nerves get the better of her.

It didn't help that she knew better than most of the other passengers on the ship what sort of shape they had finished the last leg of their voyage in. Domasa had felt the great surges and rips of anti-reality that the ship had tried to ride with and push through, which had sent it swooping back and forth, on and off its course, sudden churns that had tried to twist the ship apart like a crepe-paper party-favour, blunt surges of power that had pushed the Geller field in almost to the hull and caused the warp engines to stutter and yelp in protest. Yimora's skill had been breathtaking, the skills of the pilots in obeying him barely less so: they had turned the ship to surf the most powerful swell, spun it back to drive through the slightest gap of calmer passage in the walls of storm, ridden out every swirl in the energy flows that had seemed sure to tear the ship in two. But Domasa had sat in her cabin, hands clutching fistfuls of her robe in tense double hand-fuls, trying to remember prayers and charms that she had not used since childhood. It was what nearly every Navigator had experienced and what few non-Navigators were ever privileged to hear about: the sensation that you had looked out into the heart of the deadliest storm-cells out there in the immaterium – and something had looked back at you.

There was a sudden jab of sound in her ear, and Domasa whirled and skittered two steps to the side, spinning around to stare into the darkness around her. But it was her vox-piece, and after a moment of spitting anger at how stupid she was being she got herself under control and keyed the link on.

'Cherrick here. Utility deck, nothing. Nothing in the corridors. Nothing in the compartments we could get into. Crew habs ditto. We haven't tried to force our way into the flight sections or the enginarium, and we haven't started going through the cabins. The whole ship's on night-cycle, so if we search more thoroughly than we have done we're going to start waking people up and that's going to mean having to answer questions about what we're up to.' She ignored the sourness in Cherrick's voice. 'So unless you want us up there to help you with whatever this is…'

'No,' snapped Domasa. 'Fine. Forget it. You didn't find him, forget it. Go back to whatever you were doing.'

Cherrick broke the link without further comment and the clunk of the severed connection sounded even louder in Domasa's ear in the quiet of the deserted deck. She thought about pulling the vox-receiver out of her ear and stamping on it, stopped the thought and forced herself to get a grip again. This wasn't over yet, and she was going to need all her wits about her.

Yimora had invited her into the Navigators' perch that morning, and with the shutters safely sealed behind her she had stood beneath the armourglass bubble, carefully undone her hood and bandana and looked out towards Hydraphur. Looking into the immaterium from real space was more difficult than from a ship that had broken warp, and Domasa had only recently caught the trick of it. What she had seen from the *Gann-Luctis's* observation port had turned her guts to ice.

Santo Pevrelyi stood in a relatively small disc of calm warp space: in some places the weight and movements of planets seemed to roil the immaterium on the other side of the membrane to them, in some places such as this the effect was the opposite. But to galactic north-north-west and forty-five degrees above the ecliptic was the storm they would have to ride through to Hydraphur.

Every Navigator, it was said, saw the immaterium in a different way: some as clouds, some as swirls of colour like bands of glowing ink floating in clear water. The great Ayr Shodama had described it as a brilliantly lit room full of thick steam, swirling this way and that. Others 'saw' it

in ways that presented to their senses as patterns of sound
or even music; others saw nothing at all when they
unveiled their warp eyes, but were overwhelmed with tac-
tile sensations and perceived the movements of the warp
as breezes or cloth or fingers against their skin. For some
the warp even manifested itself as an elaborate dream,
their minds presenting what their warp eye saw as a
detailed landscape of jungle, or city, a treacherous mountain range, or an underwater reef through whose bright
coral a ship had to make its cautious way.

Domasa Dorel saw the warp as simple, depthless blackness when it was calm. Her visions of its depths and
movements were subtle, and it had taken her time to
learn to properly interpret them – her learning was
incomplete even now. She saw eddies and currents in the
immaterium as brief, slight swirls and flashes of light and
colour, often hard to pick out against the dimness, gone
almost before they were there; the kinds of patterns that
anyone could see by closing their eyes and pressing
against the lids with their fingers. She was used to navi-
gation being difficult for her, taking care and
concentration.

It took no care or concentration to see what was ahead
of them now. Towering over her in Domasa's warp-vision
was a wall of sheer coalescent chaos, not the darkness of
her normal warp-sight but a somehow living blackness,
shot through with angry, opalescent discharges of light
and power. Streaks and spots of red and green stuttered in
her warp eye when she looked that way, and flares of
strange non-colour seemed to give the thick, knitted
darkness meat and movement. Even from here both Navigators could feel the power rippling out from it.

'There's power in it,' Yimora had said. 'Whether it's living power I don't know. There's a feel to the really bad
ones, Dorel, I don't know if you've ever been close
enough to a high-calibre storm to know. A kind of
clenched, hungry feel.'

'What caused it?' asked Domasa. 'Do we know?'

Yimora had given her an odd look. You're old enough to know that there's no easy answer to that. The idea that for every little stir and gust in the warp you can point to a single thing and say "that did it" is a myth for the warp-blind. Waves and echoes have been rebounding back and forth through the immaterium since the Emperor Himself was in swaddling robes. Every thought that every living creature has adds to them, or interferes with them, or breaks them, or makes new ripples of their own. Who can disentangle what does what? I've been checking the logs and speaking to some of the others around the high docks. It's been growing steadily over the past few weeks – just chop and eddy to begin with, but there have been tides coming up from the Rasmawr Gulf that have fed into the thing and been trapped in it. It's been building up energy ever since. Three days before we came into dock it sent out a shockwave that unhinged a dozen of the more sensitive astropaths in the Pevrelyi Psykana station and gave nearly everyone on the planet screeching nightmares.'

Domasa hadn't known about this, but it explained why the shipworks had been so slow to get under way. She had been told by the captain that there had been riots down on the planet and a rash of suicides on the docks themselves. She had heard of severe warp storms leaking out into reality like that.

All she could hope for now, she thought to herself as she jerked herself out of her reverie, was that whatever menial slobs the Santo Pevrelyi dockmasters had got working on the ship were going to do good work.

Domasa pushed open the dining chamber doors and peered around. Had this been a ship belonging to the Navis Nobilite, there would always have been servants in here, ready with confectionery and soft music to soothe whichever of their masters had found themselves restless, but there was nothing here now but stale uncirculated air and more dimness. She pushed the irritation out of her mind and began a circuit of the room.

The storm ahead would have been frightening enough under any circumstances, but the storms they had already weathered between Gunarvo and here had weakened the ship. The reactions of the ship's drives had been strained and the machine-spirit that raged in the heart of its plasma furnaces had become weakened and angered. It was all the ship's own engineers had been able to do to contain and placate it, and that meant that they had found little time to examine the Geller field, whose generator had also been taxed to its limits keeping the surges of the warp away from the hull.

The toll on the field engine would not even be known for another day or two – the ship's crew could perform the rites of initiation and maintenance usual to a warp voyage but the ship's officers were unanimous that the field needed the attentions of the Adeptus Mechanicus before it would be ready to break warp again. The master engineer had told her of other things: hull stresses and power depletion, anomalies with some of the internal gravity systems that had injured several of the crew, minor things that she had not cared about. All she cared about was when they would be strong enough to face down the monstrous storm that straddled all the quickest routes to Hydraphur.

There was a whisper. Domasa stopped, cocked her head, took an experimental step. No, it had not been the sound of her skirts on the hide-skein matting that framed the rich carpets in the centre of the room. She put a finger to her vox-piece, checked the settings. No, it hadn't been anyone trying to hail her. She listened, and heard it again, grinned, and marched toward the trio of doors in the rear of the chamber behind the high table: the private dining rooms.

Varro Phrax, his wife, his chief attendant with the ridiculous metal head-frills and two others that Domasa didn't bother to try and put names to were all perched on the dining-couches. They all started up guiltily as though Domasa were a dormitory-mistress who had caught them at some kind of little game after lights out. Later, Domasa would think back on that analogy and laugh, but for now there was too much to do. She jabbed a finger at Varro.

'Master Phrax. The ship's apothecarion, if you please. Now.'

Ksana put a hand on Varro's arm, but he, to Domasa's disgust, had already stood. He really was like a puppy – snap an order at him in the right tone and he couldn't help himself.

'We were having a...' Varro shot a look over his shoulder. 'We were having a private conversation, Domasa. It's nothing you need to be present for, I assure you.'

'You may resume your *private conversation* at any point that pleases you, Master Phrax,' Domasa said. Warpspit, but the man was transparent. 'Only not right at this moment, I regret to say. You are needed at the apothecarion. Now.'

'What's wrong?' Varro's face suddenly twisted. 'Dreyder? Has something–'

'Your son is fine, I am sure. It's you we need. You're in no danger, don't worry, I'll explain on the way.'

Phrax gave what he probably thought was a knowing nod to the rest of them and stepped out of the room; Domasa could feel the others' eyes boring into her as she went after him.

'What is so urgent?' he asked as they marched away. 'Surely nobody will be there?'

'One of the ship's medicae staff is being roused on my instructions,' Domasa said, 'and he should be there and waiting for us. It took me a little while to find you, Varro, after I realised you weren't in your stateroom.'

'I'm sorry. Well, I mean, I thought we'd go elsewhere for our, er...'

'Your private conversation. Of course, Master Phrax. This is your voyage, after all, when one thinks about it.'

She caught him in her peripheral vision, giving her a dark look. Well, score a point for the man, she thought, he had more about him than she had credited him with.

'Quite right. How long have you been looking for me?'

'Some while. We checked the other decks too, or at least the main compartments. We weren't sure where you were.'

'Well, I'm sorry to have put you to the trouble. I assure you I'm safe with Rikah and Malon. And what could happen in the depths of the ship anyway?' His expression changed to something Domasa couldn't quite read out of the corner of her eye. 'Do you mean to say that you suspect more traitors in the crew?'

'It's nothing like that. Read this.' She pushed the communiqué paper at him. 'That should convince you that this is worth running about in the middle of the sleep shift for.' Varro took the paper and carefully uncrumpled it. He peered at it one way and another for the time it took them to walk down the passageway and down the forward well, where a wide curl of ramp led down through three layers of passenger decks, all deserted after Domasa's syndicate had taken exclusive charter of the ship. The walls of the well were strung with slightly brighter lanterns, in ornate spiked cases fashioned to resemble sunbursts, but even these had been dimmed for the sleep shift and Varro handed the paper back.

'I can make out references to Hydraphur and my father's flotilla. Does any of this matter? I'm sure I remember that the succession hearings wouldn't be able to start until I arrived. What's changed?'

'Did you even read the–' Domasa stopped short. After so much time clutched in her hand, the lower paragraphs were smeared into one another, and even in good light the scrawls would have been a challenge. With a small impatient noise she stuffed the paper into the sleeve of her gown and set off down the long passage, twin to the one they had just descended from, which led to the ready-room and the apothecarion.

'Alright. Our informant tells us that the flotilla has sent a sample of blood from their counter-claimant ahead to Hydraphur so the examinations to prove their half of the case can get under way. There's a line about a Mechanicus escort or something, but the message had trouble with the warp storm so some of the details got lost.'

'They must be sending it to the Mechanicus temple at the Augustaeum. That's where the tissue samples are traditionally examined when there's a contest of heredity,' said Varro.

'You knew that already, did you? Well here, Master Phrax, we do indeed have a contest of heredity, as I believe we've been at some pains to make clear to you. That's why we're marching down to the apothecarion at this damnable hour.'

'You want a sample of my blood, then. That's what this is about.'

'Well done. Presenting you in person will be a trump card for whenever we manage to arrive there, since we now know that the bloody flotilla has beaten us to the system. But we are not, mark me Varro, we are *not* going to let them have the whole thing their own way. My associates have a fast warp-runner ready to go, something that has enough power in it to skirt the worst of that storm and still make it to Hydraphur within ten days. What it's going to be carrying...'

But he had guessed. 'A tissue sample of my own.' Varro was puffing a little as they quick-marched.

Domasa had discreetly picked up the hem of her gown. 'Blood is all it should need. We've got a flask of the same pattern the Mechanicus use to transport samples so we're pretty sure it's going to arrive in the system in good condition. Given that we know for a fact that you're the Phrax firstborn, your blood should tell enough of a story to at least stall whatever the flotilla are trying to pull.' A door slid open ahead of them and white light poured out, making them both blink. 'Not nervous about having your blood taken, are you, Varro?'

'With an occupation like mine? I can't exactly afford to be, you know. Hah, all they need to do is reopen some of the weals that that Invus glasswood left me when I got careless the day before you arrived.' Some of the animation had come back into Varro's voice, and Domasa found herself smiling, rather to her own surprise.

'Before too much longer, Varro, your occupation will be rogue trader and merchant prince. You won't have to do any undignified rushing about like this, but I fear I have to warn you that you will still have people waiting around corners to draw your blood, albeit in more figurative ways.'

'That's a fact I think I'm starting to get used to, Madam Dorel,' said Varro, and walked forward into the whiteness of the apothecarion where a white-and-green-shrouded servitor was already moving forward with a syringe in one delicate hand.

THEY STOOD AT the lock and watched through the narrow port as the shuttle carrying the flask in which a vial of Varro's blood nestled slid backwards out of its berth with a brief spray of white frost as the remnant of the air in the lock escaped and froze. For a moment before it pushed itself into a new trajectory with bursts from its altitude jets they could see the distant shape beyond it of the *Noonlight Phoenix*, the fastest ship anywhere near Santo Pevrelyi, a sleek four-tiered hull with a flared prow like a snake's head.

'Wish her well,' said Domasa. 'She's carrying the opening of your claim. Throne knows I'll be sending my thoughts with her tonight.'

'I've been thinking, Domasa.'

'Oh?' Now she had her counter-gambit launched, she felt her tension lifting. She suddenly felt that she could use a good sleep herself.

'Has the charter ever been held jointly? I mean, have two members of the Phrax family ever owned it between them? I've been thinking back over what I know of my family history and I can't think of it happening, but that doesn't mean it couldn't.'

'One charter, one hand, one Phrax, one heir. I trust I'm being clear,' said Domasa as they walked away from the lock. She thought she knew where this was heading, and she had a mind to tread on this line of thought as soon as she could.

'It just seems so… stupid.' Varro sighed. 'You know? I had this whole childhood on the flotilla and then I came of age on Gunarvo and it was all wonderful in so many ways, but… well, I keep thinking that there's this other Phrax, my half-brother, blood of my blood, another son of Hoyyon that I've never known about all this time. And now that I do know about him what's the first thing that's happening? We head straight for opposing camps and get ready for war over the spoils from my father's death. Doesn't this strike you as wrong?'

'Try growing up in the Navis Nobilite,' snorted Domasa, surprising herself a little with her candour. 'The family affairs of Navigators have probably not given me a very good yardstick to judge questions like yours, but if you're thinking of letting down your guard and throwing open your arms, then I'll say think again. Stop and think, really think about what's at stake here.'

'I've thought about it. My son. That's what's at stake. *Who's* at stake.'

'Thinking about the way you will pass on the charter is very noble, and perfectly fitting for the position you aspire to, but before you can get too far with plans like that we need to make sure–'

'No. Not my son's inheritance. My *son*. He's the one I look at and remember what's at stake. As you say, Madam Dorel, perhaps your own family circumstances stop you from really understanding.' There was a tone in his voice

that set her teeth grinding. Perhaps there were things in
the universe she hated more than being condescended to,
but she hadn't found one yet.

'After all the work that I've done for you, Varro, after all
the work my associates and backers and I have done to
help you to reach Hydraphur and mount a case against
this ridiculous counter-claim, I must say that we perhaps
expected a tiny degree more co-operation and gratitude.'
Her back was ramrod straight and her shoulders back, the
way she always held herself when she was angry. 'The
effort we are making to help you is perhaps something I
need to remind you of rather more often.'

'No, Domasa, you don't.' He had stopped, now, and
waited until she drew level with him. 'I am very aware of
all the work you have done. The ships you have obtained,
Navigators, the medicae help, the support against my
half-brother Petronas. And information about him, too,
and on the progress of the counter-claim. I've noticed
that. I've noticed that all your talk about treachery and
honour when you found what you told me was a spy in
our own midst didn't stop you from cultivating this informant of yours in the flotilla. There seems to be a lot of
help that you and these backers of yours – whom you still
haven't fully named or described to me, either – are giving me that even I don't know about. How else are you
helping me, Domasa Dorel?'

'By putting your spine straight and ready to contest
your succession,' she came back without missing a beat.
'You don't know your own best interests, Varro Phrax. If
someone doesn't take you by the hand you are going to
sit there with that amiable smile on your face and let a
rival you've never met stroll by, pluck what is rightfully
yours right out of your hand and walk away laughing at
you, because you're somehow worried that reaching out
to stop him makes you a nasty person. I didn't think
there really were people like you in the Imperium, Varro.
I have trouble believing that you mean all this pious

brotherhood stuff even now. But if you do, then you're luckier to have fallen in with me and my syndicate than you know.' The lateness of the hour was finally starting to tell on her. It was the kind of private thought that Domasa would never have given voice to normally. But Varro only stood there, silent; he gave the Navigator an appraising look that was very unlike his usual one.

'I know enough to guess, Domasa, what form of gratitude you and your syndicate will be expecting. I do know that much. I believe, in fact, that we understand each other possibly a little better than you realise.'

The two of them looked at each other for a little while in the dim corridor. Domasa had seen such face-downs on rare occasions in the past, and could usually rely on the strangeness of her features to unsettle the other person enough to get them to walk away first. But, she remembered, Varro was one of the few non-Navigators she had met to whom her appearance didn't seem to be strange at all.

'Good,' was all she said in the end, and took her leave of him. It wasn't until much later that she realised she had never thought about what Varro and his wife and his staff might have been having a private conversation about, in a private room on a deserted deck in the middle of the ship's artificial night.

CHAPTER NINE

The Bastion Praetoris, The Wall,
Bosporian Hive, Hydraphur

REVEREND SIMOVA'S APPEARANCE in the court of Praetor Imprimis Dastrom was insultingly brief, an anticlimax. He had been marched into the court to testify and answer questions about how the cages had been commissioned and hung over the Avenue Solar, how Ghammo Ströon (now chained with Symandis in the dock) had been apprehended and sentenced, how the whole ordeal and the handling of prisoners worked, what his own role was. He was stunned and mortified that his mission to Trylan Tor had ended back here, scant kilometres from the Cathedral where it had begun, in a courtroom full of harsh lights and steel fittings with the cadaverous Judge enthroned high above him.

Simova was not stupid. The Ecclesiarchy worked as hard at keeping citizens' minds in line as the Arbites did, if not harder, and he knew the rituals, the settings, how to place an accused in awe. The Judge on high, the booming orders and decrees, the quieter tones of the junior examining Judges who unrolled in front of him a clever mix of what the Arbites already knew and what they suspected, lines of questioning hidden inside one another, hunchbacked scribes and blank-eyed auditing servitors recording every word. Why, had he not presided over the trials of heretics and blasphemers using exactly the same strategies?

The true humiliation: it was working. Simova had walked into the courtroom full of anger at the coarse treatment he had received at the sentry post, and disdain at the Arbites' belief that the tricks they used on common criminals were going to work on him. But still he found himself reacting the way he knew they wanted him to: wrong footed, over-anxious to explain himself and fill in the gaps in their knowledge. 'You are not on trial here, reverend,' they kept telling him, and he knew that it was a lie. This was a trial if ever he had seen one.

And it didn't help that the arrogant thug of an arbitor senioris seemed to be able to pluck his thoughts out of the air, because the first thing she said to him when he emerged from the courtroom through the four-metre-high courtroom doors was: 'That was not your trial, reverend, but it so easily could have been.'

She was standing in a carefully careless way in amongst a knot of black-armoured Arbites in the centre of the corridor. Facing her, still alone as the door swung silently closed behind him, Simova touched the gold aquila on its chain around his expansive waist, for confidence.

'Do not presume, arbitor, to even speak to me, much less to hector me about trials and what you might or might not do to me. I do not back away from a single word I have said about what will come of this. There are some things I took care to make clear to your subordinate on the flight back from that wretched tor–'

'Indeed there were. I understand that your eloquence was matched only by your stamina. There were vox-pickups in the ornithopter that brought you and your Sororitas back to the hive, did you know that? I have every point you made to my long-suffering Arbites in a data-ark on the desk in my personal chambers. I haven't listened to them yet. Perhaps I should ask one of the Bastion clerks to make a summary.'

'You are doing justice to the absolute worst of your reputation, Arbitor Calpurnia,' said Simova coldly. 'You show all the worst tendencies of the arbitrator: the oafish reliance on force, the tendency to think with your fists and boots and the barrel of a shotgun, the belief that the *Lex Imperia* is nothing more than whatever you feel like doing to whatever devoted servant of the Emperor is unfortunate enough to–'

He had scored a result, although not the one he had intended. Suddenly the tip of Calpurnia's slender power-maul was buried in Simova's navel, the spines on its tip pricking him unpleasantly through the brocade of his robe. Her black-gauntleted thumb hovered over the power switch.

'Here you stand, in our courthouse, and you lecture me on the law of the Imperium and how I may or may not go about enforcing it,' said Calpurnia. 'What an interesting thing to witness.' Her words were light but her eyes were locked on him like emerald lasers, and only now did Simova realise how furious he had succeeded in making her.

He took a step back, and she a step forward: the maul remained dug into the swell of his belly.

'You have presided over punishments for blasphemers against the Emperor, Simova. You know how literally damning words can be. Except that you forget it. You assault with words the authority of an Arbitor General of the Adeptus, something that will condemn you under a hundred different codes with every sentence you utter, and then you decide that you will lecture me on the law

that I know and enforce? You forget yourself most griev-
ously, reverend. I could execute you on the spot for what
you have just said to me and my actions would be clad in
iron by every letter of the law. There would even be cases,
were you any other man, reverend, by which I myself
could be placed on trial for *failing* to execute you. Do not
test me again.' The pressure on his gut was suddenly
gone; there was a click as Calpurnia returned the maul to
its belt-clip.

'Is that why I was brought here, then, arbitor?' Simova
made sure his tone was respectful and mildly curious. 'I
do not believe that at the time that two dozen Arbites...
removed me.' He still could not quite say *arrested*,
although that was obviously what it had been 'and my
escorts from that tor, I had said anything at all about you
or your authority, arbitor. We had not even broken the
interdiction around your fortress, although our errand
was no more and no less than to submit a claim in a
matter of law that you are currently overseeing. An
action with deference to the authority of your office built
into it, you will notice. I have co-operated and ordered
co-operation at every step. Do you think the Sororitas
would have put up their weapons had I not expressly
ordered them to? They were ready to fight for me on that
tor.'

'Where you had no right to be, incidentally, reverend.
You were required to remain here to be ready to appear
before Dastrom's tribunal.'

'To provide testimony, Arbitor Calpurnia, not as an
accused party, despite your performance to the contrary.
Read the testimony I gave in there. I am not the guilty
party, and I do not see why you needed to pretend otherwise. Or do you seriously think that you're going to find
my fingermarks on the hijacked blimp and the crane-
truck and Symandis's power axe?'

'Let's say for the sake of the argument that I don't find
you actively complicit,' said Calpurnia with a considering

look. 'The responsibility for setting up and overseeing the ordeal was still yours. If one of my Arbites dozes off on watch and an assassin gets past him to murder me, he'd be sadly mistaken to think he wouldn't be found at fault even though he didn't pull the trigger himself. Take note and take instruction. If it weren't for your particular mission and the Eparch's feelings about it you'd be in a cell already.'

'Must you drag the Eparch into this, arbitor? If you are alleging some kind of failure then kindly allege it of me alone rather than trying to besmirch the whole Cathedral.'

In reply, Calpurnia snapped her fingers and Culann placed a message scroll into her hand. Simova's nerves, which had relaxed when Calpurnia had put her weapon away, tensed again when he saw the Eparchal seal on it, already broken.

'I've had a letter,' she said, 'from the Eparch apologising for your actions in leaving Bosporian and trying to bully your way to Trylan Tor. He also says that you were merely trying your best to perform an errand that he had asked of you. I'm assuming that this is something to do with the matter of law you mentioned to me earlier, is it?'

Simova nodded, still staring at the Eparchal seal. Eparch Baszle himself had been forced to intercede on Simova's behalf, to allow him to finish the mission Baszle himself had sent him on. One little part of his mind was bidding a mournful farewell to the gold statues and lush tapestry of the Chamber of Exegetors: after this, the rest of his career would be spent supervising the cleaning rosters in a roadside shrine on some dung-splat little agri-world in the ugliest corner of the segmentum that his rivals at the Cathedral could find.

For some reason Simova always became aware of the soreness of his feet when he was nervous, and they were aching badly now. He took a breath.

'You, Arbitor Calpurnia, have been appointed to rule on the succession of the rogue trader charter passed down through the merchant family of Phrax. This charter bears not the imprimatur but the personal inscription of the Immortal God-Emperor, investing it as a relic by the hand of Him on Terra. And so in the name and by the power of the Adeptus Ministorum, I claim it as a holy relic for the greater glory of the Eparchy and Cathedral of Hydraphur.'

Culann cocked an eyebrow and looked sideways at Calpurnia's face; the other Arbites were motionless as before. There was silence in the hall while a pair of scribes hurried nervously past with armfuls of data-copy and rapped on the door behind them. The door opened to admit them, and then swung closed.

'Do you know, Reverend Simova,' Shira Calpurnia said in her most conversational tone, 'I believe that your claim is, quite possibly, the very last thing that this whole affair needed.'

The Shrine of the Machine God,
Adeptus Quarter of the Augustaeum, Hydraphur

THE HERALDS HAD gone back and forth in the form of data codes, servitors and the occasional junior adepts. The formal invitation had been, issued, received and confirmed with all due protocol. The meeting between the two respected magi of the Machine God unfolded as flawlessly as two perfectly maintained logic engines working through a data transfer handshake.

Sanja knew that there were those in the Mechanicus who distrusted people like Dyobann, considering that tech-priests spending too long in the company of extraneous influences tended to develop miscalibrations of their sacred doctrines and corruption of their liturgical beliefs. But Sanja was a genetor, a studier of biological systems that were both incredibly complex and less predictable, and such a field of study had left him a little more flexible of temperament than those of his colleagues who had embraced the inorganic for their studies.

And so when Magos Errant Dyobann came down from the Ring, alone but for two servitors and carrying an engraved flask of red-tinted steel, Sanja had met him amiably enough.

He had chosen to receive his guest in the Helispex Chapel itself. The much put-upon engine had already been dismounted for the move to Trylan Tor before it had turned out that the aforesaid move was out of the question; it had now been re-mounted in its ark in the centre of the chapel. Had there been no more pressing business at hand Sanja would have ordered the room filled with incense and a solid-state vox looping through psalms of placation, then locked with a seal placed on its door for seventy-three standard hours and fifteen seconds; this being an appropriate rite of appeasement for a machine that had been forced to endure some kind of insult to its operation. But duty and obligation awaited, and so the placation of the engine would have to wait too. Sanja had a binary translation of the Omnissiah's Catechism of Subjection loaded into the ancillary data engines that attended upon the Helispex itself, and now they circulated it constantly through the data cables lining the walls to create an atmosphere of prayerful obedience. Sanja hoped it would remind the engine's spirit of its responsibilities, at least for as long as the business of the charter took.

The chapel itself was narrow and long. Buttress-columns curving up from the floor and meeting overhead turned its sides into a procession of niches, the walls and pillars holding complex patterns of inlaid power- and code-lines ornamented and illuminated with rare metals and gems. The top and side of the ark were folded out to expose the face of the engine; the power cables running to the engraved bronze panels in the floor were adorned with ribbons, seals and strips of parchment bearing Mechanicus blessings. Behind it Genetor Sanja, in bright ceremonial robes, sat in a suspensor throne two metres above the floor. His luminant skulls hung in the air by his shoulders and his hands cradled a jewelled data-slate reader bequeathed to him by thirty-seven generations of forebears.

Dyobann left his servitors at the door and advanced with slow, deferential steps. His own garments were much plainer: red for the Mechanicus, with rows of patterns stitched into the fabric at sleeves, collar and hems to show the many disciplines of the magos errant: genetor, alchemys, metallurg, more. His head was bowed and his patchwork face was hidden by his hood.

The two luminants took the flask delicately from his hands in their webs of metal dendrites. As Dyobann knelt and prayed at the foot of the steps, Sanja's throne lowered and circled the ark, always facing in so that his back was never to the engine itself. The luminants gave little twitches of their dendrites and flicks of red light from their optics as they inspected the metal and the seals: their report, beamed into Sanja's brain through the receptors in his skull, showed all was well.

Sanja stepped from the throne and walked to them. Standing before the Helispex Engine, he felt the awe he always did: this was as great a relic of the Machine God as he would set eyes on in his lifetime. For a day and a half now he had been anointing it with oils, circulating precious incenses through the housing and meditating to clear his mind for the ritual – the preparations had left him in a state of religious concentration that bordered on trance. But now the faces were clear and cold, the air purified so that nothing might enter the engine except what he begged it to take into itself and show to him.

On the top step Sanja abased himself and set the flask down.

He closed his eyes and the world became a mosaic, a composite, like a series of images painted on layers of translucent curtains. He looked at the flask through all

the senses of his luminants and through the eyes of the
machine gargoyles that watched over the ark from the top
of every column. He watched as the luminants' dendrites,
whose grace and delicacy no human could match, carefully broke the seal on the flask and lifted out the vial
inside. Then, floating no more than a few centimetres off
the floor and with their skull-faces turned downward,
they approached the silvered face of the Helispex Engine.

The face of the engine was just that. Engraved on the
silver slab of its side in breathtaking detail, detail so fine
that without his augmetics there were elements to the
picture Sanja would not have seen at all, was a stylised
reproduction of the sacred emblem of the Adeptus
Mechanicus, the half-skull, half-cog of the *Machina Opus*.
But that had been superimposed over a larger design,
another skull, this one drawn with augmetics to the eye
and cranium that suggested a servitor or certain patterns
of junior acolytes. The skull was distended and stylised,
its mouth open, and it was into the maw of the skull that
the luminants slipped the vial.

Sanja's breath caught. He had heard the quiet click and
hum of moving parts within the engine, the sign that its
spirit remembered its duty. Moved by that spirit, the
luminants moved back and outward and the doors to the
chapel swung shut. The Helispex Engine was about to
begin its operations, calling down the mind of the
Machine God into its circuits and nanostacks, bringing
the unknowable intellect of the Arch-Mechanicus to bear.

Sanja and Dyobann both set up a buzzing, chirruping
prayer in machine-code that echoed through the chapel.
The lights in the chapel flickered and the luminants
bobbed in their places. And then, with a still and small
sound like a sigh from the depths of the engine, it was
done. The magi straightened up and looked at one
another, and the doors to the chapel, and the outer doors
beyond them, both opened again. Dyobann's servitors
stood there exactly as before.

It was time for the engine to rest before the revelation of data. The two magi stood at the base of the dais and waited.

'I acknowledge gratitude,' said Dyobann at length. 'I have seen many things in my travels with Phrax, but none compare to this. To be present at such a ritual is an experience such as I had never expected to have.'

'Genetors come from three sectors on pilgrimages to this shrine,' said Sanja with a trace of smugness. 'Seven months ago the arch-lexmechanic of the Twelfth Tech-Guard Fleet came here with gifts of servitors and scriptures and machine-parts blessed on Mars itself, for the right to pray at the foot of the dais for one hundred minutes and look upon the engine itself. The clarity of the engine's communion with the Machine God is such that it can perform seventy-six billion calculations and observations in a second, and process them in five seconds more. This is the traditional honour that the Mechanicus pays to the line of Phrax, that no less a device than the Helispex shall confirm the bloodline at each succession.'

'You are to be praised for your custodianship, magos,' said Dyobann. 'And you honour me in turn, permitting me to see the invocations for myself.' He had seemed to tense at the reference to the confirmation of the bloodline.

'Knowledge is holiness, the Omnissiah teaches us so,' Sanja replied. 'To pass on knowledge to the select and the anointed is a great sacrament and elevates us all in the service of the Machine.'

'It is as you say.'

They both stood there for a moment longer, each one reluctant to break the gravitas of the moment. Then there was a tiny sound that made Dyobann look around: the slabs of carved stone that made up the ark of the Helispex were slowly closing around the engine itself. As both magi watched they locked into place and sealed themselves, the join lines now barely visible.

'It rests now,' said Sanja. 'Tonight I will lead my acolytes in the ceremonies of cleansing as we refresh its spirit, and then we shall leave it for a time to restore itself. It has had a taxing time of these last days. Magos Dyobann, if your other duties permit you, do you wish to attend upon the engine when we do so?'

'It would be an honour, genetor-magos, thank you.' Dyobann's voice bespoke a trace of nerves, Sanja thought, but that was only natural. Then he turned as two jointed metal arms wrapped about with transmission wires emerged from the dais: the engine had passed on its insights to its attendant machines, and these in turn were ready to pass them on to the two magi. Sanja and Dyobann walked to the dais steps and knelt, each connecting to it in their own way. Dyobann extended the tiny tendril from the corner of his eye and stroked the tip of the arm until he found a receptor and slid the tendril home; Sanja had one of the luminants move forward to take the end of the other arm in one of its own and begin transmitting back to him. For a quiet moment the attendant engines performed last-minute collations on the data that the Helispex itself had vouchsafed to them, and then both magi closed their eyes and submitted to the flow of information.

In the space behind Sanja's eyes, colours exploded and swirled, sonic codes cracked and buzzed in his ears, senses no unaugmented human possessed all began to sing. The Helispex had held Petronas Phrax's blood up to the glare of the eternal Machine God's gaze, and now he saw what it had seen.

Dancing through the imagery was archive-data, the parallel records back through every generation of the Phrax bloodline. The engine remembered every operation it had ever performed, every petition that had ever been made to it. It had known it was being asked to look once again at the bloodline of Phrax, and so now the knowledge of the tests it had done on the family's every generation blossomed silently in the backs of the magi's minds as the blood-print of this new heir danced through the fore of their consciousness. Gene-prints, chemical analyses down to the molecular, down to the sub-molecular, microchemical forensics that showed every influence and impact on the heir's blood from the genes he had been born with to the food he had eaten, diseases he had had, the kinds of sunlight he had been exposed to, the kinds of vaccinations, the...

...the...

Wait.

With speed born of fear, Magos Errant Dyobann wrenched his consciousness out of the coded swirl, hissing at the flare of pain in his eye from the sudden disconnection of his tendril. At the door his servitors swivelled as he ran between them and then they fell in behind him, the sculpted metal hooves he had made for them clashing on the stone floor.

Out of the chapel they fled, through one set of doors and then another, down a reliquary hall where two young acolytes gawped at them. Dyobann fixed grimly on the end of the hall where it met the two other main halls and became a tall cave in the rock beneath Augusteum. If he could make it to the ground level there were only three sets of doors to the plaza where the mech-carriage that Phrax money had bought him was waiting. Then, alone with two lightly-armed servitors in a whole world on which he had never set foot before today–

They reached the lift-car, with a junior priest riding in it. He made to say something and Dyobann ordered him out with a gesture; he made to argue and Dyobann flicked a curt, silent message to one of his servitors which snapped a stiletto out of one of its utility-arms and stepped forward. The blade punctured the priest's skull five times in two seconds and then the car doors were closing behind him and they were on their way up to the surface.

–but he would get out, he would survive, so many years of travel with the Phrax flotilla had meant the one thing he had learned to do was survive. And here they were, the lift-car doors opening: Dyobann gave thanks that the shrine was not one of those that extended kilometres down. Had the lift ride been any longer it would have become a trap.

They ran up a ramp and through the rear hall of the shrine's central level. Could they fight their way out? He didn't know, but maybe they wouldn't have to. The circuits around the Helispex must be closed off from the rest of the shrine so the engine's contemplations would not be sullied with the mundane data. It would take Sanja some time to realise what he was seeing, more time to disengage if he took the time to do it properly, then he would have to realise Dyobann was gone–

Through the portal to the stairs, they were almost at the forechamber.

–and then he would have to leave the chapel himself to reach a system from which he could raise the alarm. If Dyobann could just survive in the hive until the flotilla arrived, he could get a message to Trazelli and have–

He reached the inner forechamber doors just in time to see the great outer doors crash closed. As he cycled up the auxiliary photoreceptors built into his eyes to make the most of the dim light, Genetor-Magos Sanja's voice boomed into him through his own ears and through every mechanical code-frequency he had open, boomed from the devices built into every wall of the chamber. The force of it nearly drove him to his knees.

'You *dare!*' the voice roared. Dyobann triggered neuroregulators inside his skull and shut down the fear impulse. Sanja was no mightier than he, he told himself. Sanja could not possibly have had to survive the things Dyobann had seen and done.

'You *dare* to bring this, this filth here? Into the place where our cult is in most abject service to the God of the Machine? This is how you serve Him?'

'…rve him?' There was a pale echo of Sanja's voice coming from somewhere, but Dyobann didn't have the time to pay it mind. He turned, looking around him at the soaring forechamber, the bronze pistons in silent motion around its walls, the ceremonial cogs hanging in gravity fields high overhead.

'Yes,' he called back. 'Yes, this is how I serve. Do you understand, Sanja, do you have the first conception of what I have done for our order with the freedom that the charter gives me? The things I have seen? Found? The relics I have brought away? I have performed works for our high priests that no magos without that flotilla to support them could ever have performed? The pieces of tech I have carried through Imperial domains with never a report or a tithe? The sacred sites I have been able to direct our explorators to? The species I have been able to treat with out of sight of Imperial eyes? The enemies with whom the flotilla has given me the resources to deal?'

'So this is the Magos Dyobann,' came that shattering voice from the walls ('…gos Dyobann,' came that slurred echo). 'A scavenger-rat in a red robe, a smuggler and thief? A murderer and a consorter with murderers? A friend of the xenos, the alien whose form mocks the pure genetics of the human template? One whose contempt for what is sacred leads him to poison a sacred engine of the Mechanicus with lies and betray the trust its keeper placed in him?' ('…in him?')

'How could you understand, rattling through endless prayers in a sealed shrine, locked away in ignorance!' Dyobann was fired with anger now, barely aware of the magnitude of the insult in the word he had just used. 'How do you dare to judge me?'

'Knowledge is holy,' bellowed Sanja, and now there were two organic voices joining in the flood of input from the walls. One was from Sanja's own throat, and Dyobann whirled: the genetor-magos had appeared in the doors behind him, flanked by luminants and servitors.

'Knowledge is holy and information is holy. We live our lives in the quest for it. The purer the data, the purer the lifeblood of the Machine and the Machine God. Purity of data is the greatest sacrament a priest of the Machine God can hope for. And now you come here with this.' He raised a vial in one shaking hand.

'...here with this.' Dyobann realised with a shock that the echo was the voice of one of his own servitors, the one he had killed the priest with. It had half-turned to him, blood and machine-oil dripping off its blade arm, and was repeating every word of Sanja's as the other magos spoke them. He'd found a way in, into its systems, had some override code that had bypassed the programs Dyobann thought he had embedded beyond all possibility of breaching. Without even a physical connection. Dyobann for the first time realised what a dangerous enemy he had just made.

'You falsified knowledge. You tampered with the data. You came here knowing that you yourself had created these impurities. You thought that you could deceive the Helispex Engine, may its spirit recover. You attempted trickery on the holy engine, attempted to use it to create untruth. An untruth which itself distorts knowledge and moves us away from the perfect knowledge of the Omnissiah. *You tried to trick us.*'

'...us,' the servitor finished. The delay in its speech was growing shorter as Sanja's control over it tightened. There was no way to tell if he had found a way into the other one. Dyobann's thoughts spun ever faster. 'Your blasphemy against the Machine God is doubled and compounded,' Sanja went on, 'and your betrayal of your holy office is nothing less than total. I strip you of your office and your name. You are forfeit.' The genetor-magos threw the vial down onto the stone floor, and as it shattered Dyobann spat a coded command at the bloody-handed servitor: '*Tikk!*' It was a word from the flotilla, the word for outsider, and the command was for

the servitor to kill everyone present who was not of the
flotilla. This was only the fourth time he had ever had to
use the command, and the secret he was protecting here
was probably the most terrible one he had ever kept.

In his heart Magos Dyobann knew that Sanja was right.
He wondered if he had ever had a chance: those short
minutes coupled into the data-stream had shown him
the sight of the Helispex was clearer and more powerful
than he had ever anticipated. But he was not going to
stand here and let them cut him down.

Sanja had almost total control of the servitor, but the
tikk command was buried somewhere he still had not
reached. The servitor loped toward the magos before
Sanja was able to halt it with a frown and a gesture, and
while it swayed there Dyobann spun and wrenched off
the other servitor's tunic-shroud. The flesh-machine
tensed as Dyobann brought it to combat-readiness and
reached for the stubby cylinders around its waist. To all
appearances they were part of the pneumatic mechanisms in its legs, but falsely so, a disguise.

Dyobann flicked back his sleeve as he heard Sanja'a
own servitors clatter down the steps, and the round collar on the end of the thick roll of mechadendrites that
had so revolted Petronas Phrax unclipped and clanged to
the floor. Dyobann's arm unplaited into a hydra-cluster
of metal snakes that plunged and snapped into housings
on the top of each cylinder. Loadout data, weapon specs
and targeting reticules unfolded themselves across
Dyobann's mind and vision as he pulled the weapon
modules free.

The servitor Sanja had controlled was spasming wildly:
Sanja must have found its combat subroutines and was
trying to suppress them. But the genetor's own weapons
were just a few strides away now, three heavy servitors,
cloned muscles reinforced by layers of exoskeleton, iron
plates carved with the *Machina Opus* or leering gargoyle
visages grafted to the front of their skulls where their

faces had been. Chainfist blades rumbled and revved; a drillspike spun so fast it was just a blurred length of shining metal in the yellow light of the lamps.

Dyobann's hydra-arm flared and writhed like an anemone and the first servitor was pitching forward, lifeless: one cylinder held a pressurised reservoir of a vicious nerve-toxin that Dyobann and D'Leste had brewed up two years before.

The second servitor hurdled the body straight into a tight-burst haywire pulse that blew out its cybernetics and sent it into a mad jerking dance. Its exoskeleton smoked and froze. The weapons in its limbs accelerated past their tolerances and began to burn out.

Dyobann backpedalled, circling out and around the floor of the forechamber. The forest of tentacles sprouting from his shoulder snaked in the air, searching for the luminants; another snapped forward and fired a chaff-pellet into the doorway where Sanja stood. There was a tiny crack as it exploded and then the doorway was full of metal-dust, heated by a tiny melta-charge and throwing out magnetic static. The sentry-servitors built into the pillars on either side of the door had been shut down as a mark of respect for Dyobann's position, something that Sanja was probably bitterly regretting now. And now, even if he reactivated them they would be blind and useless.

The third of Sanja's killing machines was grappling with Dyobann's own, and there was no time to shout out the codes: he had to use his tight-beam coder and gamble that Sanja would not detect the frequency and override it. Dyobann flicked his perceptions across the beam-link and was looking through his servitors' eyes. His vision split, the shrine-servitor doubling on itself, filling his vision as it rushed straight at him at the same time as he watched it barrel toward his servitor from four metres away.

Then his vision took a strange half-lurch, disorienting him even with the compensators built into his senses, as

his commands pitched his servitor over on its side. In the
second it took Sanja's machine to adjust, Dyobann's
servitor had hamstrung it with a low sweep of a wire-fine
blade that slipped out of a finger. A homing-dart flew
from the tip of one of Dyobann's outthrust tentacles – it
hung motionless in the air for a split second before it
lunged forward. For a moment a third layer appeared in
Dyobann's already doubled vision: the sight of the gap
between the servitor's face and shoulder plates growing
wider and wider as he guided the dart home. His vision
flashed white, then dropped to black, and he snapped the
connection back from his servitor as his dart – its outer
layer of microflechettes, inner core of pyro-acid – burst
deep in the last enemy's abdomen. Smoke and the stink
of evaporating flesh shrouded the wreck of the servitor as
it fell.

And then just silence, but for a low hoarse sound that
Dyobann realised was his own breathing. He muttered a
verbal command and his servitor clambered to its feet
and loped towards the doors. Dyobann backed after it,
fixing every mechanical sense he had on the thinning
chaff-cloud between the door-pillars. Runes danced in his
vision to show that a second homing-dart was armed and
ready, that the neurotoxin reservoir was still at eighty-
seven per cent capacity, that the tentacles tipped with
diamond-claws and tiny sawblade arrays were running at
combat revs.

There was a crackle behind him as the powered spurs
built into his servitor's forearms and wrists snapped into
operation and charged up the destructive energy-fields
that sheathed their blades. If they gave him even sixty seconds for the servitor to work on the shrine doors they
would…

Red figures poured out into the forechamber, moving
with quick, deadly precision. Their flak-gowns and cowls
were a dark, dusty red and bronze augmetics glinted and
flashed where their garments did not cover: Skitarii.

Tech-guard. Not servitors but the elite military of the Cult of the Machine.

Three of them threw short, slender carbines to their shoulders and banged off quick bursts that broke against the subcutaneous flex-plates that armoured Dyobann's torso and against the servitor's back as it hacked at the doors. The renegade magos experienced a flash of hope: they were using lightweight shatter-rounds, slugs whose breakable design could not damage the forechamber but which also robbed them of stopping power against the armoured bodies of Dyobann and his servitor.

Regaining his balance, Dyobann lunged forward to bring the two nearest Skitarii in range of the one-shot microflamer in another tentacle-tip, but the burst of white-hot vapour only splashed across the front of their gowns. Both men dived and rolled to efficiently snuff the flames, one of them firing another burst at Dyobann as he came up onto one knee. The magos errant spent a second, precious homing-dart to crumple the man's head like a gourd and flung another chaff-pellet at his feet. That was when he realised that the complex web of transmitted data dancing and tickling in one sector of his vision and in the back of his head had gone, gone at the same moment as the sounds of bladework behind him had ceased. He suddenly realised why the shots from the Skitarii had died away, why they had not thrown grenades.

Magos Dyobann spun around, the tentacles of his hydra-arm thrashing the air for a target, his non-modified hand hooked into a claw, his transponder augmetics bellowing defiance on every frequency. Even the data tendril at the corner of his eye was extended and sniffing the air.

In a flash of gold and a glimmer of bone, the two luminants whipped up and away from the servitor they had just killed. They had flown into the forechamber high over his head, hidden by the hanging cogwheels. Dyobann snapped out the tentacle that held the haywire grenades...

…but the luminants were angels of the Machine, made from components engineered to the purest of tolerances and the skulls of the most pious of the Mechanicus priest-hood – dare he strike them down with such a terrible weapon?

The hesitation wrought by that last scrap of his old piety undid him. By the time the haywire detonated over the prone servitor the luminants had arced up four metres in the air and swooped smoothly down again. One jinked to the left, and even with Dyobann's vision guiding it the third homing-dart could not turn in time to follow it and it flew on to spend itself somewhere in the darkness high overhead. The other luminant corkscrewed and rolled in the air. Dyobann's claw-tentacle snapped on air and skated by a millimetre away from its gold-leaf skin.

There was noise in Dyobann's ears, noise that hit the translator augmetics and unfolded into data: the luminants were broadcasting a simple packet of code, over and over, three times a second: nothing more than the data-seal of Genetor-Magos Cynez Sanja, so that Dyobann would know who was watching through their eyes as they delivered sentence. As one of them extended mechadendrites whose adamantine tips drove through the magos errant's armour like paper and hoisted him onto his toes, the other extruded a humming power-pack from the base of its skull. The code changed, sending a high-speed data signal on every auditory and vox channel Dyobann possessed.

The communication fed itself directly through his translator layers into his brain, so the message in all its detail unfolded in his consciousness in an instant. The message was not complex. A list of charges and four declarations. Accusation, condemnation, excommunication, destruction.

One point eight four seconds after the transmission completed, the second luminant clamped Dyobann's eye-tendril between the thick grips on the end of its power pack. There was barely time for pain: the power-pulse coursed through the tendril and through the webs of micro-augmetic filament spread through the magos's cerebellum, flashing them to white heat and incinerating Dyobann's stunned, disbelieving brain.

CHAPTER TEN

Ready-room atrium aboard the flotilla flagship *Bassaan*, En route to Galata, Hydraphur system

GALT RARELY FELT comfortable aboard the *Bassaan*. He was acutely aware of how firmly his role on the flotilla placed him aboard the *Callyac's Promise*, where shipboard routine emphasised an unhurried pace, comfort and tranquillity. The *Bassaan*, businesslike and functional, run by a curt, quasi-military crew, made him uneasy.

And that was on the better trips. With Hoyyon himself a step and a half ahead, he was always ready to serve as he watched the old man's gaze sweep back and forth and the crew blanch as though his face were a searchlight, painfully fierce.

If I could go back there, he thought, *see that contented Galt and talk to him, I wonder what he would think of what I would tell him? I wonder what the old Galt would think of the reason I'm here now?*

He watched the officers file past him down the corridor, reflections dancing across the engraved metal walls, checking their dress uniforms and fiddling with their hands. It seemed to take longer than it should – there were only half a dozen or so of them. He and Behaya had put their foot down about that: no more than a small group, and making even that concession to the travesty of an heir-apparent had driven home to both of them how bad their predicament was getting.

D'Leste stood further down the corridor, shuffling his feet fretfully. He and Galt had not spoken since Dyobann had flown on ahead to Hydraphur, and as days had passed and they had both become sure the magos would not return they had taken to avoiding each other. The flotilla meetings in the speaking chamber had given way to bitter, whispered little conferences between the masters two or three at a time in secret places. Rumours and uncertainty were spreading through all the crews. Galt wasn't surprised. A tikk could have come on board now and known straight away that something was wrong, it was that bad.

The doors to the room swung shut behind the last of the officers and Galt exhaled. They had commandeered a room near the apothecarion, near enough to get Petronas onto life support very quickly if he took a turn for the worse. What nobody was admitting was that they were nearing the point where it might not help. Dyobann was gone and D'Leste's attempts to keep Petronas stable without the magos's help had been increasingly ham-handed. Zanti and Trazelli had already promised the doctor to his face that if Petronas didn't last until the hearing they would take it out on his hide.

The hearing. That was their magic threshold, their event horizon. Just keep their heir-apparent alive until the hearing; whatever happened then would happen. Galt looked gloomily at the closed doors of the ready room. He felt the floating, fatalistic calm of someone who has made a terrible choice and is now waiting for the consequences, whatever they may be, to fall.

'How did we get to this?' murmured Behaya beside him, and neither Galt nor D'Leste had an answer.

Ready-room aboard the flotilla flagship *Bassaan*, En route to Galata, Hydraphur system

ATITH WAS THE only one who could speak as the seven of them stood around the white-shrouded bed. Phyron had fallen a place back as if what he was seeing had physically hit him, and Trichodi had put her face in her hands. Kohze, hands knotted behind his back, whooped for breath despite the smell that the perfume-mists couldn't hide.

'Nils,' said Atith in a small, broken voice. 'What have they done to you? Oh, Nils, what's happened?'

'Not Nils,' the twisted shape on the bed said. 'Not Nils Petronas. Halfway right, though, halfway. Half-right, about a half-man. Hah! Half-man. Half-man, becoming half-something else, becom–' The figure suddenly doubled over with a burst of wet coughing, trying to expel something from its chest that its muscles were too weak to shift. A medical servitor, one metre high with mask and augmetics designed to make it look like a fat ground-bound cherub, slipped through the ring of officers and snaked a drainer into Petronas's mouth. There was a short, grotesque sound and the drainer was withdrawn, slathered with something pink and translucent. The servitor shuffled back on its cloth-soled feet, awaiting the next fit.

'Petronas Phrax, that's me,' said the wreck on the bed. 'Haven't told you yet, have they? Keeping me alive for the hearing, that's what they're doing. Heard them talking, heard them all the way down here.' One of Petronas's stick-arms moved sluggishly up and pressed against his ear, then dragged itself across his temple and down over his stomach. It was impossible to tell what he was trying to point to.

'Petronas *Phrax*?' That was Kohze, who'd been one of Nils Petronas's shooting-partners when they had visited worlds with huntable fauna. 'Nils, my old friend, you can't know what you're talking about.' He looked around him. 'He's delirious from the taint. It's a miracle he's survived this long.' He took a reluctant step towards the bed. 'Nils, do you know where you are? Do you know who we are?'

The eyes were suddenly on him, and Kohze found he could not look away from them. They were clouded with sickness but glittered with energy, they danced with madness but stayed locked on his with a terrible focus that Petronas had forged by sharpening that very madness into a razor-keen, steel-cold obsession for survival.

'I know who you are, Kohze.' Suddenly it was the Petronas they all knew – all the snap and fire – lying in this bed and speaking through the wreck he was hiding in. 'I know who you are. Atith, Phyron, Trichordi, get your paws down by your sides and look at me. Omali, you tikk-loving little milquetoast, stop backing away and be a man. I need all of you. I need the help of all of you.'

'Nils, what's going on?' asked Atith. 'They told us you'd been given some kind of command dispensation, and we were going to be your crew. They said you had asked for us and that we were to… to indulge you.' She dropped her voice a notch as she finished and shot a look at the servitor as though it were writing her words down. The others took the message and began glancing apprehensively around for spy-ears.

'Forget that,' spat the Petronas-thing. 'They told you some stupid lie to make themselves think they are in control. You listen to me, now, all of you. You listen the way they are, the way they are all going to listen, the way we're going to–' Suddenly the thin body jittered and went rigid for a moment, and droplets of thick yellow liquid ran from the cracked skin at the corners of its mouth.

'I don't think I have a lot of time,' that mouth wheezed as the servitor dabbed the liquid away with a contraseptic pad, 'and that means neither do you. Those shit-gobblers outside think they're giving me a gift. I'm supposed to cry and say how glad I am to see you. I'm supposed to forget, forget all they–' Petronas spasmed and screamed reedily for nearly thirty seconds before he could ride out the pain and speak again. By that time there was a black stain seeping through the cloth beneath his legs and the gagging, sour stink of excrement filled the air.

'They think I've forgotten everything they've done. Think it's all gone the way I'm supposed to be. Hah! Hah!' The laughter made him cough again. 'Supposed to be gone but still here. Supposed to be treated and changed, treating and changed to a tumour instead. Tumour-worm, that's me. Hah! If I can go wrong in one way I can go wrong in others. Wrong plan all over. Shouldn't have been born to a whore, but even if she was a whore my revenge is still for her.'

Petronas's voice had drifted, as though he were talking to himself, and a frightening, slow-tongued slur had started to creep into his words, drifting in and out again.

'Nils, what revenge? Please, tell us what's happened to you!' Atith's voice was breaking. 'Who is this "they"? What do you want us to do?' She flinched as Petronas's eyes snapped onto her.

'Ah, little Atith. Never wanted to flirt with me, did you, even in my better days.' Petronas managed to force his face into a smile at her. Five of his teeth were missing; two of the sockets still bled. 'Nice to see you doing what you're told now, though, little girl. Alright now, no more time for pleasantries. Draw in, all of you, draw in, little children. It is time for Daddy Phrax to start explaining what he needs of you.'

And the figure on the bed bayed laughter as the junior officers, the survivors of a circle that had once considered themselves the friends and colleagues of Nils Petronas, shuffled forward to listen.

Ready-room atrium aboard the flotilla flagship *Bassaan*, En route to Galata, Hydraphur system

'WHERE THE HELL are you going?' snapped Behaya, and D'Leste cursed himself for his guilty start. He had told himself over and over that he had nothing to feel guilty about. The treatments had been experimental to put it mildly, they had all known that, and they had been Dyobann's doing anyway. How was anyone to know that the damn cogboy would see fit to disappear right at the point when the flotilla – the flotilla masters, anyway, same thing – needed him around to keep their heir stable?

He turned to face her.

'They're either going to gawp at our wonder boy and be in there an age,' he said, 'or they're going to be disgusted by him and come running out of there in a minute. Either way, the three of us standing about out here is stupid. Things haven't gone wrong enough yet for the rogue trader's chief apothecary to wait on a bunch of spotty junior officers like some damn valet. I've got things to see to before we arrive, and I suggest you might look at yourselves waiting on those people's beck and call and consider the dignity of your offices likewise.' It was hard to tell from their expressions, but he thought he'd scored a point. When in doubt, attack, attack.

And anyway, he really did have some business to transact. He had thought of something. If Dyobann was out of the picture, and D'Leste had reluctantly accepted that he probably was, then their gamble with the extra-modified blood probably hadn't worked. But with audacity and subtlety, he thought, there might be a way to smooth that mistake out.

* * * *

The Sanctioned Liner *Gann-Luctis*, in transit

DEATH HAD COME to the *Gann-Luctis* late in the voyage, as the ship tried in vain to force its way through a great thunderhead of force towards a momentary break of calm Yimora thought he glimpsed somewhere ahead. There had been pressure, crushing pressure that had made the ship's astropaths howl and claw at their clothes and skin, begging for sedation and crying out prayers. Domasa Dorel had felt it in her warp eye, like a finger jabbing into her forehead, and she had covered her brow with a phylactery containing hexagrammic inscriptions by House soothsayers on Terra, written in tattoo-ink on strips of her own cloned and cured skin. It usually helped. It didn't now.

Death came in as the ship burst free of the thunderhead and catapulted into the space beyond, not a calmer passage as it had seemed but a tight corkscrew of energy spinning through dimensions that no human sensibility could comprehend. The ship began to tumble as Yimora desperately looked for a way through and the Geller field rippled as the riptide struck it, closed on it, seemed to bite at it. It bowed further and further inwards and then, for less than a hundredth of a second which set off klaxons and bells throughout the *Gann-Luctis's* besieged hull, it flickered out.

Death came in through that tiny gap, while Varro Phrax stood in the doorway of his stateroom and watched his wife hold down their yelling, thrashing son. Even the most ignorant ship's labourer knew in a basic way that the immaterium somehow resonated with emotions: drawn by them, feeding off them, feeding them in turn. Varro and Ksana had been ready for the warp dreams, knowing what was waiting for them when they slept, and they had said the right prayers and hung the purity seals at the corners of their bed. But Dreyder must not have been paying attention when he said his prayers and allowed his words to wander, and some time after they had closed the drapes on his bed he had pitched away the little pewter aquila they had given him as a charm, playfully, absent-mindedly or in some transient pique. Warp-dreams were bad, but Varro remembered from his days on the flotilla that for a young mind they were worse. For a young mind that did not understand to expect them they must be far worse still. He remembered how blasé he had been back on Gunarvo, saying, 'He'll get a few bad nights and then he'll be used to them,' and felt sick.

'Go,' Ksana told him. 'I'll take care of him. He's awake now, but the dream got him so frightened he doesn't know it yet. I have him. You go on.' Varro closed the door.

Rikah was waiting in the passageway, leaning against one of the mosaics of capering nymphs and cherubs that lined it. He was twiddling the end of one of his implanted vox-vanes, his usual sign of nerves. That was when the klaxons went off again and both men flinched at the sudden clangour.

Death found itself born inside the *Gann-Luctis*, inside the re-established Geller field that cut it off from the beautiful warm fluidity of the immaterium outside. It had found itself born through no conscious effort of its own: in the moment the field had flickered, its essence earthed itself quickly and painlessly into a mind inside like a spark jumping across a circuit-gap and then it was in a dry, cold, glaring straightjacket of a universe, surrounded by minds imprisoned in meat that jabbered and flapped.

It didn't like the way the meat behaved, so it did certain things that its instincts suggested and the meat took on new shapes and patterned itself through this horribly constricting cell of dimensions differently and then there was no more behaviour. It did not like the way that there were ways in which it could not move, but it found it could do things to change the little physical universe it found itself in. It could unravel things and part things, and it found that rending and breaking was far more delicious here than manipulating the soft stuff of the warp. And so it went looking for more meat to break, meat whose little droplets of spirit would puff so exhilaratingly into nothing when it pushed on them.

The noise of the klaxons barely registered with it, but they terrified Varro and Rikah. Varro was three steps down the corridor before the horrifying thought hit his mind's eye and he doubled back. But inside their room his family were still alive and unpossessed: Dreyder now crying steadily instead of screaming, Ksana cradling him. Rikah touched his shoulder.

'We need to arm, Varro. Ship's drill. We're able-bodied personnel.'

'What about getting our own–'

'Best to use what's in one of the lockers,' said Rikah, glancing around them. 'Let's not show our hand yet. If we don't think we're going to get through this otherwise, then maybe. For now, just come on.' Varro followed him away. Twice he broke his promise to himself and looked back at the stateroom door.

Adeptus Arbites precinct fortress of Selena Secundus, Galata, Hydraphur system

'"THE HEIR,"' CULANN announced from the message chit he held, '"is unwell, and will not leave the *Bassaan* until the opening of the hearing. He will not be able to remain in the courthouse for longer than a certain time." What a strange way of putting it. What "certain time" do you suppose they mean?'

'I don't know,' replied Shira Calpurnia, 'and I don't care. What it means is that the heir will be out of our hair… *Stop* that, Culann, it was a slip of the tongue, not a joke. I'm not in a joking mood.'

They were standing in one of the V-shaped defensive buttresses of the Arbites fortresses on Galata, Hydraphur's moon. This was Calpurnia's second attempt at a place for the hearing, after ornithopters and air-sleds with Ecclesiarchal markers had started circling Trylan Tor just beyond where Arbites flyers were authorised to engage them. Then sea-platforms carrying squads of Sororitas had begun to appear around the tors at the borders of the interdict zone, and nervous proctors at the sentry posts had started to ask for extra squads and ammunition. Then Arbites informants in the portion of the Ring orbiting above the tor reported that more Sororitas had begun commandeering launch bays and hardpoints, and were clashing with the Ring's military crews over control of two of the giant barrage-cannon barbettes.

Calpurnia's initial, furious thought had been to simply shoot down every last one of them and haul Simova and a couple of random clerics into cells until they told her who had given the order, and she'd stepped on the urge. That the Cathedral thought itself able to make such openly threatening moves against the Adeptus Arbites showed a need for correction that Calpurnia fully intended to deliver. Later. Now, she had another duty to perform, so something else was called for.

'Guilliman could circle like a mountain-cat as well as spring like one,' was an Ultramar proverb that was supposed to date from the holy primarch's conquests that unified his domain. It meant there was no shame in manoeuvring. If head-on confrontation would cost you more, then where was the shame in marshalling and directing your strength another way? Calpurnia had muttered it just before she sent orders to the tor to batten itself as though for an attack, for the picket and sentry forces to be visibly enlarged from whoever was stationed at the tor and could put on carapace, and for the flyers to get as aggressive as they could in their flying, doing their best to unnerve the pilots the Ecclesiarchy had roped in.

Meanwhile, in one quiet shuttle-hop, she had arrived at the great adamantium tower that the Arbites kept on

Galata. It jutted out of the silver dust of the surface and
drove down deep into the cold bedrock, the winged
gauntlet of the Arbites glittering from the slab-roof out
into space. While Simova, or whoever was running the
Ecclesiacrhy's bid for the charter, was busily trying to
intimidate a non-existent hearing at Trylan Tor, Shira
Calpurnia would sit in judgement at Galata and the charter would leave in the hands of the rightful heir.

Everything about the Ecclesiarchy's campaign for the
charter made her angry. She believed in the law, the holy
Lex Imperia, not in the idea that the tools and processes of
the law were there for a flawed case – for so she knew it
to be – on behalf of personal ambition rather than any
belief in a right cause – for so she strongly suspected it to be.
It unsettled and angered her. It wasn't just the in-principle
objection to legal games, either.

She dreaded the practical implications of such a case if
it got under way. Flawed or not, there would be enough
points of order, enough contradictions between religious
and temporal laws, enough overlaps and grey areas of
authority between the two Adeptus, enough odd precedents and historical incidents to illustrate anything that
one wished to have illustrated, so a mind as cunning as
Simova's could keep proceedings running indefinitely
until the Eparch or someone working for him thought of
something else to try.

The street justice of the arbitrators was bent on brutal
control and swift consequences, but the long, slow work
of the Judges focused on enacting the most insignificant
letter of the least of every law, as decreed by the High
Lords in the name of the Emperor. Every arbitor knew the
sight of the great camps stretching away from the gates of
a precinct fortress, where supplicants lived out the
months or years it took a Judge there or on some more
distant world to decide their case. Some went into the
decades as books of precedent and case histories had
been shipped in from a thousand other worlds to make

sure the verdict stood foursquare on the rock of Imperial
law. Calpurnia had even heard of Judges and advocates
who had had been given leave to raise a new Arbites on a
case so successive generations could take over the arguments when their originators had died: mere mortality
would not slow the great engine of Imperial justice.

Had the Ecclesiarchy a stronger case, Calpurnia would
have heard it. The idea of overriding valid law for her own
convenience would have revolted her, had she taken a
moment to entertain it. But after Simova had been shipped
back to his Cathedral he had sent an envoy straight back
with a written copy of his claim, which had gone to
Calpurnia's chambers and then to the great complexes of
archivists and lex-savants in the Wall's second bastion. Her
initial appraisal of it had been that there was no case, and
every fresh examination by savants and Judges reinforced it.

That helped her feel better about having faked them
out and slipped away to Galata to hold the hearing. But
not so much better that she wasn't spending more time
than she should have running through her analysts' latest
reports on the Simova claim and muttering the Guilliman proverb to herself over and over.

For a moment she wondered what the shape blotting
out the left side of her vision was, then she realised to her
embarrassment that it was her hand. It had crept up to
run a fingernail down the scar-lines on her forehead. She
put it down, feeling the twinge in her shoulder: she had
fallen behind on the exercises she was supposed to do to
keep it limber.

'Ma'am, one more message, and then I'll go and check
on those dock-security protocols you asked me to look at.
A reply from Genetor-Magos Sanja. It begins with the
same formalities as the last one, and–'

'I'll take your word for the phrasing and the formalities.
Is he telling us anything we wanted to know?'

'No. Um, he makes it pretty clear that he's not going
to, either. He repeats what he said after that first blood

specimen went to him. Circumstances which he may not reveal have placed the Helispex Engine beyond the reach of these proceedings, but the oaths and duties of his office prevent him from explaining why. He also says that he's empowered to offer some kind of compensating obligation by the shrine and will meet with you to discuss this, but not for ten days from the sealing of that message which was about an hour ago.'

'And an explanation of why exactly the Helispex Engine is unavailable for the first time in thousands of years?'

'No ma'am.'

'An explanation of what happened to that blood sample from this heir who came in with the flotilla?'

'Nothing, ma'am.'

'A clue as to what's going to happen to this second blood sample from Varro Phrax, which is apparently coming in on a dromon from the Higher Tetrajin Gate?'

'No clue at all.'

'And I suppose I don't even need to ask what he says about the tech-priest from the flotilla who went marching into his shrine with the heir's blood and hasn't been seen since.'

'Indeed, ma'am, you do not.'

'What do you think happened, Culann?'

'I couldn't say, ma'am, I've been with you the whole time.'

'I was being serious, though,' she said, turning those green eyes on him. 'I'm interested in hearing it. I like to know how my colleagues' minds work. Go on.'

'Something happened, ma'am.'

'Oh?'

'The Mechanicus are zealous about their privacy and their mystique. If something had happened to the Helispex there's no way any of them would come out and say so even to many people inside their own order, given the disgrace it would mean to Sanja as its custodian. I don't think it's because of that trip out to Trylan. He was worrying about what effect travel and non-consecrated ground was going to have on it, but I don't think the engine itself left Bosporian. I think something happened after he got back, maybe related to the flotilla cogboy, sorry ma'am, tech-priest going there to visit him. Unless he left by some way we don't know about.'

'We have a pretty good idea what goes on around most of the Augustaeum, Culann, and I'm as confident as I can be that the only way out of that shrine is through the main doors. Me, I think Dyobann is dead, either because he had something to do with why the Helispex is unavailable, or because he found out something about it and the other adepts killed him for it. I'm fairly well-disposed towards Genetor-Magos Sanja, but I have no illusions about what he might be capable of if he gets his blood up. Did I tell you about the Mechanicus cell we had to deal with on Don-Croix?'

'No, ma'am. But your thoughts about what happened to Dyobann match mine.'

'They do? Then you should have said so, Culann. Candour between an Arbitor Senioris and her staff is important. I need to know I'm getting every thought that passes through your mind.'

'Yes ma'am,' said Culann, standing at attention, his spine vibrating with pride.

'Alright, then. Go and check those protocols. There apparently are appalling warp storms between here and Santo Pevrelyi and it's holding up the heir's ship. The other one, that is. But meanwhile, I have to go and announce that the blood vial of Varro Phrax that this emissary brought through those storms is actually of no use now. I'm sure he'll enjoy hearing that. Apparently the passage here is not one to wish on your worst enemy at the moment.'

CHAPTER ELEVEN

The Sanctioned Liner *Gann-Luctis*, in transit

'YOU'RE STAYING BACK here,' said Domasa Dorel. 'Cherrick, get in front of him.' She would have blocked the way herself, but the hellish storm outside the hull meant that too much of her strength was spent keeping herself upright and her thoughts her own. There was thick, migranous pressure on her temples, and the flashes of power against the Geller field showed in her warp eye like a flash of red through closed eyelids. She sagged against the plain metal wall of the crew-deck.

'No ma'am,' said Cherrick and, after the initial disbelief Domasa's burst of anger on top of what was already in her head made her dizzy. 'All available able-bodied hands have been ordered to hunt this thing down,' he went on. 'One of the oldest shipboard disciplines there is.' Cherrick eyed Varro and Rikah's short-barrelled lasguns as he spoke, his words underlined by the clanging alarms in the corridors around them.

'And you're not going to order me away from this, Madam Dorel,' Varro put in. Behind him the mini-squad of the *Gann-Luctis's* troopers muttered and looked at each other. 'I left my son in my wife's arms eight decks above us. Believe me when I say I'd rather be with them than here. But Cherrick's right, this is an obligation.'

'You're the heir,' said Domasa, but with little spirit. She hadn't the energy. 'Anything happens to you, the whole point of the voyage gets flushed. Won't that be nice?' A dozen ratings, white-faced and gasping along to a prayer their overseer was chanting, clattered by, heading down the ramp behind Varro. They mostly clutched ships' tools to fight with: oxy-torches, heavy wrenches or tool-hafts, buzzblades on heavy forearm mountings. For all the good it would do them.

'It's an obligation,' Varro repeated. He was pale with fear, but there was no give in his voice at all. 'That's all. Now if you're coming with us, Domasa, then let someone help you. Otherwise we'll see you to somewhere safe.'

'Nowhere is safe at the moment,' she said, and as if on cue there was a momentary shudder as the ship bucked in the warp flow faster and harder than the gravity plates in the deck could smooth out. The tremor boomed through the dim halls all around them: where they stood, at the intersection of four great fifth-deck thoroughfares, it was like muffled thunder welling out of the darkness on every side at once.

'You're right,' said Rikah, 'and as long as this thing is loose inside the hull we're less safe than ever. And we're still standing here talking.' He tilted his silver-frilled head towards the ramp down to the second-order crew-decks. 'Let's not allow it any more time, shall we?'

Cherrick nodded with grudging respect, wheeled and strode to where the ship's soldiers, overhearing them, were going over their weapons once again. Most wore bulbous combat bridles holding the targeting visors over their eyes, vox pickups at their jaws, and dangling amulets and purity seals at their temples; their faces, what could be seen through all the hardware, were grim. Cherrick knew they had been trained and conditioned to trust in one another, and having to follow him and Domasa around was galling. Cherrick himself was no better off: distrust of anyone but his own handpicked people was ingrained so deeply in him that he had insisted on having at least one of his own troops at a dozen strategic points across the ship. He was feeling their absence now, though, and he muttered obscenities under his breath as they readied themselves to move.

'Can somebody tell me,' slurred Domasa as she leant on Rikah's arm, 'why we all have to club together like this? I thought it was only bad melodramas where any dangerous mission required all the most irreplaceable members of the crew to gang up.' The ship lurched again and a tight, coherent current of warpstuff scraped down the side of the Geller field. Rikah and two of the ship's troops jumped and looked around as though they had heard a voice calling to them, and strange transparent spots danced in Domasa's vision.

'We're not leaving,' Rikah countered by reflex, and then calmed himself. 'Varro and I are here because we're able-bodied personnel and we're obligated to do what we can to defend the ship. The troopers are here for the same reason. Cherrick, well, I suppose he's here because he's the chief of your staff and he's responsible for you, but you, Domasa, if there's anyone here who should be somewhere safer–'

'She's here because she's our bloodhound this evening,' called Cherrick over his shoulder. 'Except with an eye in her head instead of a nose on her face. So to speak. She's how we knew to follow the thing down here.'

'What it is,' Domasa condescended to put a little more weight on Rikah's arm as she spoke, 'is… like a little, thing. A piece of what's out there all bundled up with what's in here.' She swallowed as the ship bucked and the internal gravity lurched for a sickening moment. She wasn't sure, but she thought they might just have been tossed end over end. 'It's like... little fine threads working their way in, then being tied into a knot. Or something from outside seeping in and then crystallising in here. Or something from outside spurting its seed in, which grew into something in here. All of those things and none of them, I can't... *Ahhii–*'

Two murder-black whirlpools of force had merged right on the ship, and the force of them wanted to wring it like a yard-fowl's neck. Every man on the deck around Domasa felt his skin crawl. Cherrick was suddenly caught in the memory of his first kill and realised that he was a murderer. Varro remembered the first time he had truly feared for his son's life, in a watercarriage crash on Gunarvo's canals. Domasa thought nothing at all, the thoughts chased from her mind by bursts of filthy urine-yellow light, hot and sour as old hatred.

'Are you alright?' asked Rikah as he gripped her arm. A tiny drop of blood trickled down from his nostril. 'Can you stand?' Domasa muttered something. 'I'm sorry, Madame Dorel, I didn't catch that.'

'I said Throne protect Yimora. If this is what this is doing to me in here, then... eagle's beak, he's perched out there in the Navigator's roost. Throne protect him.'

Rikah helped her stagger down the ramp after the rest of them. Two more ship's troops ran past, one toting a flamer and one pulling an outsized fuel-cylinder on a trolley.

'Can't... afford,' she said. 'It's up ahead. Strong one. Saw it clear as day. It flared up in sympathy when we hit... that last... whatever it was.'

'If it's that strong, Domasa...' Rikah began, but Cherrick turned and interrupted him..

'If it's that strong we need to weaken it and damned soon,' he snarled, 'because if it's that strong then by the time it uses up all its own punch it's going to have gutted the ship from prow to tubes and any of us left alive will soon wish we weren't when it breaks down the hull and we get our souls torn out of our bodies. You want to wind up in some nightmare's gullet before you get a chance to come before the Golden Throne, Rikah, then find your own way into it. Domasa?' She nodded, wearily.

'He's right, Rikah. We're going to finish it off. It can't be more than a few compartments away, coming towards us. Let's find it and get this over with.'

It didn't seem like much longer before they were close enough to hear the screaming.

A man ran back past them, one of the ratings they had seen earlier. The buzzblade he had carried was splayed out into streamers of metal, some of them threaded into and out of his flesh in a way that stitched his arm to his body. He was howling, scorched, almost naked, insane, and Cherrick felled him with a point-blank hellshot. Varro groaned, but nobody argued: broken minds were a threat in a warp storm.

The ramp brought them to an assembly area, rows of benches across the hall and order-sheets pasted to the walls. Now the benches were overturned and broken and a crowd of crewmen were coming the other way, screaming and shoving, trying to have someone, anyone, their enemy or their best friend or the man from the shift-crew whose name they barely knew, anyone to get between themselves and death.

Death came behind them, framed in the archway where the assembly area split like the arms of a Y into two low corridors. It capered and flopped on the red-slicked deck, pausing with each little leap or stamping step as though the sensations of its lacerated feet slapping against the metal were odd and delicious. It had been unfamiliar with the limitations of the meat it had somehow become snagged in at first, and by the time it had learned that the pitiful little extremities the meat owned were supposed to move only in certain ways most of its joints had been broken or dislocated by the inhuman will moving its muscles. There was a point when it had wanted to pass through a hole it had managed to make in a bulkhead that the meat had to run around, but the hole had been barely wide enough for one extremity to fit through, so it had crumpled the hard little bone frame the meat was strung up on and fed itself through the hole like a snake. The frame had not reassembled on the other side, and trying to hold it in place through will was tiring. Now its skeleton was a mass of bone fragments and splinters all clicking and grating as it moved. Its feet either splatted on the metal with the sound of raw meat or clicked like a dog's foot from the bone jutting through the sole.

The midshipman's uniform it had worn when it had still had the human mind it had been born with was soaked red and dripping, but not all of the blood was its own. With a crackle of tearing flesh it shot out an arm, the skin popping as the limb distended, and a hand that looked like a cudgel spiked with bone thudded into the back of one of the rearmost crew. Only Cherrick, standing his ground at the head of the formation and clubbing crew aside as they ran at him, actually saw the red shape drag its catch back. Suddenly more bone splinters sprouted through its skin: first just their points like droplets of hard white sweat and then their whole length like bloodied cactus-spines, and it took the screaming crewman into its embrace. He screamed for a moment longer, then the red thing let him drop and gave out a gargling wail that could have been triumph, disappointment or something else beyond human thought.

The sound was enough to redouble the panic, and in another moment most of the hunt-and-destroy squad had disappeared up the ramp, all thoughts of drill and duty forgotten. Perhaps half a dozen were left, knocked sprawling or tangled in the benches or cowering by the walls. One shrieked and writhed in Cherrick's arms and

two more were grappling with the troopers. Varro and
Rikah both backed away, trying to protect Domasa from
the brawling before the troopers realised it wasn't worth
the trouble for people obviously so determined to run.
They let them go and two sprinted away, one cannoning
into Varro and then on up the ramp. The other curled
against one wall, weeping.

The metallic scratch-click of shells being rammed into
a shotgun snapped Varro's attention back onto what was
in front of them. In amongst the wrecked furniture, three
crew were making a stand. The two they had seen with
the flamer-cart crouched behind an upturned bench and
worked frantically on a fuel connection – they had lost
their trolley, but a little metal egg that must have been an
emergency reservoir hung from a hose on the side of the
casing. The sound he had heard came from the woman
next to them, frantically reloading a snubby, wire-stocked
shotgun as the red thing loped out of the arch.

Varro walked shakily forward, feeling as though his
body was going to tear itself apart in the way the red
thing's seemed to be: the instincts branded into every cell
of his body wanted to propel him back up the ramp even
as his horrified, disbelieving mind told him he had to go
forward. His gun trembled as he raised it.

The red thing took a half-step and reached for the men
with the flamer, but this time its arm seemed to have
trouble stretching and a shower of blood and bone splinters pattered down onto the deck. The woman with the
shotgun panicked and set off one blast, stunningly loud
in the low metal space. Shot rattled and stung off the
metal roof and blew out two of the lamp housings; two
more began to flicker and spit erratically, and the sudden
sporadic light gave everyone's movements a staccato
quality that only added to the dreamlike horror.

The red thing staggered another step. Even with his ears
ringing from the shotgun blast Varro could hear the sickly
tearing sound its neck made as its head tilted up to look

at the flickering light. One of its eyes was gone, a wet flap of skin and hair from its exploded scalp hanging over and partly sucked into the empty socket. The other eye, turned glistening black like a basalt pebble, bulged as though some unimaginable pressure from inside was about to burst it and it glittered madly in the light from the broken lamps.

The crewwoman took a breath, steadied herself and fired again as the snaking, wavering arm veered towards her. This time her aim was true, and the arm turned into a blood-spray that painted the ceiling and wrecked the half-broken lamps. Suddenly the room was almost light-less. The thought that the red thing might be advancing on them in the dark threw Varro into a panic. His hand clenched the trigger, more fear-reflex than aim, and the room was lit by a quick flurry of dim red stabs of light as Rikah joined in. At a shouted order from Cherrick two of the ship's troops opened up too, and then the rest of them, with Cherrick at their head, darted ahead into the assembly area proper, fanning out in a line, planting their feet and adding their own fire.

'Split!' Cherrick was shouting. 'Split up! Make sure if it gets near you it only gets near one of you!' And indeed, the other troopers were spreading out. Varro, his nerves and instincts screaming again, forced himself to move into the room and around the opposite wall, aim and fire again.

The thing in its coat of blood watched them silently, the single black ball of an eye catching the light of the las-bursts as they struck it. They did not knock it backward: normally even a laspistol shot would feel like an impact as explosive vapourisation of part of the target's surface imparted backward momentum. But the shape in red stood there, its jaw hanging slack on broken and dislo-cated hinges, as shot after shot burst puffs of vapour off it. They did not seem to be penetrating as they would a human body, they simply cratered its front, as though something were binding its meat into a barrier far more dense to the bursts of incinerating light.

The shotgun did better work. Under cover of the lasfire around her the crewwoman crept forward through the wrecked and tumbled benches, clamped the stock to her shoulder and sent three more booming, flaring shots ripping into the already stippled flesh. Domasa could see it happening, see the hurt, although she could not communicate it: the thing throbbed in her vision like an ulcer and it was all she could do not to drop onto all fours. But her warp eye could see it starting to come apart. The shotgun was what it needed: lasfire was a weapon for living creatures, a way to inflict trauma on a live metabolism to the point when it could not continue to function. But to fight something like this you needed a weapon that could not only break up a body but demolish it, physically rip it apart until the knot of will that held the flesh together was exhausted. The clot of warp stuff inside the corpse opposite her was starting to leak and lose cohesion: already it was having trouble stretching its limbs and the shredded flesh of its neck and shoulders was starting to settle and slump. The wretched heir was still playing the damn-fool hero, though, the way she had specifically tried to stop him from doing. Who did he think he was?

The barrel of Varro's gun was smoke-hot and icons were flashing down the length of the case: power cell low, mechanisms overheating. But he still ran forward. The shotgun woman was reloading again and the daemon-corpse's attention was on her; the flamer crew would not get there in time. Lasfire and shouts from Cherrick and the troopers passed over his crouched back; Rikah was two paces behind him, his own weapon approaching overheat level as he tried to cover them both. The corpse still had not moved. Its other eye had taken a hit and ruptured; its front had been cooked black as the bolts hit it, and Rikah saw places where the bone had started to show. All Rikah could think was, 'How can it not die?'

It wouldn't die, and Cherrick hated that. The thing stood there, flesh sizzling and crackling, and didn't waver or fall. He had spent a long time learning how to break bodies and take lives, and with his mind charged and twitchy from what was going on outside the sack of meat in his sights was starting to look more and more like a calculated insult, a rebuke to his skills. Roaring wordlessly, forgetting what this thing was and what it could do to him, he advanced. He wasn't going to be resisted by the mockery in the spreading red pool, and he wasn't going to be shown up for a fool by the merchant-brat who was rushing right through the field of fire. He spat, and his saliva sizzled on the heat-sink fin of his custom-crafted hellgun as he ejected the spent cell, kicked it away across the floor and slammed in another. He stepped over a broken bench as the two flamer-men were lugging their weapon into position, kicked one of them in the ribs and bellowed at him to move faster.

The thing in the corpse had noticed the nature of things around it change. It could not understand that this was because its eye had gone and with it the last crude analogue of physical sense, and that it now possessed only psychic sense blunted by its looted flesh. It had never had the experience of material form, knew no way to differentiate one material experience from another. But it was starting, in some way, to sense a danger: it was now an effort to move and hold the meat together. It wanted to pop open these new bundles of inflamed emotions that were surrounding it, but it did not like the sensation of having to grip and hold the stuff of itself together – every last aspect of that sensation was utterly alien.

So it turned, but it was hard to move. It realised after a moment that there was something in the way, and just as the line of humans firing at it were starting to think that perhaps it was weakening as it walked face-first into the bulkhead, it twitched and heaved and stroked one ragged forearm-stump down the metal. The steel bulkhead parted and peeled back at the motion, like stretched cloth parting under a knife, and the meat-shape stepped through.

On the other side of the bulkhead was just air, the upper half of a double-high passageway through to the mess and to the lower decks' chapel. Tearing open the bulkhead had opened a hole in the upper part of its wall, and the thing from the warp made its meat-vehicle fall slowly, end over end, what was left of its crude senses relishing the curve and tumble – only a sad echo of what its home had been like, but good enough. Then it stopped, and what little the thing understood of the rules of its new home seemed to mean that it would have to get up and move under its own power again. It got its arms and legs under it, lurching and slipping on broken joints forced to work at inhuman angles, and found out that it seemed to move much better now. It liked being away from the attackers and their odd sensations, but it hated being away from the strange, exhilarating taste of their souls. It tried to think of a way it could do both, but making its thoughts work in the sack of meat was hard so it picked a random direction and wandered in it, waiting to see what would happen.

Rikah had been first to the breach it had made in the bulkhead, and at first Cherrick and the others thought that he had been attacked by the way he staggered back from the opening with his mouth working. But each of them when they looked through the opening had to fight down the same visceral response at the sight of the once-human body walking away from them in a kind of dragging scuttle, its palms flat on the deck and its knees and ankles both bending through right-angles in the wrong direction to bring the soles of its feet onto the floor. Its head hung limply down, almost brushing the floor as if it wanted its ruined face to watch the bloody prints its hands and feet left on the deck behind it.

'Can't,' gasped Rikah, breathing harshly in between dry heaves, 'can't we wait? It... has to be dying.' But Varro and Cherrick were already shaking their heads.

'Not an option,' said Cherrick without his usual unkindness. 'They sometimes die, they sometimes get stronger. And if there's another accident and this happens again there is no way that I'll have two of them about at once. I've never heard of anything like that happening on any ship that survived its passage. See to Madame Dorel if you can't come with us.' He turned to the crew and troopers behind him. 'Who's got climbing line?'

One of the troopers started to reach for the kitpack at the small of his back, then froze, arm twitching and mouth gaping under his combat-bridle. The others were reacting the same way. Varro had taken a convulsive step back and Rikah had clapped a hand to his mouth. Cherrick registered this in a half-second; a half-second later he heard the sticky sound of something wet encircling his helmet and smelled blood and burnt meat. A half-second after that he punched the quick-release on his helmet strap and sucked his body down toward his boots, and as he toppled into a clumsy roll and came up scrabbling he heard the splintering sound as the warp-thing crushed his helmet between splayed and distended fingers.

It had disappeared from sight below them, then wriggled about and walked easily up the wall and back to the tear it had made: now the sac that had been its head hung in the gap while its fingers snaked around the helmet trying to find why there was no mental death-spasm as the ceramite and fibroc shattered in its grip.

There was a boom and hand and helmet both vanished: the crewwoman had reloaded her shotgun again. Too confident, though, and too far forward. The thing's head split open like a lamprey and sprayed hot blood and flechette-sharp fragments of skull with every bit the force of the shotgun blasts. The fountain of red decapitated the crewwoman and three slivers of bone went through the face of the trooper behind her: both pitched backward as Varro jumped forward with a yell and jammed his gun into the dripping stump. The barrel sizzled in the meat, and then he began to pump the trigger as Rikah and Cherrick both tried to drag him away.

Varro was lucky that the cell of his gun was so low, because when the clogged and overheated barrel finally hit flashpoint and exploded there was little enough power behind it to be soaked up by the warp-thing's body. The thump of power was still enough to send him staggering back, though, his face, chest and hands painted with blood.

What came swarming through the hull breach behind him was no longer remotely human. It leaked and stank and moved on a collection of limbs, some its old human ones and some sucking tendrils of flesh that it had extended from its torso.

The thing hurled itself out of the breach, past Varro, Rikah and Cherrick and straight at the troopers who were the ones right in front of it, knocking them flying. One died immediately, gouged in a dozen places by bone claws, one thrashed two metres backwards with his throat open before he gave one final kick of his legs and lay still. There were three quick las-shots in succession that sent bursts of reeking steam up from its skin, then it leapt again.

The slow, almost thoughtful pace of its moves was gone now, now it was all predation and deadly speed. Two more dead by the time a third shot had been squeezed off. Cherrick leapt up and pelted back toward the ramp, Rikah dragging Varro away from the wails and crackling bone. The flamer crew were both screaming at them to get aside, and as Varro passed them they managed, finally, to produce a spurt of white heat that lit the assembly area ferociously and brought the stink of melted plastic to the air as three benches slumped down into pools of slag.

Acrid smoke made a wall across the room, and as the firelight died the after-images added to the dimness.

There was only silence, and Varro had time enough to collect himself and look around for a replacement weapon before the thing flew out of the dimness and sprawled over the flamer crew. They screamed in unison, their voices sounding eerily alike, like brothers, and then Cherrick took careful aim and snapped off a single hell-shot.

He hit exactly what he was shooting at, the weak spot where the hose coupled the flamer to its reservoir. There was a tiny flare as the seal was breached and then Cherrick flung himself flat as a roaring orange-white cloud filled the room. The flamer crew didn't scream – they didn't have time. But something howled as its flesh was incinerated and the lattice of thoughts it had tried to hold together were left with nothing to anchor them. Domasa and the three men felt the scream begin in their bones, build through their forebrains and finish somewhere in the writhing subconscious – on nights to come that scream would still reverberate through their nightmares. As Domasa saw the knot of force finally untangle and melt away, the flames swirled and all but guttered: weaving in and out of the pools of burning plastic, paths of hoarfrost glittered in disturbing patterns before they evaporated. The last of the lights blew out, and in the darkness the whispering echoes of that death-scream seemed to echo and slink through the smoke for a long time.

Lower decks of the sanctioned liner
Gann-Luctis, in transit

'WE HAVE TO find out who he was,' Varro Phrax said dully. He was sitting crosslegged on the deck, head bowed. 'There won't be anything left of him here but we can piece it together somehow.'

'Why?' asked Cherrick. Varro couldn't see him, except in occasional silhouette from his shoulder-torch as the man prowled about the scorched wreckage.

'We all need to pray for him. It frightens me to think where his soul must be. We need to pray the Emperor will find him in the warp and carry him safely home.'

'There are some dead people around here who might suggest that that's being a little gentle, Varro.' The sneer was back in Cherrick's voice. 'And I personally don't believe in praying for the souls of things that have tried to crush my head like a chew-seed.'

'That wasn't him and you know it!' retorted Varro. 'You know it as well as I do. That man was the thing's first victim, as much as the rest of us!'

'I don't care.'

'Well, I do. And I don't care if you don't care, because we're going to break warp and hold a funeral for these people. All of them. Even the ones it didn't kill itself.'

The torch-beam swung around and Varro blinked as it fell on him. The disc of white grew larger as Cherrick stamped closer until Varro was sitting and looking up into the light like a schola progenium child waiting to be let out of a repentance closet.

'That sounds like an accusation. Don't you think that sounds like an accusation, Madame Dorel? I think it does. And I think it's odd that there's an accusation being made here, considering I did exactly what needed to be done to save us and the ship.'

'Think what you like, Cherrick,' Varro told him. 'I'm the heir apparent. I'm the leader of this mission and the reason for it. And I say we break out of this storm and hold our funeral, and do whatever work we can to make sure that we can travel the rest of the way safely.'

'We go on.' Domasa's voice, unexpectedly firm and strong. It made Varro jump, and Cherrick gave a hoarse laugh. Her face, swimming out of the gloom and into the torch-beam, unnerved him even more. The shadows emphasised the mutated, distended bones and the pallor of her skin, the feverish hostility burning in her eyes. 'We came into this storm knowing the risks, and those risks have not changed, and I say we go on. If we broke out now it could mean months of drifting in real space, and months we do not have.'

'But we–'

'No, Varro. No. My backers are keen to help you, as am I. But my backers are keen to help because they know you are going to help them in turn. And you are going to help them,' and Varro cringed at the feel of Cherrick's gun-barrel pressing into his temple, 'by going to Hydraphur and getting your damned inheritance. And after that we shall go on to decide what our working relationship is going to be. And if you are good to us, and behave, and your charter is useful, then we will even allow you to do the occasional deal or authorise the occasional trip yourself, Varro, won't that be nice? And if you *really* behave, if I am left with no doubt about your desire to co-operate with House Dorel by the time we come away from Hydraphur with our little document, why then I will even have Cherrick control his baser urges and let your wife and brat continue to live with you instead of aboard a Dorel barge as my guests and hostages. And I know you'll agree that that will be nice.'

There was a long silence. Rikah watched, his skin cold and crawling, until Varro quietly dropped his eyes to the deck between his feet.

'I see,' said the heir. 'Well, then. At least we have certain things out in the open now. The cards are all played now, at least.'

'I didn't want to have to get so ugly with you,' Domasa told him with no real regret that Rikah could see. 'But if you're going to pull at the collar and force things, well, I don't have much alternative, do I?' The ship twisted and groaned again, and she winced. 'We're still in the storm. I'm going to my quarters. Cherrick, report this in, will you? And you two, it's quarters for you, and quickly, please. See how trusting I am? I'm not even going to send someone with a gun at your back. Don't let me think

you're having second thoughts about that co-operation
we discussed.'

They walked away from each other in the gloom, and
as they came up the ramp Varro and Rikah exchanged a
look. Behind them Domasa said something quietly and
Cherrick brayed with more laughter, but neither man
flinched. They held the look for a moment longer, then
Rikah gave a tiny nod, imperceptible to the two at the
bottom of the ramp, and Varro returned it. Then they
walked away, not speaking, faces thoughtful, as the ship
twisted and the warp storm howled and flared.

CHAPTER TWELVE

Adeptus Arbites precinct fortress of Selena Secundus, Galata, Hydraphur system

AFTER ALL THE angst and preparation, thought Shira Calpurnia, it seemed odd to finally look through a window-slot and see the *Callyac's Promise* seeming close enough to reach up and touch, its spine of steeples raking the black sky. Above the *Promise* in turn loomed the grey bulk of the Punisher-class cruiser *Baron Mykal*, keeping watch with gun bays open and batteries armed. The rest of the flotilla had been herded by the Navy to dock at Hydraphur's Ring, putting almost the whole of the moon between them and the fortress, and Naval patrols combed the space in between.

The fortress itself was in lockdown by Calpurnia's orders, and Odamo, who had spent half a day prowling the upper levels with a team of his own auditing every security feature he could think of, had reported himself satisfied. The lower levels were sealed and guarded, the

courtroom itself garrisoned by arbitrators from the
fortress and the Wall. The levels between the hangars and
dromon docks, the courtroom itself and the surface, had
been stripped down beyond even their usual ascetic furnishings and filled with guards.

And somewhere out there, according to the message
chit Culann had just come in with, the battered and
bruised liner *Gann-Luctis* had finally lurched out of the
warp and into a long, exhausted coast toward Hydraphur,
in formation with a watchful Navy escort. And something
else too, apparently.

'A dromon runner carrying an Ecclesiarchal delegation,
if you believe that,' said Umry, who had spent some time
monitoring vox chatter from the Ring and requisitioning
travel papers from the airspace and orbit controllers.

'Oh, I believe it,' Calpurnia replied, still standing at the
window with her hands laced behind her back. She was
enjoying the view. Hydraphur sunlight made everything
orange-yellow and hazy; she liked the way that the airless
surface of Galata gave everything outside a bright and
knife-sharp precision. 'The bad blood hasn't gone away,
Umry, it's just in remission. At the moment they don't
feel that they can stop the Ecclesiarchy flying out on such
an obvious mercy-mission to a vessel in distress.'

There was a faint satisfaction in her voice: Calpurnia
had been intimately involved in the events that had seen
the long feud between the Cathedral and the Navy chiefs
fall off into a grudging truce. 'Innocent though I'm sure
they are, I trust you got a full passenger complement.'

'Of course, ma'am. As registered at the Ring on departure, there's a party of preachers and lower-order acolytes
from the Vicariate Astral, a full pontifex in charge, appropriate religious supplies for purification and benediction
masses. And a dozen Sisters Hospitaller with a
respectable load of medicae supplies. Exactly the sort of
mercy-mission you'd expect in the circumstances. If the
reports of what they flew through to get here are a tenth

correct then I'd be wanting to hear some hymns and smell some incense at the end of it too.'

'Is that all?'

'One here that I don't recognise. A Sister Palatine of the Sororitas. Sister Elouera Krovedd. Order of the Eternal Gate. Don't recognise them as a Hospitaller order. And not Militant, either, not on Hydraphur.'

'The Eternal Gate. Hmm.' Calpurnia sorted through her memory for a moment until it hit her. 'One of the Orders Pronatus. They're a minor order, or a minor range of orders. Their responsibility is tracking down and obtaining relics and sacred items to bring back into the Ecclesiarchy's care. I knew I recognised–'

Umry was ahead of her: Calpurnia saw the expression on the other woman's face a moment before she caught up with her own words and realised their import.

'*Damn* it,' said Shira Calpurnia as she motioned Umry to pick up a data-slate and began giving out a new set of orders.

Rogue Trader craft *Callyac's Promise*, Low docking orbit over Galata, Hydraphur system

'THIS GETS WORSE and bloody worse,' muttered Kyorg as they waited for D'Leste to show up. The others looked at him with barely-concealed contempt and said nothing.

'Well, don't you agree? I mean, is this how it was meant to go? Am I the only one who realises there are going to be whole swarms of tikks tramping about here? What are we doing about this?'

He had meant the question for Trazelli, but it was Beyaha who answered.

'I suppose,' she said sweetly, 'that we were rather trusting that our Master of Envoys was up to the job of meeting with this Arbitor Calpurnia and persuading her to rethink this ridiculous idea. Wasn't that foolish of us? Trusting you to be up to doing your job, that is, Kyorg.'

Kyorg flushed. He had never had any illusions about what the rest of the flotilla masters thought of him, but there was an etiquette to what one did and did not say. A line had just been crossed. He made sure his expression betrayed nothing and ran his fingers over the heavy rings on both his hands. It wouldn't be long now.

Then portals from the docking bays rumbled open and the first of the Arbites stepped over the high threshold. The floor of the reception deck was beautiful polished bronze, the walls gold leaf, the ceiling overhead great sheets of softly lit amber, and all inlaid with wire-fine lines of jet to form a line-drawing of the view from the High Mesé at Bosporian Hive, facing toward the Cathedral. It did not usually fail to make an impression, but the arbitrators paid no attention.

'Who presides here?' demanded one of them, with a pistol and silver trim to his uniform, as D'Leste came hurrying from the stairs that led up to the primary deck. Like all of them, he was in full and formal garb: an ornate grey and white tunic that fell to his thighs, soft black boots and frock-coat with silver braid in which threads of scarlet, denoting him a physician, caught the light. Like all of them, he wore a tapered black hood-cap decorated with chitin-quills from a Vassilian spark-glider and a rosette with the Phrax emblem.

'No one of us presides, respected arbitor,' said Galt, pointedly ignoring the apothecary's entrance. 'We are the masters of the bureaux and offices within the flotilla, operating in a caretaker capacity for the voyage back to Hydraphur. We meet and welcome you aboard in that capacity.' He bowed, as did they all.

The head arbitrator thought about this for a moment, then muttered into a vox-pickup and more Arbites poured into the *Callyac's Promise* like black beetles. Kyorg winced at the way their hard boots scuffed the finish of the deck. To the flotilla masters, used to even their lowest menial being uniformed and decorated with fastidious care, the Arbites were underdressed to the point of being comical in their simple carapace and flakcloth and their impassive mirror-visored helmets. The smell that came through from their ship was metallic and sharp, the smell of armour and efficiently-filtered air, coarse after the delicate perfumes circulating through the *Callyac's Promise*.

'Is this necessary?' That was Galt again, making a second small bow. 'My recollection of previous inheritances is limited, but I do not recall an Arbites presence on our own craft on previous occasions. When the late and mourned Master Hoyyon succeeded the charter, we carried the charter down to the very surface of Hydraphur ourselves.'

'Special circumstances,' said the arbitor curtly. Eye coverings had never been in fashion aboard the flotilla, and it was disorienting to Galt to hold a conversation with someone whose eyes he could not see. 'Attempts to interfere with the succession are at a level without recent precedent and Arbitor Senioris Calpurnia has ordered an Arbites watch on each claimant's ship for the duration. Notify your crew.'

'The crew in this matter fall under the fiat of my colleague, Madame Behaya,' Galt replied coolly, and Behaya took a step backwards and closed her eyes. A loose silk scarf was wrapped around her neck but Kyorg could see her throat working as she subvocalised into the microbead in her neck. A second whisper from another direction confused him until he realised it was D'Leste trying to attract his attention.

'It's all under control,' he muttered to Kyorg under the tramp and clank of boots as the Arbites began spreading out through the deck and the ship.

'I'm sorry?'

'All handled. I knew I'd find a way to balance out the advantage.'

'D'Leste, what exactly are you trying to talk about here?' Kyorg looked over his shoulder: Zanti, Halpander and Trazelli were walking over to them as well. D'Leste

gestured to them and the little group shuffled out of the
way of the flow of grim arbitrators.

'Dyobann!' said D'Leste in an urgent, pleased murmur.
'Whatever happened to the old freak, I don't think that
doctored blood sample he took on ahead did very much
to help us. There was another sample due from Varro, of
course, but the warp storms helped us there. It got
delayed and I don't think–'

'It got delayed and it's not necessary anyway,' snapped
Zanti. 'Because the Mechanicus got something stuck up
them in the last few days and brought the shutters down.
No blood-printing, barely any of the tissue-printing we
were bracing ourselves for, for us or the heir. Dyobann's
scam may not have done the trick, but I think that he
somehow got things so stirred up down there that he's
done just as well.'

'But anyway,' put in Kyorg, delighted by the apothecary's crestfallen expression, 'what was this thing you had
taken care of, D'Leste?'

'I used some connections from your resources, Kyorg,'
D'Leste answered, returning the sally. Kyorg tried to make
it look as if he had known that D'Leste had been giving
orders to his people. 'It wasn't too hard to find out when
the ship that was carrying the blood ahead of Varro came
in and where it docked. It flew right in and disembarked
at the Ring itself, I don't know who had the contacts to
pull that off, but we should have the same ones.' D'Leste's
voice was picking up as he got excited again. 'Kyorg's
office had all sorts of contacts and getting an agent who
could move around the Ring was no trouble.'

'I think we get your drift, D'Leste. You took care of
things.' Trazelli gave a meaningful tilt of the head to the
Arbites swarming around the rest of the room. None
seemed to have heard them, but D'Leste saw the point
and moderated his voice.

'All I wanted to pass on was that I made sure that a particular possibility, presenting a possible if minor threat,

has now been closed off. I shall so inform Galt and Behaya when they have finished conversing with the, uh, commander over there.'

'Here's a better idea,' said Zanti. 'You go back to the heir's bed and make damn sure that he manages to stay alive until the hearing. All this closing-off of possibilities is no good to us if our claimant's dead by the time we walk in there.' D'Leste, chastened, touched his cap and hurried away again.

'What happens if he dies?' Kyorg had assumed that even if Petronas wasn't going to recover from the treatments, at least he would still be around to contest the hearing.

'Then we improvise,' Trazelli told him. 'As far as we can tell, Varro's built up quite a syndicate of his own, too much of a power base for us to housetrain him. We may have to bring him in anyway by force, and break that power base somehow. Zanti and I both have plans for that. Maybe you'd like to consider whether you have any capacity to assist.'

'Of course, colleague,' said Kyorg, bowing and ignoring the open insult. 'Everything depends on having the successful heir in the right hands. I shall, as a matter of fact, pursue the possibility this instant.'

He walked away, his mind revving and whirring, barely noticing the squads of arbitrators filling the halls and decks of the *Promise*. He didn't have much time. It wouldn't be long until the hearing, not long at all.

The dromon *Omicron's Dart*, En route to Galata, Hydraphur

It was not the arrival Varro Phrax had dreamed about.

He had fantasized about flying down to the Augustaeum in a richly-appointed shuttle, his wife on his arm and his son running ahead of them as they walked through the Adeptus Quarter, admiring the minarets of the Monocrat's palace and the great spire of the Cathedral. They would stand before the Arbites the way his father had done, the way one of the giant paintings in his manse on Gunarvo showed: Hoyyon Phrax standing in a ray of gold light that lanced down through a high window, head back and noble profile tilted into the light, one hand on the crystal dome beneath which the book of the charter lay open.

The reality never stood a chance. He looked around him now at the long, narrow passenger hall of the dromon that the Adeptus Ministorum had sent out to collect them. Only four metres wide and two levels high, the walls opened into regular flights of steps up to the outer galleries, from which windows looked into the passenger deck in turn. The furnishings were mainly benches along the walls – it was more like an alley between buildings than a room on board a spaceship. There was still a residual taint of incense in the recycled air, left over from the clergymen and Sisters who had filled the ship on the way out.

Their presence had seemed like a true blessing at first, a mercy mission. There were plenty of systems where mission-ships circled the outer reaches ready with healing and spiritual strength for crews coming in from bad warp-passages, and Varro had been delighted to find one here.

He had been surprised but not alarmed when the fat priest had come aboard and addressed him by name, but he had felt a chill when a sharp-eyed, shaven-headed Sister Palatine had followed him and he saw the pistol holstered under the shoulder of her purple-black robe, its grip and barrel matching the gunmetal grey of the aquila at her throat and the chain of office around her waist. He had not led his wife and child into the court on Hydraphur: 'Do your duty, my husband, I am proud of you,' Ksana had said, and Dreyder had hugged him, and then the Sisters had escorted him away.

Now he sat despondently at one end of the compartment with Rikah next to him. Further down was Domasa, silent and hunched over: the start of this trip was the first time he had seen her truly afraid. The Sororitas and their grim reputation toward mutants, Navigators or no, had her pulling her cowl over her head and her sleeves down until barely any of her was visible under the black and russet cloth. She looked almost as though she were praying; more likely, Varro thought, she was regretting having left Cherrick back aboard the *Gann-Luctis*.

'Domasa,' Varro hissed, to no answer. He moved closer. 'Domasa!'

The cowl slowly turned toward him.

'Shut up, Varro, I'm thinking.'

'What about?'

'About a way we can manage this situation, you little pissbrain. I can't believe that the issue hasn't arisen before, and it must have been dealt with because the charter is still in circulation, but I don't know enough history to know, so I have to improvise. If you don't have anything useful to add you have my cordial permission to leave me the hell alone.' Varro had heard no news about Yimora but he had seen Domasa recover from the warpvoyage with terrifying speed, and this was a Domasa Dorel he barely recognised. Not the courtly and obliging woman who had come to him on Gunarvo, and not the sick and exhausted woman of the voyage. This, he supposed, was the Domasa Dorel that had lived underneath those two, all steel and poison.

'The Ministorum, you mean? I remember my father carrying relics for them once, when I was very young. We flew into a war zone in the Ophidian Sector where the sanctioned traders couldn't go and brought stones from some old shrine back to Avignor to be made into altars. That's all I know of.'

'And they didn't try to snatch it then, at least not in any way obvious to a toddler. So there probably won't have

been any clashes recent enough for a decent precedent.'
Domasa was talking half to him in the way one might use
a child or a pet as a token listener while they sifted ideas.
'Alright then. If they were really confident about the charter they wouldn't have come for us, they would just have
taken it. If they're here with us it means they think they
need us. And that means we can make them negotiate.
And if they'll negotiate…' Domasa took a deep and satisfied breath, 'then they won't know what hit them. At least
until we're safely away with the thing, methinks.' She
glanced at Varro and shrugged, half to herself. 'I'll have to
keep improvising, but that's alright. Nothing about a
bunch of pious little cloister-monkeys that I can't handle.
And I've had news that the stupid fake heir the flotilla
crew are putting up may even keel over dead before long.
They're panicking, and that's good. Just *you*, Varro,
remember not to try anything on with them. You owe it
to yourself to bear in mind where your wife and son are,
and that Cherrick is there with them.'

'I know the situation,' Varro said softly, and backed
away. He thought again of Ksana and Dreyder, and wished
he could have left Rikah back aboard the *Gann-Luctis*. But
Rikah was his aide and retainer, his close companion for
the whole voyage, and leaving him behind would have
been suspicious. And they could not afford suspicion, not
now. After all, it would not be long now.

Adeptus Arbites precinct fortress of Selena Secundus, Galata, Hydraphur system

'DO WE SEPARATE them, ma'am?' asked Odamo, slapping
his gauntleted hands together. 'We've got more than
enough boots on deck to be able to face the Sisters Militant down. And this rock is tough enough to fend off
anyone who comes after them, too, until we choose to
give them up. Just let them try and stand over this place
like they did with the tor.'

Odamo had been offended by that, Calpurnia knew, and had been looking for a way to bend the Ministorum's nose by way of retaliation. And then – she smiled at this – there was the gravity. The fortress used deck-plates to boost the moon's weak gravity, but they were still a little below Hydraphur gee. Odamo was finding it much easier to get about on his usually stiff augmetics, and it was making him feisty.

'He's got a point,' said Umry, walking alongside. 'Simova's not stupid, and this Sister Krovedd won't be either. They'll be using the flight to try coat-tailing their way into the hearing, but if we know that that's what they're doing, as we do, then why should we allow it?'

Calpurnia did not answer for a moment, but touched her signet to the Arbites icon in the centre of the door in front of them and stepped through into the courtroom.

This was a smaller, plainer court than the great chambers in the Bastion Praetoris, there because every Arbites fortress was required to have a courtroom within it. Unlike the more grandiose chambers it was built for function, not pageantry and exalted spectacle. It suited Shira Calpurnia perfectly.

'I believe we will let them enter, and speak their case,' she said, walking out onto the high pulpit from which she would oversee the trial. She stood five metres above the courtroom, above walls of smooth black metal at seventy-five degrees to the floor – had she wanted to walk to the far side of the court from here she would practically have to rappel down first. 'One heir will stand on each side of the centre-aisle, with whatever retinues they have brought, and Simova and his delegation central and further to the back.' She turned to face the others, whose rank did not allow them to stand in the pulpit: they peered in from the other side of the door.

'I didn't think this could be the first time that the Ecclesiarchy would have made a grab for a relic as precious as this,' she said, 'and I was right. Umry, it was you who made the report on the last documented fighting, wasn't it?'

'Yes ma'am. The Ecclesiarchy tried to bail up the flotilla while it was in orbit over Mayinnoch about a century and a half ago, and had a confessor and a quasi-independent order of warriors called the Fraternal Order of the Aquila try and demand the charter. The Arbites garrison stopped that attempt in its tracks.'

'Because…?' Calpurnia asked.

'It took any number of years before a ruling was sealed – went up to the high precinct command for judgement. But the verdict was that while there's a pretty damned complicated stew of law and tradition that allows the Ecclesiarchy a heavy hand in acquiring sacred objects, this particular sacred object contains express direction as to how it is to be disposed of and controlled. Express placement in the hands of temporal law and the Arbites takes precedence over its origins including it in the broad subset of things that mostly-implied law gives the Ecclesiarchy control over.' Odamo was nodding, Culann was blinking.

'Thank you,' Calpurnia answered. 'And the fact that this current attempt seems to have been made with no knowledge of the previous one is heartening. It strikes me that Simova, and the Eparch too, are blinded by ambition for a unique relic and haven't done their research.' She looked out over the courtroom again, with its high-sided boxes and dock, the aisles cut into the floor, the stacked galleries around the walls. As an arbitor senioris she was at the lowest rung of the arbites general, where the Judge and arbitrator hierarchies recombined. Just as arbites generals promoted from the Judges had to get used to donning armour and commanding actions in the field, she was having to get used to presiding over trials and ceremonies. She, she thought, had the better deal.

The doors to either side of the pulpit swung wide and bailiffs from the courtroom garrison saluted up to her and began setting up the dais on which the charter would sit. She was prepared and confident of herself against the Ecclesiarchal claim now. She had the counter-arguments and the precedent, whatever Simova might think. And once his interference was cancelled out, the heirs could put their cases. And when she had heard those, she was confident that the right judgement would be obvious. Whatever had happened with the flotilla tech-priest might have traumatised or scandalised Sanja into seclusion, but that was a loss she was sure she could handle. It was nothing she couldn't handle. She was starting to feel eager for the courtroom to fill up, eager for the hearing to start.

Patience, she told herself. It wouldn't be long now.

Main landing hangar, Selena Secundus, Galata

HER UNIFORM WAS grey silk that whispered when she moved; her hood-cap was of the same grey as her eyes and the veil that fell across her face made her look at the world as though through a fog. The other nine were dressed alike, in paler, simpler versions of the ceremonial uniforms the flotilla masters were wearing. Through the veil, when Atith had looked around, her companions looked like ghosts.

The ten of them stood in the cold air of the hangar bay, breathing the acrid smell of propellant smoke from the tubes of the ship's boat that stood on six landing-legs behind them. They stood with antique long-barrelled autoguns, held outward to show where the ammo clips had been removed, and slender formal daggers thrust through their grey silk cummerbunds at precise angles. They stood in a ring, all facing outwards, and in the centre of the ring: a simple dome of dark metal, perhaps a little over a metre across, catching the light dully.

None of the ten wavered or looked around as the circular platform on which they stood began to move. On growling treads it carried them to the broad hangar doors, to the broad passage leading deeper into the fortress. It was lined with black-armoured Arbites, all with shotguns held at arms, their faces as invisible behind helmet visors as Atith's own was behind her veil. For the first time, she wondered if she would come out of this alive. Ten of them, only ten. The seven who had come out of the soul-branding meeting with Nils in the medicae, three more they were sure they could trust. Ten of them, ten whom Nils (Petronas Phrax, she corrected herself, he was Petronas Phrax now) had insisted on for the charter's ceremonial guard. Ten to help him get his revenge.

She breathed out and snapped through the motions of the drill, dropping her empty gun into the ceremonial position in the crook of her arm and falling into step as four heavy servitors, their thick augmetic limbs shining with filigree and fluttering with ornamental grey silk, lifted the dome and began carrying it toward the courtroom.

Not long now, she told herself. Whatever happened, she would help Nils. They all would. That was all she had to remember. Not long now.

The dromon *Omicron's Dart*, Low orbit over Galata, Hydraphur

THEY WERE BEING flown straight to Selena Secundus, and Simova was delighted. Arbitor Calpurnia didn't seem to want to stand on formality, and the charter was being conveyed to the courtroom as they were flying in. It meant that they would be able to walk almost straight into the hearing in the company of the heir, and although Simova had spared some time for a moment of dutiful indignation at such an offhand treatment of such a precious relic, the whole affair couldn't suit his purpose better. Or the Emperor's, he assured himself, or the Emperor's.

Sister Krovedd had seemed confident, too, when he had instructed her in the basics of the case as his second, and he more than trusted the Sisters Militant to emphasise the Ecclesiarchy's determination. He was even willing to let the heir make a statement or formally hand the thing over or whatever he felt like doing, if propriety allowed. He wasn't sure why the horribly deformed Navigator woman was tagging along, but that was probably why there were guards with them, so that Varro could order her contained if she tried anything. Not that she would; he was sure the abhuman knew her place.

He gripped the landing harness in sweaty hands as they coasted in under the giant shape of the *Baron Mykal* and towards a docking bay in the side of the fortress. He was looking forward to this. Not long now.

Not long at all.

CHAPTER THIRTEEN

**Adeptus Arbites courtroom,
Fortress of Selena Secundus, Galata**

THE HONOUR GUARD from the flotilla, ten young officers in
pale uniforms and veils, stepped aside with empty
weapons pointed down, and the servitors removed the
metal cover and carried it away. Shira Calpurnia leaned
over as far as dignity and the high-collared formal uniform would allow, but there seemed little to see: a small
square of cloth, a closed book. It was only knowing what
was in those pages that made her breath catch.

'Bring in the heirs and claimants,' she said. She had
been mildly surprised that the terms of the charter laid
down no formal legal liturgy for the hearing itself, but
she was taking advantage of it. No ornate ceremony.
Respectful, plain, functional as an arbitrator's kit. It was
her way of paying the charter her respects.

Simova was first to bustle in, of course, at a pace that
had Calpurnia expecting him to trip over his robe at any

moment. His arbitrator escorts halted him well back from the two raised boxes and he stood there, scowling, stymied.

Varro Phrax came in next, a tanned, nuggety man with cropped black hair, wearing a suit of deep green that Calpurnia considered a little too dishevelled for an occasion like this. He had a broad, likeable face full of deep laughter lines, but his expression was tired and haunted. He was followed by two retainers in heavy armoured shipsuits and a slender shape in a deep-cowled rust-brown gown that Calpurnia took to be one of his Navigator backers. A third retainer, with odd silver ridges inlaid into his head, had turned away at the door and walked back out into the atrium as Varro and the cowled shape stepped up into the box.

The third party, the second heir…

…the second heir was nothing like she had expected. Three junior flotilla ratings, in simple bodygloves with blinker-harnesses and mouth-stitches to show their indentured status, pushed in a medicae carriage on silent suspensor cushions. There was something behind its curtains, something that twitched and wheezed. The man hurrying beside the carriage, with the face of a slum-thug and the elegant uniform of a flotilla master, had his eyes riveted to the flickering life-sign runes on the diagnostors floating by the curtains. Others in the same uniforms filed in behind the carriage: two women, one tall and gangling, one hunched and sour-faced, an elderly man with a lugubrious hound-face and a slender metal staff, the next bald, with a blade of a nose and darting, suspicious blue eyes, the last a bull of a man with a plaited red beard.

They were grim, tense, and when the curtains retracted Calpurnia understood why.

'THAT… THAT'S MY half-brother…' Varro's words were disbelieving, and not quiet enough. Domasa heard him and snorted. But most of the court's attention was on the wasted travesty nestled amongst the soft white cushions.

The thing was dressed in Phrax livery, more ornate than the flotilla masters'. But surely no uniform had ever been tailored for a body like that.

Its lower limbs were fluid-swollen and elephantine. On its torso weeping tumours strained against the cloth, ribbed or folded like brain coral. The arms were sticks, the hands gripped into fists that the thing began to flail in the air: the skin and flesh on one seemed to have melted the hand into a single uneven lump. The other opened into a hand, but the flesh between the fingers had split so deeply there was barely even a palm now, just cracks where the hand was splitting right up to the wrist, lined with a red-black crust. The head above the ruffed collar looked like a skull covered in runneled and melted white wax, clouded eyes glaring blindly. The final touch, which nauseated Varro all the more for its banality: such a head should have been hairless, not bearing such a mane of tawny hair.

A shudder seemed to pass through the flotilla guards. Varro heard someone cry out. The female arbitor with the green eyes was leaning forward again, staring down.

WHAT WAS LEFT of Ensign Nils Petronas beneath the hate and the tumours and the agony-induced psychosis could dimly make out the woman leaning over to watch him, high, high above. He idly wondered if it might be his mother looking down, or one of the women he had killed in that alley. He was trying to focus on her when he heard D'Leste's voice buzzing in the aural feed they had fastened to his head to make sure he could hear them.

'They're looking at you, Petronas. Be careful. Can you understand me?'

Somewhere in his mind, down past the dreams and hallucinations, a switch was tripped. This was it. The moment. Mad, scrambled thoughts spun and tumbled.

Then, rising up through his fevered mind like an iceberg surging to the surface of a stormy sea came lucidity, clear thoughts forced together by a monstrous effort of will.

D'Leste moved a vox-pickup in front of his face.

'I… am…' His voice was a death-whisper, barely his own. For a long moment his thoughts wandered and he tried to remember whether his mother's eyes had been as green as this woman's. Then he shuddered and coughed and squeezed his eyes shut.

'I am Petronas Phrax, the son… the son of Hoyyon Phrax, Phrax the… the elder.' It was broken up by wheezes, but he recognised it. It was his own voice. His own body and mind had been taken away from him, but he still owned his voice. That pleased him and he grinned, and above him Calpurnia flinched: his teeth were a gapped and snaggled ruin, but white new teeth were trying to push themselves out of the fronts of his gums. 'I am here… here. For the inheritance. Father's charter, mother's… mother's, mother's satisfaction. My doctor knows about that, although he doesn't know really. That's what my friends are here for.' Petronas giggled and his split hand rapped and drummed on the coverlet. D'Leste, face white with nerves, bent over his equipment and muttered orders to the diagnostors. 'It all makes sense if you know what… what…' something seemed to puzzle him and the blind head began questing to and fro.

'My… my lord-in-waiting Petronas Phrax has become unwell, arbitor, as you see,' said Zanti, thinking fast and stepping forward. 'And we made all haste to Hydraphur so that the legacy of the great Hoyyon could be placed in his hands. Once we are able to return my lord to his ship we shall be able to help him rest and regain his strength.'

'This is a travesty!' boomed Simova, striding forward under Zanti's furious gaze. 'That a holy relic of the Emperor should be turned over to such as that? The harbouring of the mutant is an abomination unto the Emperor and this shall not stand!'

'Back in your place, Simova,' Calpurnia warned him. 'You are here on sufferance, not in charge. You.' She pointed at the man with the ruffian's face, and he looked fearfully up at her.

'I am D'Leste, madam arbitor, physician to the Lord Phrax.'

'Does the Lord Phrax have the ability to understand what is going on, for a start? And will the Lord Phrax submit to a genome trial before an Arbites medicae, as we shall demand of his rival?'

'Lord Phrax!' cried the wriggling thing on the bed. 'Yes, Lord Phrax will undergo your genome trial, for the trials that have already been visited on him through his genome have given him no reason to fear one more!' The thing grinned again. One of its lips split open and pinkish fluid began to drizzle out. Behind the carriage the flotilla masters were leaning into an urgent, whispered conversation; by the carriage the veiled heads of the charter's honour guard were turning too.

'A trial by genome is farcical,' declared Simova. 'By the authority vested in me by the priesthood of sacred Terra and the Eparch of Hydraphur I–'

'Back in your place, Simova. Now.' Four armoured arbitrators stepped away from the wall. Simova glared at them and started to back away.

'The Mechanicus will not conduct a gene-trial for us on the occasion of this succession,' Calpurnia told the courtroom, 'but a trial there will be. Trial by genome and trial by testimony. Let the two heirs and claimants come forward. The *two heirs* and claimants, Simova, and you disgrace these proceedings and shame yourself that I have to say it to you. Restrain him if you need to.' Her voice was ice-cold. Simova of all of them she had expected to know how to behave in a court, but the man was arguing with the arbitrators and shooting glances back over his shoulder at the Sisters Militant, who were looking to Sister Krovedd for direction. D'Leste was guiding the carriage forward to just below the pulpit, beside the charter; the honour guards were following. And with the noise from one and the grotesquerie of the other, it took Calpurnia a moment to notice that Varro Phrax had not moved.

'MOVE IT, VARRO, that's your call. This is as good as over. Look at that joke. The charter's ours, go fetch it.' Domasa's voice was low and pleasant, not carrying even to her guards. She looked at Varro for a moment as he stared at the floor between his feet. He had laced his hands together to stop them shaking.

'I said move. Are you going to make me kick you?' He could feel the Calpurnia woman's eyes on him as well, as cold as Domasa's. And then for a moment it wasn't Domasa he thought of or the little blonde woman in the pulpit, but Ksana, Ksana's beautiful dark eyes looking into his. He looked at the chronometer at his cuff. It was nearly the time they had agreed. Rikah would have things moving by now.

'Varro Phrax,' said Calpurnia, 'as an heir and claimant–'

And Varro stood, and opened his mouth. What came out first was dry and rusty, but then he managed it.

'I am the eldest son of Hoyyon Phrax. I was told his charter was mine. But I have had enough of blood and murder and greed and scheming. If that is the Phrax legacy then I am well rid of it. So, if it please the most learned and respected court: *I will not claim the charter.*'

ATITH AND THE honour guards didn't really register the words. They were focused on the wreck of Petronas, ready for the signal, ready to keep their promises.

D'Leste barely heard it either. He was almost weeping with fear. Petronas dead in the courtroom would mean his own life within the hour, he knew it, and as rune after rune on the diagnostors went into the red he scrabbled through his memory for something, anything that Dyobann had said that might help.

The other flotilla masters heard the words but were too stunned to react to them. The look they exchanged was simple. It said: what does this mean for us now?

Kyorg felt a burst of fear, the sudden certainty that he had taken the wrong bet.

Domasa Dorel felt like a trapdoor had dropped open under her: the lurch in her gut was like falling. She felt her muscles tighten and her third eye start to throb.

'I hope you know you've done it now, you little bastard,' she told Varro aloud. Now that everything had gone in a heap it seemed stupid to care about disrespecting the courtroom. 'You knew what we arranged, and if you think you've seen—' That was when she realised that it might indeed matter what she said there, and without a word she turned and strode out of the courtroom, her two guards falling in behind her. One of them paused by Varro and gave a leer from under his visor and an obscene little fist-in-crotch gesture that Varro did not acknowledge. Then the tall doors swung shut again and they were gone.

'Someone's got to keep an eye on her,' muttered Kyorg to Halpander and hurried out after them. He didn't care if his exit had sounded convincing. By the look of things, points like that were going to be distinctly moot soon.

'On behalf of the departed—' Simova began. He had belatedly remembered that he was here because he had supposedly joined the Phrax entourage as they flew in. He was wondering when Arbitor Calpurnia was going to get things back onto an even keel so that he could begin his arguments. Then Krovedd pushed past him and walked forward level with the carriage.

'Let's neither of us fool ourselves, Arbitor Calpurnia. One heir refuses to claim, the other won't last another day barring the hand of the Emperor Himself touching him. If the charter passes to this Petronas there'll be another hearing soon and, if there's no line, then I think—' but she was interrupted by a scream from the carriage.

'Rogue Trader Petronas!' the thrashing thing howled. The violence of its movements tore its skin in half a dozen places and fluid stained the grey of the coverlet and the white of the cushions. 'Even better! What a time! What timing! Mother, are you listening? Pay close attention, be proud! Rogue Trader Phrax knows no laws, we all learned that, didn't we! Goes where he wants, does the rogue trader! No more sneaking, then!' It snapped upright and suddenly its mummified face was staring point-blank into D'Leste's. His scream cut off as Petronas's split and bleeding hand gripped his neck with terrible, feverish strength.

'Rogue Trader Petronas's first order!' the thing screamed into his face, and D'Leste felt something warm splash out of its throat onto his skin. Something bounced off his lip and onto the bed: a tooth. 'First order is avenging! First order is justice for mother-killers! First order is...'

Petronas stopped. For a moment he had felt wonderful. There had been terrible pain in his hand, but he had felt his fingers sinking into something and his blurred, doubling, tripling vision had shown him the doctor who had done all this, the doctor who had stood over the bed, the doctor, the doctor was dead.

He dimly heard shouts. There were others he had meant to see to, weren't there? The sound of flesh being struck. It sounded good. He could feel his body slumping, hurting, as his tissues rejected once and for all the genetic disguise that Dyobann's brutal experiments had tried to stamp onto them, as his cells blew out and broke down, as his flesh sloughed away. He looked at the doctor's face. He wondered if it still counted as revenge, even though he was the one that this one had hurt and not his mother, and while he was wondering that, he died.

'GONE FEET-UP,' Behaya had said. 'No heir at all, now.'

'If we can get the charter onto the ship,' Galt had muttered, 'we might still have a chance. Get Trazelli.'

So Zanti had left them in the courtroom and hurried out through the doors, their closing swing drowning out the screeching as Petronas finished whatever he was doing to D'Leste. Incompetent idiot. They should never have trusted him to look after Petronas after Dyobann disappeared.

'You.' She snapped her fingers at one of the armoured figures in the corridor. 'Get a message to the boat from the *Callyac's Promise*. The message is–'

'Arbitor Senioris Calpurnia commands us,' the arbitrator told her bluntly. 'Not you.'

'Arbitor Sen–' Anger would not let her finish the sentence, and there were things to do. Red with humiliation, she hurried on until she thought she was in range of the hangar, then keyed the vox in her wrist-amulet. 'Trazelli. We're going to be leaving with the charter soon but things are bad. Has Kyorg reached you yet?'

'I saw him on the dock level,' came Trazelli's voice in her ear, 'but he didn't come here. Not yet.'

Zanti squeezed her eyes shut for a moment and forced clear thoughts through the anger. Waited for connections to click, for data to–

'*Bastard*! Trazelli, four men to meet me at the first set of steps in the courtroom hallway. Now.'

Trazelli knew better than to try and ask why.

ATITH WAS SOBBING as she and Kohze and Trichodi led the charge. They had hidden magazines full of low-density undetectable rounds for their ceremonial rifles, but there was no time to load them as they closed in on the flotilla masters, the people who had betrayed Nils, Nils who was the rogue trader now. Mutiny. Revenge.

Her long dagger was in her hand and red-bearded Halpander was in front of her. He batted her first thrust away with a swipe that laid the back of his hand open along the dagger's edge, bellowed and flicked the sleeves of his coat a certain way. Two shining flaps of micromesh chainmail dropped out, set with odd ridges of metal; then Halpander made fists and the ridges snapped into rows of spines along his now-armoured knuckles.

Next to him, little long-faced Galt flipped up the end of his staff and there was a shimmer in the air as a micronthin carbon blade took the head off the man next to her. Then Halpander's fist crashed into her mouth and she was on her back. Phyron stepped over her, yelling and swinging his empty gun in an arc that smashed Halpander's collarbone before the microblade in Galt's staff took his arm off.

Sobbing and spitting blood, Atith scrambled back. She wanted to call out to Nils, tell him that they were fighting as he had told them to, but he was limp on his bed. Then she was in a crouch and powering forward and her dagger punched through the flakcloth layers under Halpander's coat, sending him over backwards to sit and gape at the hilt jutting from his sternum.

There was a rapid cracking from behind her: Trichodi had taken the time to find her magazine, load and empty it into Galt's face. That was enough for the Arbites: they had been moving in to break the brawl up with fists and boots and shotgun butts, but after Galt went over without a sound Calpurnia shouted an order as she vaulted the pulpit rail and the arbitrators took aim. Trichodi was knocked three ways at once by blasts of shot – she pirouetted and fell. An Executioner shell smacked into the side of Kohze's head as he tried to load up to get a shot at the fleeing Behaya. Atith scrambled to cover under Nils's bed, and thought she might be about to make it before there were more shots and two bodies collapsed onto her, pinning her to the ground. When she shook them off and stood up again there was an arbitor on the other side of the bed aiming point blank at her and she opened her mouth to say–

TRAZELLI CAME DOWN out of the boat from the *Callyac's Promise* at the head of two dozen armsmen, pounding through the portals along the route that the charter had taken to the courtroom, leaving four armsmen and nine arbitrators lying dead in the boat and on the hangar floor.

'Zanti, sir!'

'What?'

'I just saw Zanti, sir,' said the armsman, 'heading into one of the cross-corridors!'

'Get after her,' Trazelli said, thinking of the last exchange over the vox. 'And you and you and you. Make sure she's alright. Get her into the boat and then wait for my orders.' The four armsmen peeled off and the rest of them ran on.

The hall sloped down into the guts of the fortress, then flattened and widened and rose up in half a dozen broad steps to the double doors of the courtroom. That was where the next garrison of Arbites were. They were just closing ranks across the corridor when the doors swung open and Behaya burst out between them, holding up her skirts and running as fast as her long legs would carry her, as from inside came a roaring chorus of shotgun fire.

'Halt – now!' bellowed an arbitrator in the centre of the line, gold rank-trim glittering as he held up a hand. But one look at Behaya's face was enough to make Trazelli decide. He flung himself flat, high-bore autostubber already whining and clicking as the loader cycled up. Behind them Behaya gave a yell that distracted just enough of the arbitrators for just long enough–

'KYORG!' IN THE narrow side-passage leading to the dromon docking-sockets, Kyorg jumped guiltily and spun around, his bald head catching the lights. Behind him, Domasa Dorel shuffled a couple more paces back toward the airlock where the *Omicron's Dart* was docked, wishing she'd had the chance to bring the toxin needler with her. She had sent one of the guards ahead into the ship to get a transmission back to the *Gann-Luctis* on what to do with the hostages, and now she motioned for the other one to get between her and the confrontation.

Stamping toward them was a woman in the garb of a flotilla master, a black-haired old biddy with a hawk-beak nose and the shine of augmetic sockets visible under the edge of her hood. Domasa could see the terror of her in Kyorg's eyes. She should probably leave them to it. She backed up a pace more.

'Oh, and didn't I just *know* it would be you, Kyorg, you treacherous little tikk-fondling...' Zanti was spitting with fury, every word flying out like a bullet. 'That's how they knew to send a blood-sample of their own, that's how they knew we were counter-claiming. You told them everything, didn't you. Is that who that freak works for?'

'I was doing what I had to,' Kyorg squeaked, backing away from Zanti. 'You think I didn't know you people had it in for me? You think I didn't know I had no future with the way you all joined against me? Bypassing me, talking about me?'

'You bypassed yourself, you incompetent little tikk! If you'd ever thought of doing your job instead of coasting on Hoyyon's work...' She tailed off as four armsmen in white-grey-green livery came pelting up behind her. 'Ah, good, I don't have to handle all this on my own. I think what I'll do, Kyorg, is drag you back to the *Callyac's Promise* and fly you back with us so we can tell–'

The threat of humiliation before the flotilla did what the other threats had not. Kyorg pistoned out both hands in front of him and his ornate rings flared with energy. Zanti, wise about hidden weapons, backed and turned away in time, and the two hindmost armsmen were protected by their visors. The other two caught the full blast and staggered away, howling and clamping their hands to their faces. Another ring spat a needle-fine laser that lanced through the third man's throat just below his helmet's chin-strap and sent him reeling and choking against the walls.

As Domasa reached the ramp of the *Omicron's Dart* her own guard shoved Kyorg aside and raised a snubby little shotcaster he had drawn from a pouch in the small of his back. His mistake was to pick the last armsman as the major threat: in the time that it took for him to aim and fire, Zanti pinched the front of her floor-length coat firmly in her fingers and flicked it out. The braids of memory-wire woven into the hem curled up for a moment and then whipped savagely back, trying to regain their original shape, and the metal weight in the hem cracked the guard's kneecap. As he lurched and stumbled the second flick hit him between the eyes with more force that any movement that brief should have been able to muster, and the third connected solidly with Kyorg's temple with a sound like an apple hitting concrete. As both men sagged to the floor, Zanti plucked the shotcaster from the guard's limp hand, fired it into the guard's face, checked the load, sighted on Kyorg's head and emptied the rest of the magazine.

ONE OR TWO arbitrators swung around to cover Behaya as she barrelled through the courtroom doors, but most of them were intent on Trazelli's armsmen as they began exchanging fire. Behaya ripped off her heavy uniform medallion and hurled it away, hearing the crack as the casing fragmented then the hiss as the filaments from the xenos weapon they had captured long ago, the filaments it had cost the lives of two techs to extract from the teleporting warrior's strange gun, popped clear.

They touched and tangled and, when the Arbites tried to brush them or pull them away, they cut and bit through armour and into flesh. The air in the hallway was suddenly filled with screams, scarlet droplets and the thick smell of blood.

But three armsmen had fallen to Executioner shells already, and as Behaya ran forward two more were punched off their feet. She raked a hand down the front of her coat, ripping off the ornamental buttons, and scattered them to one side as she ran: a couple were dummies, but more exploded in white heat. Two arbitrators died instantly, arms and faces incinerated and their bodies flash-cooked inside their carapaces; three more staggered and fell as the lethal heat sucked the oxygen out of their lungs. In a few seconds more the tiny incendiary pellets had burned out and Behaya ran on through the smoke and the cauterised blood on the floor.

There were still shapes moving in the thick haze behind her, and the armsmen began a steady suppressing volley. She tried to call to Trazelli, but her voice was lost in the gunshots, the hooting of a fire klaxon and the rumbling of shutters sealing the courtroom off, triggered by the heat and smoke.

'What? Get behind me and speak up, Beyaha.'

'I said everything in there is gone. Zanti and Kyorg are clear, that's all, we have to–'

The first Executioner round came arcing through the smoke and caught her in the small of the back. The impact thrust Behaya's hips forward, then the second round hit the base of her neck and sent her to the deck in an ungainly sprawl of dead limbs. Trazelli bawled a curse and banged off a burst of stubshots into the smoke, barely aware of how many of them were coming back past him in vicious ricochets. It seemed like an hour of firing, rolling, reloading before he realised that nothing in front of him was moving. He stood in the corridor and reloaded in the sudden silence with shaking hands, looking around him at his surviving men, trying to work out what to do. He had walked forward, slowly, picking his way over the corpses, when the courtroom door began to open again.

CHAPTER FOURTEEN

Courtroom, Adeptus Arbites fortress
of Selena Secundus, Galata

VARRO PHRAX HAD started for the door after the tall
woman in the grey when the brawling changed to shooting. He veered off, hands over his ears, as the Arbites cut
down every last one of the white-veiled guard who had
inexplicably turned on their masters. Then he heard a
clank behind him and looked around: the green-eyed
arbitor had vaulted the edge of her pulpit, hung by one
arm for a moment, and then slid down the almost-sheer
side, hitting the floor and rolling. She disappeared out of
sight for a moment behind the box Varro had stood in,
and then she was there beside him. There was no malice
in her stare, but little pity, either. Still looking at him, she
motioned the other Arbites toward the courtroom doors,
but as they began to move there was a chorus of shouts
from outside, then a storm of gunfire and an odd thump-
ing roar.

230

'Stand up,' Calpurnia said. He did. She was shorter than he, smaller than he had thought, the three scar-lines running up from her left eye flexing as she scowled.

'You chose not to inherit,' she said. 'Why?'

'I told you,' Varro said dully. 'The things I've seen people do, the things I know people *think*. This can be a terrible universe, Arbitor Calpurnia. Why should I make it worse for myself and my family by putting myself in the middle of... of...' A wave of the hand toward the bed and the corpses summed it all up.

CALPURNIA TILTED HER head as though she were considering another question, and made a statement instead.

'That Navigator wasn't an ally.'

'No.'

'She was using you.'

'Yes.'

'How did you stop her? Stand up to her here?'

'I arranged it with my chief retainer before we came in. He's gone back to the dromon. He has people working to protect my wife and son back on the ship.' Animation started to come back into Varro's voice. 'They're the ones I need to get to. The *Gann-Luctis* was following us in more slowly, that's where they are. They're who I need to get to. Not this charter. We'll go back to Gunarvo, to the house there. Away from this.'

'I don't think you'll be able to get away from this,' Calpurnia told him, 'not now that you're indisputably the only heir. There won't be any getting away from that, not even if you formally renounce your succession. Too many people will want to make you change your mind.'

'Then what do I do?' Varro's voice was low and hopeless.

Calpurnia looked at him for a moment, then stood up and walked across to the dais. Simova was standing over the charter, licking his lips, trying to muster the courage to reach out for it. Calpurnia drew her pistol and knocked him to one side with a sidearm hit to his temple, picked up the book without fuss and walked back.

There was only the faintest shake of her hands as she opened the book to its last page. Varro looked at the marks without really understanding them; Calpurnia stared at them for a long moment before she spoke in an unsteady voice.

'A long time ago, Varro Phrax, the God-Emperor walked across the galaxy choosing men and women to lay the foundations of His Imperium. He came to Hydraphur where there were great fleets ready to strike out into the unknown for Him and He looked at all the masters of spacecraft and who do you think He chose, Varro? He chose the line of Phrax to carry His word and His charter. I don't pretend to know your life or your mind, sir, but I know about family legacies and I know about traditions. Don't drop this burden in the dust. For good or ill, Varro, this is yours as it will be his. The legacy is his and yours and your father's and the Emperor's. Don't betray that.' She looked at his expression. 'Varro, you don't want any part of your legacy to fall into the hands of people like that. Nor do I. I know about minds like that as much as you do. So take the charter. By the authority invested in me, I name you heir. Take the charter and keep it safe from the schemers and the thieves and the murderers. Take it.'

He stared at her for a long moment, another. Finally, his hand reached out, his fingers closed around the plain cloth of the charter cover. They rested there for a moment, then his grip firmed and he took the book from her hands.

'What ceremony do we need for this?' he asked.

'We've had it, I think,' Calpurnia replied. 'You're the Rogue Trader Varro Phrax now.' She stood up. 'And my obligation is to see you safely to your ship and out of Hydraphur. Let's get the flotilla organised and get your wife and child picked up. Get those doors unsealed, please, we're going to the hangar. Sister Krovedd, your bodyguard still have their bolters unloaded? You may give them permission to reload. You Arbites, all of you, with me.' She keyed her vox-torc. 'Culann, vox a message that the escort ships for the *Gann-Luctis* are to stay on heightened watch. Have the *Baron Mykal* stand ready too, we're going to – what? Say again.' She paused glowered again, swore. 'Fine. Have a pinnace ready from the *Mykal*, and fast. We're moving. Varro, come on. Now.'

The doors were opening. Calpurnia walked over to Sister Krovedd and saluted her.

'Let's just abbreviate our whole disagreement, Sister. There is not the legal case that Simova thinks there is. The charter has been handed on. This is the Emperor's will as laid down in His law. Will you help us honour it?'

The Sister Pronatus's head bowed, and she murmured something that Varro didn't catch. Calpurnia did, though, and gestured for him to open the book. The Sisters Militant stepped up behind Krovedd and all stared at the marks: the letter, the spot of blood. A single small tear slipped out of Krovedd's eye and down her cheek.

'It's enough,' she said in a small voice, and they turned to go.

The mood was broken an instant later. A moustached man dressed in a flotilla master's uniform stood staring at them, the loader on his autostubber whirring.

Trazelli never pulled the trigger. A shell from one of the Sisters' freshly reloaded bolters took him in the solar plexus, lifting him and carrying him backwards through the air and over the steps before it detonated inside him half a metre above the hallway floor.

'Let's move,' said Shira Calpurnia.

Ecclesiarchal dromon the
Omicron's Dart, Galata space

As THE *Omicron's Dart* closed its hatch on the gun-toting harridan outside and blew itself free from the docking socket, Domasa Dorel found her second guard lying dead

outside the cockpit doors, next to the alcove that held
controls for the dromon's communications arrays. His
helmet was askew and there was a single neat las-burn in
his cheek, opening a cauterised tunnel up into his cranium. She had no doubt as to who was to blame. It had
been Rikah, the metalheaded no-hoper, on behalf of his
worthless, treacherous runt of an employer.

There was no sign of him in the gallery, nor in the central passenger alley as the little ship turned and
accelerated up and away from the base. She could not
hear him over the soft sound of the ship's systems, and
when she made her quiet way through the forward compartments to the cockpit there was no sight nor sound of
him. She felt the absence of the needler at her arm, but
she was not totally defenceless: she reached up and
pushed the hood back from her high-browed head and
loosened the headband that bound her warp eye shut.

'Rikah?' she called as she padded along the gallery that
ran down the port side of the ship. 'It's over, Rikah. You
lost. Come out. It's all done. Just you and me now.' No
answer. She wondered if he had taken refuge in the
cockpit or the enginarium, but no, she had ordered the
crew to seal themselves in.

'We'll be back at our own ship soon, Rikah, and Cherrick is waiting there. You do know you've failed, don't
you? Whatever you were planning, I can stop it. Give it
up, Rikah, it's over.'

No answer. Domasa shrugged the tension out of her
shoulders, looked forward and back, and stalked carefully on through the softly-lit corridors.

Docking level, Adeptus Arbites
Fortress of Selena Secundus, Galata

ZANTI HAD BARELY survived the dromon's takeoff, scurry-
ing backwards as the sirens went off and the docking seal
cracked. She could see the Navigatrix freak silhouetted in

the cockpit dormer as the gravity plates powered down and the *Dart* began to withdraw its prow from the docking socket – a dromon was too big to fit in a hangar. The dropping gravity and growing tide of air gave her a moment of utter terror and then she was through the portals and gripping a safety rail as the seals thundered closed.

Zanti didn't bother trying to get to the window to see it climb away. She hung onto the railing, breathing in hoarse gasps, until her heart slowed and her head was clear.

She didn't know how many of the rest were alive, so she didn't think about it, her thoughts stripped to the most simple and brutal. Survive and get out of the fortress. Survive and get to the *Callyac's Promise*. Survive and get to the flotilla. After that there were too many variables. She would deal with it when the time came. And deal with it she would. By then there would be arguing and second thoughts and the kind of woolly thinking that would give Zanti all the opportunities she needed.

She had been too intent on chasing Kyorg down the switchbacking passages between the main hall and the dock to have remembered her way, but it wasn't hard to find her bearings once she concentrated. She hurried back to find her ride back to the *Promise*, the little shot-caster gripped in her hand, and after a few more turns she was close enough to the boat to vox out the name and vector of the *Omicron's Dart* for forwarding to the gunnery officers on *Promise* and the *Bassaan*. She grinned savagely as she ran on towards the boat. See how far the little milksop heir got with his Navigator sidekick dead and his dromon destroyed.

Ecclesiarchal dromon the *Omicron's Dart*, En route to the Gann-Luctis

THE CAT-AND-MOUSE could not have been going on long, but long enough for Domasa to be struck by the silliness of the image in her mind: the dromon speeding through space, a handful of crew sealed behind blast-doors in each end, and in the long central corridors these two enemies stalking round and round and round. She had found Rikah's cast-off boots in one of the lower galleries – he must have shed them to try and be quieter – and she saw the occasional footprint marked out in sweat, but she hadn't been able to close with him. It had taken effort to keep her mind sharp, to push away idle thoughts like the picture of them chasing each other in circles or the growing temptation to just start stamping down the corridors and galleries yelling his name. That would be the way to walk into an ambush, and yet she had been too keyed up to want to simply wait in ambush herself.

That was when she heard him in the communications alcove. For a moment her heart froze, and then she licked her lips and went towards the sound, tugging the bandanna away from her forehead. Her unveiled warp eye glistened in the low light, looking out into blessedly calm space. Domasa licked her lips as the noises became louder: Rikah's voice and the chitter of message tape. She almost held her breath as she closed on the doorway and then almost laughed when she stood in it.

The idiot must have decided to die. He was turned away from the door, pistol dangling in his hand, the ridiculous silver ruffs on his head quivering as they communicated with the comms panel.

'Sir, you are going to have to change course closer to the formation! They're coming around Galata and from what I can tell they'll be in range. No, not good enough, we can't evade them for long enough to get to the *Gann-Luctis*! Are you even listening to me?'

'Rikah.'

He spun around, eyes wide.

'Domasa, please you have to help, we have to co-operate now.'

'Do we? No we don't. Ask your master about co-operation, Rikah. Do you know what he did? Don't even bother answering, you revolting little insect. Do you know what's going to happen to me? Answer: nothing that can be worse than what I'm about to do to you.'

'LOOK!' Rikah shouted into her face, and despite herself she glanced over at the message tapes in his hand. Most of it was gibberish to her, but she knew enough to pick out authorisation codes for the Phrax flotilla and the Imperial Navy.

'They're going to fire on us!' Rikah yelled at her. 'They're coming around Galata, the whole bloody lot of them! They think Varro's on this ship, or the charter is. They are armed and they are going to try to destroy us! There's a Navy squadron covering us, we need to get into their range! Are you *listening* to me, you stupid woman?'

As they glared at each other there was another chitter from the panel and another tongue of creamy-white tape spewed from an engraved bronze dispenser as the words crackled out of the panel.

'...*Kovash Venator*, ordering you to power down your weapons immediately and redirect to the vector our astropaths are providing. I say again to the Phrax flotilla, this is the Imperial Battlefleet Pacificus warship *Kovash Venator*, ordering you to power down your weapons immediately and redirect onto the vector we are transmitting.'

Domasa leaned over and snaked a long finger out onto the internal vox switch.

'Maintain course, pilot. Just bob and weave a bit.' They felt the floor start to gently undulate under them as the crew obliged. 'If you can plot a fast course to the *Gann-Luctis* that takes us through Navy cover then do it. If you can't, then don't. We're not going to lose any time.'

'Ships of the Phrax flotilla,' came another crackling voice, 'this is the Battlefleet Pacificus warship *Voice of the Seraph*. Power down your weapons *now*.'

'You heard, Rikah,' said Domasa, turning to face him. 'The Navy are moving on them. We're in the middle of Hydraphur, you stupid man, did you think they would get away with this?'

'We're going to turn in and head for the Navy squadron,' said Rikah, his voice trembling. He had remembered the pistol in his fist and was aiming it at her chest. 'I can tell you what's happened on the *Gann-Luctis*, we saw to you. We had it all worked out before we even reached Hydraphur. So you can, you can just–'

'Did you work out *this*?' asked Domasa, and looked at him.

To Rikah, it suddenly seemed as though a freezing wind laced with sleet and vapour was scouring at him. There was roaring white noise in his ears, and the metal ridges on his head seemed to burn. The augmetic receptors buried in his ears burst into life, registering static that sounded like keening voices, and in his vision the woman's warp eye grew and grew until it filled his sight with purest blackness–

It took a second and a half for her gaze to blow out every synapse in Rikah's brain and send him spasming to the floor. She put a foot on his wrist to make sure the gun could not flail up at her and go off, and waited for the last twitches to subside.

The chatter between the ships had fallen silent, or switched to a different frequency that the *Dart* could not pick up, and there was silence in the alcove now. Domasa grunted to herself and stepped into the corridor. There were viewing ports studding the outer wall of the highest of the galleries, and she headed there to see what she could see.

Just as she was emerging from the stairs all the viewports were lit up with a dazzling yellow-white light as the plasma shells from the *Bassaan's* cannon began to burst around them, and the ship shuddered and bucked under a miss so near that Domasa was catapulted down the corridor.

* * *

Ship's boat from the *Callyac's Promise*, Galata space

ZANTI REACHED THE boat from the *Callyac's Promise* at the same time as Calpurnia, Varro, Odamo and half a dozen arbitrators, and suddenly the plan was in her head as though she had known it for a decade. She made herself nod and smile and bob while they made all their pompous tikk noises about 'by authority of the Adeptus', and let them think they were commandeering the boat to take them to the *Baron Mykal*. She acted horrified by the carnage in the courtroom. It sounded like Galt and Halpander had gone first. Behaya and Trazelli might have had a chance if they hadn't gotten stupid. And D'Leste, D'Leste had deserved every scrap of it.

She fawned and scraped and agreed that of course they must fly to the *Mykal* and then she used her flotilla seal to let herself into the boat's cockpit and told the crew, 'The *Promise*. Dock anywhere but the *Promise* and I gut you.' She knew they would obey, and she knew that once they were back aboard the *Callyac's Promise* things would be different. She knew that once the heir was aboard she could get him into the charter shrine and then who would know, really, what he had to say? She would carry his words out, his orders that the Arbites leave the ship, the orders that the flotilla form up and leave the system, and if he were alive to deliver those orders then fine, and if not, fine too. And then there would be the matter of selecting a new team of flotilla masters, and she had just the people lined up...

'Reverse the order, please.'

Zanti was not used to being in a reverie, let alone having to come out of one, and it took her a moment to realise the green-eyed scar-headed arbitrator woman was standing in front of her, one hand on the butt of her pistol. Varro stood behind her, framed in the arch that led to the boat's main compartment, clutching the charter to his chest and staring. With an effort Zanti pulled her gaze away from the little book and looked the other woman in the eye.

'I gave no order, my esteemed lady justice,' she said, bowing even lower than her stoop normally made her. 'I was ensuring that the crew had the wherewithal and the experience to dock with an unfamiliar craft such as your illustrious warcraft to which you have so wisely redirected–'

'You gave an order for the crew to fly us to the *Callyac's Promise*. Reverse it and maybe I'll try you after this is all over rather than executing you where you stand.'

Zanti stared at her. She could kill the woman easily enough, and then all she had to do was keep Varro from raising the alarm for a ten-minute trip to the *Promise*. Once they were there she would have the resources to take care of the rest. These thoughts took about a second to go through her mind, and then she stepped forward.

Varro saw the grim-faced woman in the cloak-gown grasp the hem of her garment in an odd, tense way and start to move it up and forward, then a pistol-shot made him start. Zanti, pop-eyed with astonishment, doubled over and skidded backwards into the red stain that had appeared on the cockpit doors behind her. As she fell forward onto her knees Calpurnia stepped forward and fired another round into the back of her head, bursting it and sending the metal augmetic plugs popping out of their mounts and scattering across the floor.

As Varro looked on, his face stricken, Calpurnia stepped over to the body and nudged the cape-hem with her foot. It writhed and straightened itself as she pushed a curve into it.

'Memory-wire and weights,' she said. 'Popular blue-blood weapon on Hazhim. You can put a pock-mark into steel plate if you're good enough with it.' She sighed. 'For nothing, too, that was. There are far more of us aboard the *Promise* than I think she knew about.'

She turned back to Varro.

'Make sure the crew get the order that our destination is the *Baron Mykal*. This is your ship now, after all.'

Near Galata space, Gyre Aurucon,
Inner Hydraphur system

THE FLOTILLA HAD come around the curve of Galata, blasting itself forward and out of proximity with its Navy and Arbites shadows. The *Bassaan* and the *Magritta's Arrow*, the two most powerful ships with the most aggressive commands, were the first to surge away after the fleeing *Omicron's Dart*.

The slowest, the *Sounding of Aurucon* and the *Proserpina Dawn*, had it worst as they lumbered about to follow. The Navy had not forgotten the flotilla's conduct on its arrival and when the *Bassaan* powered up and discharged its first burst at the *Dart*, that was enough. The *Voice of the Seraph*, a Furious-class grand cruiser whose gun batteries rivalled those of some battleships, opened up first, using barely half its firepower to cripple the *Proserpina Dawn* outright. As the sleek container craft that had been Halpander's home for nineteen years coasted away from Galata at a drunken angle, bleeding burning air from the wounds in its hull, the light cruisers which made up the *Voice's* squadron-mates equally deftly scythed through the *Sounding of Aurucon's* enginarium with a co-ordinated lance salvo that sent plasma from its drive room coursing through ruptured bulkheads and incinerating three-quarters of the crew.

The *Gyga VII*, the fat nugget of a ship that had housed Magos Dyobann's secret chambers, wrapped itself in layers of void shields that not even the flotilla masters had known it possessed and opened its engines, trying to accelerate through the middle of the flotilla formation and past the Navy ships. But by putting up its shields it made itself a target to one of the few vessels that could both keep pace with it and do it damage. The *Kovash Venator*, a spear-slender Long Serpent-class cruiser with powerful engines, sped out to intercept the *Gyga* and flanked it for another hour, battering at its shields with plasma and macroshells. Finally, its hull crumpled and drives damaged and with another Navy squadron closing in from its patrol route on an intercept course, the *Gyga* accepted its fate, burned retros, dumped off its velocity and prepared to be boarded.

The *Magritta's Arrow* tried to run too, followed by the little escort-sized *Kortika* that had been Zanti's home and domain. *Kortika*, not built for speed, tried to skim over the surface of Galata to hide behind the moon's curve. Her captain realised that Galata was as fortified as every other body in Hydraphur when a great battery of plasma silos in the surface swatted the shields off his ship with contemptuous ease and a trio of giant lance turrets came to bear to finish what the guns had started. *Kortika* blew out in a storm that sent static and interference screaming through unshielded systems for twenty kilometres around.

On the other side of the planet, torpedo bays had slid open their shutters in artificial rift-valleys and six mammoth spikes of adamantium tore through space after the fleeing *Magritta's Arrow*. Two burst as they tried to fly through the heat of its exhaust, and another disintegrated under fire from the *Arrow's* point-defence arrays, but the final three plunged into its hull like lethal hypodermics, exploding deep in the layers of decks they had torn through. The dark, smouldering hulk that had been *Magritta's Arrow* tumbled on through space for another seventy thousand kilometres before four Firestorm escorts drew alongside it and methodically broke the wreck down with their batteries into fragments no bigger than the pulpit Calpurnia had stood on in her courtroom.

Last was the *Bassaan*, which at least had the minor victory of smashing *Omicron's Dart* to pieces with its second and third salvoes before answering fire from the *Baron*

Mykal and *Voice of the Seraph* stove in its shields on both sides and left it crippled and fighting to stay functioning.

Aboard the *Callyac's Promise*, stranded above Selena Secundus and cut off from the flotilla, there was a brief and abortive struggle as a third of the crew tried to fight their way through the *tikks* and get the ship out to join their fellows. The Arbites put it down without mercy, and the summary execution of every rebel crewman and the news filtering through of what was happening to the rest of the flotilla was enough to put pay to any more ideas.

There was mopping up, of course, salvage and arrests, damage control around Galata and the recovery of a saviour pod from the *Omicron's Dart* containing a badly injured and barely conscious Navigator who was hastily collected and spirited out of the system by agents of House Dorel. This was generally considered to be the end of the Phrax Mutiny, and that was how it was entered in most of the Imperial records. For Shira Calpurnia, it didn't end there.

The sanctioned liner *Gann-Luctis*, outer Hydraphur

THE CHARTER LAY on the table, unheeded. Varro Phrax knelt on the floor, Ksana cradled in his arms as Dreyder was cradled in hers. The blood from their death-wounds mingled and pooled under them, and slicked Varro's chest and arms as he tried to hold them both to himself at once. Tears trickled from his face and mingled with their blood.

Shira Calpurnia stood a few paces behind him, hands laced respectfully before her, head bowed. They had passed signs of the fighting, where staff and crew loyal to Varro had tried to wrest the ship from Domasa's agents and the delegation of Gunarvo's governor; that was as much as she had been able to piece together. For the most part they had succeeded, and the *Gann-Luctis* had let the

Baron Mykal close and the shuttle carrying Calpurnia and
Varro to board with no resistance.

They had succeeded except for here.

'Cherrick' had been the name on the tags of the man
lying on the floor in the middle of the room with the
gunshot hole in his gut. The name was not one that had
appeared in any of Calpurnia's dossiers. There was a
hellgun lying by his corpse, but when he had come in
here to kill Varro's family he had used a knife. She didn't
pretend to know why, but that seemed to be what had
given Ksana Phrax the chance to draw and fire. She supposed she would never know exactly what had
happened here.

Varro wept on and on, the sound with little rise or fall,
the low, constant crying of a man whose spirit was broken. He had bent forward over their bodies, his face in his
wife's blood-stringed hair.

Calpurnia's vox-torc buzzed, and when she stepped out
into the corridor and keyed it open she heard Odamo's
voice from the *Baron Mykal*. She turned away, as much so
the *Gann-Luctis* crew waiting outside in the corridor
wouldn't see her expression as for privacy of speech.

'Ma'am, you asked for surveillance of the ship.'

'Yes? What of it?' Even as she asked she felt a telltale
rumble of power through the deck and the lights for an
instant went dim.

'We're picking up power to the drives, ma'am. They're
getting ready to move and there's a signature that the aus-
pex crew tells me is consistent with power to the warp
coils. We think they're going to try and jump out of the
system from here.'

Impossible. That was her thought. She had seen the
reports of the state the ship had been in when it came
into Hydraphur. And now it was undercrewed, and did
they even have a Navigator left after that last voyage?

She rounded on the crewmembers, who quailed under
her look.

'Abort this manoeuvre instantly. Now. Get word to the bridge. This ship is not going into warp.'

'Master Phrax gave the order,' said the middle officer defiantly, a rangy man with a cascade of grey hair. 'He gave the order as he was coming up here. He told us that we would break warp for Gunarvo, no matter what the consequences.'

'That's insane,' snapped Calpurnia. 'You of all people know that it's not survivable. This far in-system? With this amount of damage? How could he give the order?'

'He gave it as he came to the stateroom,' the officer said again. 'I think he knew what had happened even then.' The other two nodded agreement.

'Then you know he's not of sound mind. Abort the order. Now.'

'Varro Phrax means more than just a new master to us, ma'am,' said the grey-haired officer with a lift of his chin. 'He risked himself to fight a warp-daemon. He was our luck when we voyaged here. And now he carries a charter signed by the Emperor. We fought for him. We put our trust in him.' The other two nodded their agreement. Calpurnia stared at them for a moment, then strode back through the door and to the kneeling trader.

'Varro? Varro, listen to me. I know what you're feeling. I know what you've been feeling since you did what you did in the courtroom.' He didn't seem to notice her kneeling by his side or her hand on his shoulder. His face was hidden. The smell of blood was thick. The weeping went on and on.

'Varro, you don't have the right to take this whole ship and everyone else on it to a terrible death. They somehow don't believe it will happen, but it will. You owe a duty to the living, Varro. Listen to me!'

Then the ship rumbled with power again, a rumble that rose in pitch as the warp engines struggled to work. Calpurnia's torc buzzed and screeched and through the

interference from the charging engines she could hear
Odamo's voice frantically calling her name.

It was a decision that she would hate herself for for a
long time, but there was nothing else she could do. She
stood up.

'Emperor walk with you, then, Varro, wherever you
may end up.'

And she ran.

VARRO PHRAX DID not hear the warp engines fire to their
highest output, and his only reaction when one of the
coils began to flicker and overload and send shudders
down the length of the ship was to grip his murdered
family tighter and tighter, terrified that the embrace
might have to end. He wept, uncaringly, as the proximity
alarms went off in response to the *Baron Mykal* passing
insanely close to grapple in the saviour pod that Calpurnia had managed to reach before it blasted its way past
on full engines and sped out of the danger zone. He wept,
unhearing, as the main warp engines, weakened from the
terrible strain of the storm, broke and overloaded. He
wept, unseeing, as the hole in space opened, not sharp
and bullet-precise but a great, ragged, spreading wound
into which the ship slid like a reptile into a tarpit.

He kissed his wife's cold cheek as the screams began
from the crew, as the Geller field crumpled and the stuff
of the hull began to ripple and fray; he stroked his son's
hair as the walls of the stateroom began to softly undulate as though they were curtains in a breeze. He did not
see the colourless nothingness filling the *Gann-Luctis's*
corridors and rooms or the death-throes of the crew as
curious, malicious fingers of ether began to pick at their
flesh and their minds and finally whirled them out
through the disintegrating hull. He heard the whispers at
the corner of his mind that got louder and louder until it
was a hammering in his skull and he felt the room spin
and fade around him and his own flesh teased out into

threads and clouds, but he accepted it and rocked his wife and his child. Maybe they would not reach Gunarvo, but maybe he had known this ever since he had seen the faces of the crew when he came off the shuttle with Calpurnia. Maybe he had always known they would never return to Gunarvo, and so all there was to do now was stay here and rock his wife and child until it didn't matter any more.

THE BARON MYKAL sped away from the unholy death of the *Gann-Luctis* with all engines open; it was an hour before its captain felt it safe to shed velocity and start to bring the ship about. No one had any illusions about finding survivors.

Shira Calpurnia went to the bridge and stood there in silence as they passed the spot where the rift had been. After they had passed it, and as Galata loomed large in the forward windows, she left and walked down to the ship's chapel. She did not pray there, but sat in a pew before the golden aquila. She sat with her head bowed in silence, sat there for a very long time.

EPILOGUE

NOBODY KNOWS WHERE the story started, nobody knows who is supposed to have seen the events unfold. Some versions tell of a crewman, some of a woman, one last survivor who looked out from a saviour pod and into the wound in reality as it closed. Some are stories of an astropath or a seer somewhere on Hydraphur, or even a nameless rating in an opticon deck aboard one of the ships was in pursuit. The story was rumoured to have been heard in a drinking-nook in the crowded decks of the Bescalion gate-stations, or told to a medicae team aboard the Ring, or whispered to a priest in a shrine somewhere in the Augustaeum, or screamed in desperation in an Arbites cell, or revealed in the Imperial tarot, or printed onto a thousand sheets of grubby paper and pasted onto walls or passed from hand to hand in the lightless alleys of Constanta Hive. The story came from everywhere and nowhere.

But no matter who the witness is supposed to have been, when the embellishments of the various tellers are stripped away the story remains constant. It tells that as the gash in the stars closed, leering and bleeding colours that could corrode the mind, shadowy forms closed on the doomed *Gann-Luctis* as it came apart, closing like sharks on a swimmer, wolves on a traveller, nightmares on a child's bed. They slid around and into the ship like oil flowing into cracks, as the stuff of the hull began to fray and come apart.

Some versions tell of giant talons tearing the *Gann-Luctis* to fragments, or that the edges of the rip sprouted teeth of purest darkness and macerated it like soft meat. There are versions that say that the ship's death-throes were lit by bright hell-light that seemed to come from everywhere and nowhere on the other side of that rent in space, or that the ship disappeared into depthless, mindless patterns of living dark but that images of it still, somehow made their way out, as though the sight of the ship was arriving in the mind without passing through the eyes.

Every form of the story relates that something was left behind when the rip closed and writhed and left nothing but empty starlit space, something that simply passed through the sides of the rip as they closed, or whose presence seemed to push the rip away across space as it shrank. But most of the stories tell instead of a silent howl of pain that came bellowing out of the gap in space, as though some great animal of that other world had tried to grip white-hot metal in its fingers and felt its flesh being burnt away, and that it came hurtling as though its presence in the turmoil on the other side of the rip was unbearable, as though it were poison being spat from a great gullet.

The more restrained storytellers will leave the matter there, and refuse to be drawn on what it might have been that did not follow the *Gann-Luctis* into oblivion. But there are others who insist that that nameless observer saw something drifting past the window of the pod or across the lens of the opticon. They say it was a book, a plain book, cloth-bound, turning end over end in the vacuum. Some go as far as to say that it passed close enough for the watcher's eyes to see the momentum spread the pages, and for light to spill from them, light that died as that observer looked on, as though the discharge from some powerful reaction was only just dying away, light that surrounded a tiny mark like a spot of blood on the final page.

Whether anything really escaped the destruction nobody knows. There are tales that the book flew towards Hydraphur's sun and burns there still, or that it now coasts silently through the vacuum of interplanetary space. Some say that it was caught by a mysterious ship that disappeared like a ghost, or that it flew towards Hydraphur itself and now is locked away in a dark cell beneath the Cathedral, or the Wall, or the Inquisitorial fortress in the planet's furthest land mass. There are stories among the survivors of the flotilla that say that the ghosts of Varro and Petronas Phrax roam the warp around Hydraphur and that one day they will meet and fight for their charter, tales that say that even the memory of the charter is cursed and that every living soul who voyaged with Hoyyon Phrax is doomed.

The last of the flotilla ships has been broken up now, the remnants of the crews imprisoned or dispersed. There is a small memorial garden to Ksana Phrax and her family on Gunarvo, erected by her brothers after the *Gann-Luctis* was lost. All records of the existence of Nils Petronas were erased when he became Petronas Phrax, and he is not now remembered.

The documents of the Phrax succession now lie in one of the archiving houses in a remote corner of the Wall, on a metal shelf in a rockcrete cell, waiting for a servitor to mark and store them. Maybe they will one day be stored, maybe not. Shira Calpurnia, Cynez Sanja, Essach Simova and the others might look back on the strife at Selena

Secundus now and again, but there are new challenges, new concerns for all of them now, every day.

And so now the only monument to the ten-thousand-year Phrax succession is legend, the twisted, exaggerated, fanciful tales of heirs and rivals, daemons and poisoned mutants and cold puppeteers, traitors and victims, that travel from ear to ear across Hydraphur to this day. The line of Phrax is gone; this alone is their legacy.

ABOUT THE AUTHOR

Born in 1970, **Matthew Farrer** has spent most of the subsequent period in and around Canberra, Australia, and is a member of the Canberra Speculative Fiction Guild. He has been writing since his teens, although he didn't break into professional sales until 'Badlands Skelter's Downhive Monster Show' appeared in *Inferno!* a few years ago. Since then he has published his first novel, the Shira Calpurnia adventure *Crossfire,* and a number of short stories. He was shortlisted for an Aurealis Award in 2001.

Arbites officer Shira Calpurnia finds herself in the
thick of the action when she investigates a series
of assassination attempts in the dockyards of the
Hydraphur system. But can Calpurnia avoid the
crossfire and bring her faceless enemies to justice?

ISBN: 1-84416-020-3

www.blacklibrary.com

GAUNT'S GHOSTS

In the war-torn Sabbat system, the massed ranks of the Imperial Guard battle against Chaos invaders in an epic struggle to liberate the enslaved worlds. Amidst this carnage, Commissar Ibram Gaunt and the men of the Tanith First-and-Only must survive against a relentless enemy as well as the bitter in-fighting from rival regiments.

Get right into the action with Dan Abnett's awesome series from the grim far-future!

INFERNO!™

Inferno! is the Black Library's high-octane fiction magazine, which throws you headlong into the worlds of Warhammer. From the dark, orc-infested forests of the Old World to the grim battlefields of the war-torn far future, Inferno! magazine is packed with storming tales of heroism and carnage.

Featuring work by awesome writers such as:

- **DAN ABNETT**
- **BEN COUNTER**
- **WILLIAM KING**
- **GRAHAM MCNEILL**
- **MATT FARRER**

and lots more!

Published every two months, Inferno! magazine brings the grim worlds of Warhammer to life.